ROOTIN'
FOR
THE CRUSHER

CARL HENDRICKS

Published by
Professional Business Consultants

Formatting/Cover Design
By Chris Ebuehi - Graphic Options

Published and Distributed by:
Professional Business Consultants
1425 W. Manchester, Suite B,
Los Angeles, California 90047
(213) 750-3592

First Printing, January, 1998
10 9 8 7 6 5 4 3 2 1

ISBN 1-881524-17-5

"Men will always prove bad unless necessity compels them to be good."
- Niccolo Machiavelli, THE PRINCE

DEDICATION

To Marie Mccarthy who always believed; to Stu Schwartz, who said this could happen; to the late Alfred Matthews Sr., who said this would happen; to Les Farr, who was there when a machine failed; and my late mother, who understood toward the end.

ACKNOWLEDGEMENT

The help provided by the East African Wildlife Society for the Kenya segment is greatly appreciated.

ROOTIN'
FOR
THE CRUSHER

A NOVEL

CHAPTER I

A NEST OF THE NETHERWORLD

They were showing it again. The same cartoon all week. The credits had finished, the action was about to begin.

Simeon's son looked up as a hulking figure ran across the Mitsubishi Diamondvision scoreboard in hot pursuit of a rabbit. "Come on, Crusher! I'm rootin' for ya! Kick the rabbit's ass!" he yelled.

Sprawled in his beer vendor's uniform, as still as shark bait on a sea of blue stadium seats, Rollo Boyce popped an eye, glanced up at the cartoon and went back to doing what he had been - sitting with his eyes closed, listening to the pock-pock of batters warming up, wondering how he could let any woman - even a redhead - make him feel so dizzy, while he waited for the fans to pour in. Along with every food and beverage vendor in Yankee Stadium, he was hoping for a feeding frenzy today. Down to a man, they needed the money.

"Come on, Crusher! I'm rootin' for ya!"

Rollo Boyce opened his eyes.

As the Crusher gained on the rabbit, the teenager hopped up and down in his seat. Rollo shook his head in disgust. He might only have a high school diploma, but Rollo Boyce wouldn't root for a cartoon character. What did they teach these kids in college anyhow?

Suddenly the Crusher grabbed Bugs, but he escaped in a flash, humiliating the Crusher.

"I can't take it anymore," Simeon's son said. "I don't know what's worse - watching Crusher get whipped day after day, or having some lazy fan ask me where his seat is when all he has to do is look at his ticket. What a way to make a living! I don't see how you vendors stand it. Damn. Here they come. I'm outta here." The kid

1

pulled his legs off the seat in front of him and sprinted for the commissary behind the lower deck as the fans began to pour into Yankee Stadium.

Rollo watched the kid disappear. As far as he was concerned, Simeon was wasting his money sending the kid to college. The sun went behind a cloud. Goose bumps covered Rollo's arms. Observing he was the only person present in a vending uniform and wanting to escape needless questions, too, Rollo stood up, stretched, and made for the warm commissary. He figured there was just enough time to get warmed up before selling beer.

Inside the commissary Simeon's son sat in a caged-off corner on top of peanut boxes. Simeon, the checker, wasn't present yet. Errol, Uranso, Brad Brown, and Stacey Oasis were. They were there because it was cold for the last Sunday in April, and they were relying on the lighted stove, the closed door and their huddled bodies to keep them warm while they plotted how to spend fortunes they didn't have and might never earn. A popular preoccupation during downtime.

"I don't care how it is for you guys this year. You're going to have to give us porters good subway, or we're not going to break our asses for you," Errol said. "Uranso and I pump your beer and cook your dogs, and we are entitled to a share of the tips." He pulled out a box cutter, examined the blade for dramatic effect, then threw it at a cardboard box near Brad Brown's head.

"Chill out with the knife! Or I'll pull out mine," said Brad Brown. "What you mean break your ass? The fans say the beer's hot, tastes watered down, and there're black specs at the bottom of the cups. For that you want 'sub'? Forget it. As much subway as you want, you can rent a limo," said Brad Brown.

"Forget rent. With the amount they're demanding, they could buy a limo," Rollo said.

"Forget this a limo shit. They could buy an entire limo service and quit this gig," said Brad Brown.

Errol's eyes became as big as eggs, the irises diminishing to laser dots in the sea of white behind his glasses. As his smile widened, his dimples grew into dark brown golf balls. "That's not a bad idea, but you know I couldn't leave you guys."

"That's because you'd really have to work then. If you hit the lotto or the number, your ass would be gone," said Rollo Boyce.

Errol grinned. "You people know if you take care of Uranso and me, we take care of you. When August comes and it's like a furnace in here, who serves you lemonade? Feeds you when you're hungry? We keep things running smoothly. If it wasn't for us, you'd dehydrate and go broke. All we want is what we deserve."

"There's only a slight problem. You and Uranso always think you deserve more. You're never satisfied. Sometimes you even collect beforehand," Rollo said.

"Funny things happen between the third inning and check out time. Vendors leave early, lose money or get suspended. And I end up not seeing a dime." Errol reached into his pants back pocket.

"What you reaching for?" Brad asked.

"I wish I could say it was money." Errol smiled, brought out losing lottery tickets and ripped them up. "I only needed two more numbers to win last night."

"You going to keep on trying?"

"Might as well. All I got to look forward to is pumping beer." Errol turned toward Simeon's son. "Hey Junior! Did I tell you your father wants to see you in management's office? You better go see him." He watched Simeon's son leave. Junior gave a middle finger salute before disappearing.

Rollo Boyce kept silent. Pumping beer might be Errol's fate, but Rollo had other aspirations; however, when he mentioned his aspirations to most people - including his own flesh and blood - they thought him absurd, fantasizing. This reminded him of Einstein's statement: "Great spirits have always encountered violent opposition from mediocre minds." He vowed to keep quiet, be quietly effective, and steadfastly pursue his goals no matter what.

"Hey, and if vending or the lottery doesn't do it, there's always Kelso's business proposal," said Brad Brown, peeking outside, making sure Simeon's son was gone. "I'm glad that sneaky, ferret faced motherfucker is gone. I don't want him yapping to Simeon about Kelso's plan."

"You take Kelso's proposal seriously?" Errol arched his eyebrows.

"Have you ever known Terence Kelso not to take making

3

money seriously?"

"No, but that doesn't mean his ideas work."

"You going to the meeting at the Renegade's club to discuss Kelso's proposal?" Rollo asked.

"Sure. Isn't everyone going to Beezer's place?" Errol answered.

"Yeah. Lenny Mo Dinner, Oasis, Copperblum, Rod Somer, Andy Metzger are going. Even the guy who helped the priest distribute those inspirational books'll be there. Kelso's idea must be deft," said Brad Brown.

"Wait a second. When you analyze it, most of them got to be there: Lenny Mo worships him. Oasis always needs more money with four daughters to feed on a correction officer's salary, and Andy Metzger is always curious about schemes," Rollo said.

"True, but even the guy - what is his name - the one who helped the priest is attending. Looks like Kelso may have a winner this time," Errol answered.

Rollo planned to attend, but he wasn't going to be greatly surprised or disappointed if things didn't work out. Unlike Kelso, making money wasn't Rollo's greatest passion. He wanted to achieve meaningful goals. He had had his fill of working nine-to-five, being a good employee, giving his all for the company so he could get laid-off or fired when the company didn't need him anymore. He was tired of being an assembly line employee with no room for individual expression.

Determined to be a successful Rhythm & Blues songwriter and producer, he knew he possessed the skills to bring these plans to fruition. Radiating charm and charisma was a skill he had cultivated since childhood. He figured the only thing that kept him from achieving his goals was a lack of discipline. But in the end, if it became obvious he wasn't going to succeed - he had a brief mete-oric brush with success in his early twenties - he'd move to a trop-ical island, find six women to keep him company, breed and only return to the States to sell beer during Baseball season.

Rollo didn't consider the vast quantity of time he invested in establishing relationships with beautiful women as a detriment to his success. Other men devoted a lot of time to relationships and suc-

4

ceeded. Why hadn't he? Of course Rollo wasn't exactly pursuing vestal virgins. The sexier and sleazier the object of his affection, the more motivated he became, and although his success in obtaining intimacy with females was enviable, running after this type of woman did take a heavy emotional toll. His mother asked why he didn't bring girls home to meet her. His friends questioned his moral stability. "How could you go with someone like that?" they often asked.

Of late, he even questioned his own values. He found his failure to achieve a successful career intolerable. He was aware life would go on despite his predicament. He told himself he must persist, get control of himself, be more disciplined. He didn't want to wind up at Yankee Stadium for the rest of his life.

He'd be glad when working there was a memory. The money he earned at the ballpark was obscene; people got soused and waved cash around as if it were Kleenex. Just the other day, a fan showing off to his friends gave Rollo a seventy-five dollar tip to appear every half inning with a fresh beer tray. Rollo had no problem with that; yet, when he considered how many destitute people there were, it felt wrong. Even though he enjoyed the comraderie of the vendors, some of the guys and the entire management were despicable. Still, he told himself, the day would come when if the Yankees were home or on the road wouldn't matter. It was for this day he lived.

Meanwhile, until his deliverance, he'd view America's pastime behind a vendor's badge to have stories to tell his children and grandchildren. Their arrival he was sure of. Of exactly when, he had no idea. The sooner his songwriting success was assured, the quicker he'd have an idea about procreating offspring. He had already penned hits for Elston King and Mary Memphis, two popular R&B artists, and written half the songs on 'The Cliches' triple platinum album, "The World Belongs to Lovers." Now he needed to build and expand on his past musical success. He had also made love to numerous women, but now he wanted to find one worthy of having his children. How he managed his wants and needs would go a long way toward determining how soon he'd have the opportunity to see Bugs Bunny kick the Crusher's butt on a personal-sized Mitsubishi Diamond Vision scoreboard - on his own island.

5

While the men were discussing Kelso's meeting, Uranso, the porter who worked with Errol, had kept quiet. He was ready to attend but was enjoying curried goat and Jamaican bread and didn't want to be disturbed. Suddenly, the commissary door banged open and another vendor, Rod Somer, entered.

"You guys are crooks and thieves," Rod Somer said, pointing at Errol and Uranso as he entered. "Over at Shea whatever subway I give the porters they're happy. Here, a day doesn't go by without the demand for more, more, more. No matter how ma-much or how little the fans ba-buy." Mini spit bubbles pierced the air in front of Rod's mouth.

"Yo, Rod, you four eyed studderin' motherucker. If you don't want to hook us up that's fine; we know how to deal with it," Errol said. "But, if you call us crooks and thieves again, you'll never walk out of here with a tray fit for human consumption. Your beer cups'll be half filled. If you're on dogs, they'll be raw."

"You bloodclot," said Uranso, his West Indian accent causing Rod to turn a shade of red he didn't care for.

"You're not getting another dime out of me," said Rod.

"That dime going to do you any good when the fans stop buying your beer with dirt specs in it?" Errol helped himself to some of Uranso's curried goat.

"I'll talk to management."

"Yeah? You better maneuver your ass carefully or you're going to be an outcast in a second commissary. We can be just as mean as that porter who gave you half filled cups and warm beer." Errol wiped curry gravy off his lips with the back of his hand.

"You guys would do that?"

Uranso finished picking his teeth, pointed the toothpick at Rod and curled it back to himself. "Despite how everyone feel about you, Rod, I like you."

Rod smiled, buckteeth showing. "Wha-what's not to like about me?"

"You can barely talk, mon. When you do, you don't know what ta say. You have that psoriasis of dee elbow rash. People *feel* you speak to them because of your spit. You need for me ta go on?"

"So why do you like me?"

"When I look at you and see what you've accomplished in spite of yourself I know there's hope fa everyone. No, seriously," said Uranso. "You're married, take good care of your wife. Even though you can't speak too well, you stand up for what you believe in, and you like everyone despite their hating you. I know it seems far away, but eventually good things'll come to you, mon."

Rod hugged Uranso. "Don't worry I'll take care of you from now on," he said and moved toward the beer tap.

Uranso winked at Errol and whispered, "It shame he sucker for dat 'good cop, bad cop', routine."

"How come you always get to be the good cop?" Errol asked.

"Aren't you always saying you a 'baad mon'? Well a bad mon can't be good cop, right?"

The University of Notre Dame's fight song blasted through the commissary, silencing conversation as Simeon, the checker, arrived and began to direct traffic. "Peanut vendors go out first," he yelled over the organ music. "Then soda and ice cream guys, then hot dogs and beer. Let the fans taste that golden juice!"

Simeon puffed on his Parliament like a general deploying his troops. The years had been good to him. He had a solid build, and if not for his gray hair, he and his son, the college matriculating cartoon lover, could have passed for brothers. But Simeon was not liked by the men. He had a cruel streak and seemed to enjoy torturing the vendors.

Rollo stood up, psyched himself for the first tray. He was approaching the same age as Christ when he was crucified, but since he worked out religiously and was careful in his eating habits, he could still pass for twenty-three, the age when he wrote songs for: "The World Belongs to Lovers." He had gone to bed with enough women that there was no doubt he wasn't ugly; even the girls who wouldn't sleep with him said he was handsome. They claimed personality clashes, family or personal honor prevented them from copulating. He saw these for what they were: stated obstacles created to prevent him from getting in their behinds. When he was younger and sex was a greater preoccupation, he'd do what it took to overcome the obstacles and harvest the rewards, but as he approached his thirty-third birthday, fucking was no longer the dri-

ving passion in his life. Also AIDS was approaching epidemic pro-
portions. He now practiced temperance, most recently with a redhead
who reminded him of a television star. It wasn't easy, but, he
reminded himself, if he was to achieve a successful songwriting
career, it was necessary. Squandered time was irreplaceable.

"Beer men, everyone else has cleared out. Get going!" Simeon
yelled.

Rollo and the other beer vendors picked up metal trays holding a score of beer cups, placed them in plastic, spill proof trays and
told the checker their names as they left the commissary. Since
Yankee Caps were being given out, Rollo knew beer sales would be
slower than a weeknight game, when most fans attending were men.
Giveaway days attracted family crowds. And the Yankees were
playing Cleveland, not one of the league's better crowd-drawing
teams. With the overcast sky and abundance of children, yelling,
despite the chilliness, he had guarded optimism. Still, the beers
were sold out in no time, and Rollo and Brad Brown found themselves
heading back to the commissary for more. "What's the matter?" Brad
asked. "You got a blank look on your face."

"I'm not into it today," said Rollo, wishing he hadn't started
thinking about the redhead again.

As Rollo and Brad Brown entered the commissary, Uranso,
stood idly by the capping machine, having finished his curried goat
and Jamaican bread brunch.

"You haven't pumped more beer trays yet?" Rod Somer asked.

"Errol's down in dee ice box, fixing dee lines. You tink you
really going to sell a lot today Somer?" Uranso asked, resentful tone
in his voice and moved toward the spigots.

"There's only five of us," said Rod. "A-a-and they're givin'
away caps - to everyone."

"Mon, it's col' out dere. Beside der still be a lot of kids here."

"Weather has never stopped beer drinkers from coming.
Besides, kids come with adults."

"Uranso moved fast and soon had three beer trays of twelve-
ounce plastic cups sealed and set in their metal racks. "When I have
two more done, Somer you get de fuck outa here," he said.

Somer rubbed his hands together. If Uranso and Errol could

supply beer to meet demand - or let demand slightly exceed supply - he and the other beer vendors would earn a small fortune. All in a little more than two hours. The prospect of selling to 25,000 fans seated in the lower deck on Cap Day, despite the Cleveland Indians, chilly weather or not, filled his mind with illusions of selling twenty-five beer trays. Five beer vendors were covering the third base side at the field and main level.

Rollo picked up another beer tray and went outside still not caring about Cap Day, how many trays he sold or who won the game. Only, the redhead expressing an interest would make him joyful at the moment.

As Rollo worked his way through the seats around his commissary, a man with a little boy called Rollo over. As Rollo handed the father his beer, the youngster looked at a baseball card and then at Rollo. "Matty Alou! Matty Alou!" He held out his scorecard and pencil.

Rollo looked at the youngster.

The father placed his beer cup on the ground, took the scorecard and pencil and turned to Rollo. "Sign it!" he said. "He thinks you're Matty Alou."

Rollo didn't want to lie; he didn't want to break the child's heart either. When he was a youngster, he and his friends used to wait outside the players' gate after games to see if they could get autographs. He recalled the euphoria when a ballplayer signed his name to whatever he held out, the despair that permeated his soul when a ballplayer walked by as if he weren't there. Rollo put the pencil to the scorecard and quickly signed in an illegible scrawl.

A smile as wide as the outfield came over the child's face. He put his small hand in Rollo's palm, and they shook hands. Rollo returned the youngster's smile, picked up his beer tray and left. He might sell one less beer tray, but he wasn't upset. He had earned something far more valuable than money today.

The Yankees won Cap Day, 8-3.

Rollo was having work done on his Puegot's carburetor. "Copperblum, can you give me a lift to St. Ouen Ave.?"

"Sure, its not out of the way," responded Copperblum, in the union vendors locker room.

Jared Copperblum was disappointed. He had made more money than most vendors who worked Cap Day, more fans ask for him than anyone - including the ballplayers, and had company for the ride home.

"Why am I being deprived of the right to earn as much money as I possibly can?" asked Copperblum. "Why is management depriving me of one of my rights as an American? Am I ever going to sell beer again?"

"It is going to be a long season, but you'll rate beer before it's over. And besides, there's Kelso's business plan," said Rollo.

"What makes you think that has a chance of working?"

"Businesses more shady and simple work. Why can't his?"

"Nobody likes him."

"A lot of people don't like people they do business with. Business still gets done."

"We'll see. You ever seen so many kids at a ballgame?" Copperblum's Stanza inched ahead, trying to get onto the clogged Deegan expressway.

"Wait till Bat Day. You'll see even more."

"You heard Iggy Biggy threw a soda tray at a rookie who acted like a wise guy?"

"No. I didn't," said Rollo.

"The tray had filled soda cups in it, too."

"Iggy's a strong son-of-a-bitch. Some guys have trouble lifting a soda tray and he's throwing it."

"The rookie wasn't no smart alec after the soda tray knocked him down."

"Was he seriously hurt?"

"Had the wind knocked out of him and coke syrup stuck to his skin, but he was able to continue vending." Copperblum arched his thick eyebrows. "You still seeing the girl you went with last season?"

Rollo said he was not.

"You found a new girl?"

"Last week I met a fine girl on the subway. She's from the Dominican Republic and resembles a red-headed Lisa Bonet."

"You don't meet nice girls on the subway, but why quibble. Did

10

you get her phone number?"

"She doesn't have one, but she gave me her address without my asking and kissed me."

"I don't want to listen to your exploits. Besides, why waste your time with a girl who doesn't have a phone?"

"Did you hear who I said she looks like?"

Copperblum drove with greater deliberation. "Who are Tuesday's starting pitchers?"

"Why are you so concerned about starting pitchers?"

"Because I'm a baseball fan and if the Yankees win, enough fans'll come for me to rate beer again."

"Spoken like a real patriot."

"Fuck you. When are you going to go out with a girl you'll be proud to take home to your mother?"

"I was. That wasn't all it was cracked up to be."

"Why's that?"

"It was almost like going out with my mother."

"What's wrong with that?"

"I'm not into those Sigmund Freud theories."

"So you keep scoring with girls of questionable repute," said Copperblum.

"Funny. You're the only one who questions their repute," said Rollo.

"That's because I care about you." Copperblum smiled and dimples appeared.

"Oh, I'm moved. But you gotta get out there and see more of what the world has to offer. These girls you speak so highly of, there's a very fine line between them and the ones you say I should forget about."

"Does that mean you're hopelessly devoted to this Lisa Bonet look-a like?"

"I want to find out what she's like. She might be more scrupulous than what I'm accustomed to. You can't prejudge someone because you meet them on the subway, right?"

Copperblum rapped his knuckles on the steering wheel. "Yeah, yeah, yeah." The blood rushing to his face subsided. "Well, I still think you should forget her, but perhaps she won't go through men

11

like Epsom salt."

"Good. I'm glad I got a C.P.A. to agree with me." Rollo gave Copperblum a friendly knock on the shoulder, noticing as he did that Copperblum looked better than ordinary. Copperblum wasn't cover boy material, but whatever inefficiencies were on his face were overcome by his personality. Rollo knew it was Copperblum's warm personality that allowed him to compete with better looking beer vendors. Fans actually confided in him. This made him and his product far more in demand than vendors who simply sold their beer, collected money and were off seeking the next sale. As Dale Carnegie stated: "If you want to gather honey, don't kick over the beehive."

The Stanza arrived at a destination where Rollo could catch a cab. He gave Copperblum two dollars, told him he'd see him on Tuesday, got out and slammed the door.

CHAPTER II

LISBETH

It was easy for Copperblum to forget the Lisa Bonet look-a-like; it wasn't for Rollo. It was the day after Cap Day, an off day. If Rollo could contact the redhead it would be an off day he could savor. When Rollo first saw her he was mesmerized. Not only did she resemble Lisa Bonet, she was blessed with a figure that wouldn't quit: large round breasts, trim waist, succulent butt, and though she was wearing jeans, he could see she had well contoured legs. He decided he would not leave the subway without talking to her.

He had seen her get on the #2 train at 96th Street. The express was closing in on Times Square when he knew he had to find a way to approach her. As the train pulled into the crossroads of the world, he saw she was making every sign of getting off. He hoped she didn't go upstairs. Not only did he not want to contend with the relentless pressure of Times Square as he approached her, but if it turned out she worked in a porno establishment, it would break his heart - knowing all the lechers that frequented such places were staring, drooling, masturbating at and possibly fondling her. He found it ironic. He wanted to avoid girls who reminded him of those working upstairs, yet the first one to come along, he locked onto like radar.

The train's doors opened. Rollo followed her, keeping his eyes glued to the succulent butt. She didn't have the hard look most girls who did porno had, so he remained hopeful as she walked down the tunnel toward the exit near the Port Authority Bus Terminal.

The moment of truth was fast approaching; only a few yards separated her from the Port Authority Exit to 42nd Street, or the stairway to the A,C & E trains and Rollo. She was within an arms length of the

13

Bus Terminal Exit. Her body tilted toward the Exit gate. Rollo's heart wilted. She was about to enter Times Square's dens of iniquity. Suddenly, her body swerved to avoid a rancid derelict and then she was past the exit and continuing on down the staircase to the trains. Rollo made sure to keep close enough so that if a train were there and she jumped on it, he could, too.

When he reached the Uptown Queens platform no trains were there, but the girl with the fiery red hair was. He fought to contain his glee as he walked toward her. "Did anyone ever tell you you look like Lisa Bonet?"

"I want the E train," she said in broken English.

Having learned Spanish while matriculating, a smile enveloped Rollo's countenance. He had an inner glow, a gut feeling this was going to work out fine - just fine. The E train arrived. They got on.

They made small talk as the train sped toward the young lady's stop. He discovered her name was Elizabeth; she would soon be going back to the Dominican Republic for two weeks to visit her family. She lived in an apartment building on West 181st Street in Washington Heights. She didn't tell him what kind of work she did; she did tell him she worked from 8P.M. to 4A.M., five nights a week. Rollo smiled. It was better than no work at all.

As the E train pulled into Parson's Boulevard, Elizabeth got up. Rollo asked if he could carry her pink gym bag. She nodded. Rollo picked up the gym bag. He grimaced. It was heavy. He wondered what was inside.

There were no men on their car as they exited, but that didn't stop every women's head from turning their way.

When they were upstairs and outside walking along the Boulevard, the admiration continued. Above ground the admirers were male and theirs was a different type of admiration. Rollo noticed when the women on the train stared, they were admiring a loving couple; the men on Parson's Boulevard were staring strictly at Elizabeth - some attempting to turn their necks one hundred eighty degrees to catch a glimpse - and wishing they were taking Rollo's place. Rollo was elated; confirmation that he had a find was taking place right before his eyes.

They stopped at a fruit stand. Elizabeth bought a pear, an apple and a banana. She asked Rollo if he wanted anything. Rollo shook his head. It wasn't fruit he wanted. When they walked another half a block, Elizabeth asked Rollo for a pen and a paper. She took them, wrote her name and address, gave them back to Rollo and kissed him. Rollo gladly accepted her hospitality. He looked at the paper, "No telefono?"

She shook her head and went into a small walk-up building.

"I'll see you when you get back from the Dominican Republic," Rollo called, but she was already out of sight.

The two weeks were a moment and an eternity to Rollo. An eternity because it seemed to last forever and a moment because he felt as if they were already together, bonded by magnetism even though they were half a continent apart. He wondered how intense his feelings would be when they were next to each other, caressing each other, kissing each other, doing the natural deed.

The night of her anticipated return Rollo was at the apartment on West 181st Street with a bouquet of carnations - he thought of flowers too late to find a place selling fresh roses. He didn't recognize the person's voice who buzzed him past the lobby door. When he got to Elizabeth's apartment and rang the bell, a short chunky-looking women answered and told him Elizabeth was working - he had forgotten about her 8P.M. - 4P.M. working hours. He handed her the carnations, asked her to tell Elizabeth he'd be back the next day after 5P.M. and sped back to the Puegot in a smug verve. It would be a matter of hours before the eternity would cease, and the moment would hopefully last as long as they wanted it to.

When he arrived home, he climbed into the queen sized platform bed and slept. He didn't have any nightmares. He wanted to be well rested and coherent when he saw Elizabeth.

When he arose the next morning, the day's menial tasks seemed more menial than ever, but he vacumned, cleaned the dishes in the sink and scoured the bathroom - she might want to come to his apartment instead of remaining in hers. After he was finished tidying up, he showered, dried himself, and put on cream white silk linen slacks, a pink polo shirt, a double breasted ventless cream white sport jacket and a pair of chalk white espadrilles. He splashed on enough Lagerfeld cologne that she would have to notice - if she didn't, he'd have to ques-

15

tion her sense of smell. The grooming took place after he had penned two songs he knew would be hits; he was psyched.

The train screeched to a halt. Walking up to Elizabeth's street, he felt as if he were ascending to heaven.

Elizabeth lived in a hub residential neighborhood. The towering George Washington Bridge Bus Terminal was the neighborhood's axis, dwarfing the nearby brownstones, small apartment buildings and housing projects. Every conceivable business that could infuse vitality and make life more pleasant could be found. There were no automobile dealerships, no firearms stores and government buildings were at least a mile south. It should have been a model of urban splendor, but crack dealers were everywhere, seeking customers without even bothering to hide their aggressive tactics. He wondered if she would prefer to live with him, but it might not be long before the same business activities were taking place in his neighborhood. Perhaps they would be smarter to find a new neighborhood in which to begin their coextistence.

He went in a flower shop half-a-block away from Elizabeth's. The roses looked shabby, so he purchased tulips instead. As he walked out the florist shop, he felt everything had been taken care of: he was dressed to impress, had flowers to warm her heart, a twinkle in his eyes and charm to do the rest.

He recognized Elizabeth's voice on the intercom. The buzzer rang. He burst past the door, blood surging. He felt transformed, as though he had passed the Pearly Gates and was going to meet the Archangel Peter to see if he belonged or if he would be thrown back from whence he came.

He knocked on Elizabeth's door. A petite girl opened it and gestured for him to enter. He found himself in a small hallway leading to a large living room with yellow walls. As he turned to the right, Elizabeth stood in the bedroom door, looking even more impressive than when he had met her. She wore a white blouse with gemstones sprinkled across her chest, a red leather mini-skirt and lace pantyhose. The sight of the black lace pressed against her red-brown skin brought Rollo's blood past the surging stage; his arteries felt pounded by a tidal wave. Elizabeth told him to take a seat on the couch. He did. She returned to the bedroom but left the door ajar, planting herself in front of the mirror to further prepare.

As he took his seat, he noticed the girl who had opened the door cradling an infant. She turned her back toward Rollo, pulled her t-shirt up to her shoulders, removed her breasts from her bra cups and placed a nipple in the infant's mouth. Must be a very open family he thought. He spoke what Spanish he could with her. They understood each other for roughly half of the conversation.

Elizabeth then emerged from the bedroom and held out her hand. As he gave her the bouquet and kissed her, she turned her cheek.

"Thank ju," she said. "These are nice. I haven't gotten flowers this good in a long time."

Rollo smiled, glad that she liked the flowers, but mystified by her coolness.

She took the flowers to the kitchen, put them in a vase and took them to the bedroom. He waited for her to return.

After fifteen minutes he was still waiting. The intercom rang. The petite girl carried the baby to the intercom, pressed a button, asked who, heard an acceptable response, pressed another button and returned to her seat.

The door bell rang. A petite, middle aged woman walked in. They weren't introduced. After looking her over, Rollo considered her entrance inconsequential.

Elizabeth came to the bedroom's doorway and rolled her head for the middle-aged woman to follow her. They went inside the bedroom. A loud discussion in Spanish ensued. Eliazabeth came out of the bedroom and asked, "Could ju wait outside, please?"

"Why?" Rollo asked.

"Just for a few minutes," she said.

With great reluctance, Rollo left and waited in the hallway. He wondered why Elizabeth was ambivalent. She was the one who initiated their keeping in contact. She kissed him when she left. Had she forgotten him? She wouldn't have let him in the apartment. Was she scared? She wouldn't have asked him to wait. Why had her demeanor changed when the middle-aged woman entered?

Elizabeth and the middle-aged woman finally came out.

"Bye, honey. I'll see you. I have to go," she said.

Rollo's eyes bulged to the size of Kiwis. His chin sank like a dropped bomb. "What?"

"Bye, honey. I'll see you. I have to go."

Rollo couldn't accept such a terse farewell. He walked right beside her and the woman. This continued until they were a block and a half away from the apartment. Then Elizabeth and the middle aged woman made an effort to move away. Rollo despised following anyone, but he had to get an answer. "Elizabeth, what's going on?" he called out.

Elizabeth stopped. The middle aged woman said something in Spanish so quickly that Rollo couldn't catch it. Elizabeth turned and said, "You've got to leave. This woman's my mother-in-law."

"What!"

"This is my future husband's mother."

"You didn't mention this."

"I didn't think you'd come see me."

"You gave me your address. Remember?"

She started walking away.

"Are you serious?" Rollo asked.

"The baby you saw in the apartment is my son."

"Where's the father, your future husband?"

"In Santo Domingo."

Rollo stopped walking. Now everything was clear. Rollo watched the succulent butt and the well contoured legs sashay away, wondering what might have been. Then he walked to the subway, put a token in the turnstile and went to the downtown platform. It didn't take long for an A-train to pull in. He got on and sat down. Why had Elizabeth led him on? Could it be possible she was only putting on a show for her mother-in-law? What difference would the answer make. She wasn't free. As the train approached the next stop, Rollo noticed a familiar face. It was Elizabeth - on the platform alone.

She didn't notice him. She got on the car behind his. Rollo let one stop go by, then went to Elizabeth's car. He stood beside her seat, looking down at her. She didn't look up. As the ride continued, it became apparent she didn't realize he was there. When the train pulled into Rollo's station. he walked off and turned for one last look. As the train door started closing, Elizabeth looked up and gave him an ear to ear smile as a farewell present. Then she was gone.

Rollo stood there staring at the empty tracks, wondering if any body at the Stadium would believe what he had been through in the last four hours. He wasn't sure he believed it. In the triumphant days of songwriting, events like this had occurred, only then he didn't dwell upon them. He moved on to the next girl and the event was viewed from - a more objective perspective: as part of history. Sometimes things did work out fine - just fine - just not as fine as one expected.

CHAPTER III

ALOUISCIOUS

It was a new homestand's first game. Three days after Rollo last saw Lisbeth. Seated near the Men's Locker Room, his back against the wall, Rollo was thinking about Lisbeth, wondering how what had seemed so encouraging could turn into an illusion, when he saw Alouiscious walking through the vast tunnel toward him. Rollo closed his eyes and shook his head. One man's problem was another's opportunity, wasn't it? Alouiscious would console Rollo. It wasn't the type of consolation he preferred, but Alouiscious would make him laugh and shift his train of thought.

Alouiscious, intentionally or unintentionally, made people laugh. It could have been his appearance: thick nappy hair; a smile that revealed, if he was brushing his teeth, he wasn't using tartar control toothpaste. He had a respectable build but wore either cheap clothing or clothes that would have been chic if he were still living in the early 1970's. It could have been his odor; his funk was so rancid people considered donating him to a zoo. Or his pretentiousness; he swore he was God's gift to women and never failed to boast. For all his acumen in wooing females, no one had ever seen him with a pretty girl unless he was serving her a beer. He had bragged he had taken wives from their husbands. Yet, when Rollo saw him with one of these 'woomens' it appeared more like the husband was getting rid of a malady or someone about whom he was now asking himself - "I walked down the aisle with that?"

Alouiscious tapped Rollo's foot. "What's the matter? You look like you want to go to outer space."

"Maybe I do. I just got back from the Twilight Zone."

"You meet any girls there?"

20

"Funny you should ask." Rollo explained what happened at Washington Heights.

Alouiscious laughed. "Now if that was me that never would have happened."

"I know. You would have used Alouiscious pull, swept her in your arms and carried her home, right? What makes you think she would have given you the time of day, much less let you touch her?"

Alouiscious flexed his arms. "I could have given her more than she ever had."

"More what? More funk than she's ever smelt before?"

"You know what I mean."

"No, I don't know what you mean. Explain yourself."

"The baseball bat I have between my legs. You know some of the players want to use it the next time they come to bat."

Rollo shook his head. "Stop bullshitting yourself. If any player touched what you got between your legs, he'd be out of the major leagues."

"Say what you will, but that girl would have gone head over heels for me."

"To get away from you she would have gone head over heels, bent over backwards, o.d.ed on drugs. Need I go on?"

"When you see me out there tonight with four fine ones and at least six phone numbers, you'll regret those words."

"Fine what - girls or animals?"

Alouiscious smiled, brownish-yellow teeth and tartar clearly showing.

"You're jealous. There's only one Alouiscious and all the 'woomens' want me."

"I'm jealous, huh? How come you've never introduced me or anyone else to these 'woomens' who want you?"

Alouiscious shrugged. "They only want to be with me. No one else."

"I've seen the ones that only want to be with you. Thank God they only want to be with you."

"Jealously is the sign of a weak individual."

Alouiscious saw one of the female vendors and started walk-

21

ing toward her. "Hi sweetheart. Got a moment?" She continued walking away from him. "Don't you wanna hear what I have to say?"

The girl, a black teenager with cornrows reaching her shoulders, kept walking.

Rollo giggled. "It don't look like that babe wants to be near you. When's the last time you took a bath?"

The following morning on the plus side of 6A.M. the sun was already making Rollo glad the Puegot had air conditioning. It felt more like August than April. He was ordering breakfast at a drive thru McDonald's in a despair ridden section of Hunt's Point and debating whether to go home or to the beach. If he went home he'd probably continue thinking about Lisbeth. He might do the same at the beach, but he might also run into a swimsuit-clad woman who'd make him forget her. The beach it was then. He gave the cashier money, received his food and change, closed his window and turned on the air conditioning. The ride to the highway was enjoyable: cool air, fine food and soothing music. Three of his senses felt fine. Once he put his foot to the gas, two didn't.

As he drove along, he saw row upon row of gutted buildings, buildings that looked like they had survived a war. For every new or renovated building amid the rubble, there were two or three gutted ones with holes in the walls and all the windows broken out. The eyesores were multiplying like fungus. The Bronx, for as long as he could remember, was the borough of the swift and the strong. The swift and the strong had always fought through adversity and peril, but proliferating drug traffic now made the Bronx a haven of the ruthless, cunning and hyper-immoral. Rollo wondered how anyone could contemplate raising a family in such an environment. He thought of Lisbeth and how she seemed so close and was yet so far. And wondered when he'd get to raise a family - anywhere. He reminded himself that patience, self-control and discipline would lead to a successful songwriting career and hopefully, to finding someone who would make hit it and quit it girls a thing of the past.

As the Puegot stopped at a red light, a skinny yellow girl with a short natural approached the passenger side and tapped on the window. Rollo took a sip of orange juice, leaned over and lowered the window.

"Can I join you?"

"Didn't your mother tell you not to talk to strangers?"

"Would I have any friends if I took my mother's advice?"

Rollo opened the passenger door. "Come on. Any girl who doesn't follow her mother's advice isn't all bad."

The girl was in the car before Rollo finished speaking. What had come over him? This certainly wasn't the kind of girl to be sought after if he wanted to resume his songwriting career. It was difficult to imagine the beach not having better prospects. Then he remembered: "A bird in the hand is better than two in the bush." Still, he would have preferred an eagle to a pigeon.

At every red light Rollo turned to look at the girl, hoping she would be more attractive than the physical surroundings. As the sun rose higher, he saw that she was, but not by much. What struck him immediately was how thin the girl was. She wasn't emaciated, but she didn't have much further to go. She was wearing shorts and shouldn't have: her legs looked like a spider's. She wore a halter top, even though what she had to work with under it wasn't going to halt anyone. He bet they resembled pancakes with raisins on top. When the girl took off her Foster Grants, and Rollo got a close look, her eyes were semiglazed.

"What's your name?" he asked at last.

"Lucinda."

The quick response surprised Rollo. After seeing her eyes, he doubted she was coherent. "Hay un momacita es linda pero flaco," said Rollo. "Flaco Lucinda."

She laughed. "What's your name?"

"Tito," Rollo answered. There was no way he was going to tell this one his real name. "Flaco Lucinda. Flaco Lucinda." He said it as if he were singing.

"Kill that Flaco Lucinda chant. It's dry now. Can you give me twenty dollars so I can buy some Pampers and milk for my babies?"

"If you have kids, why the fuck aren't you with them at 6:20 in the morning instead of out here on these streets?"

"My mother looks after them."

"Hopefully she's doing a better job with them than she did with

23

you. What you got, boys, girls or both?" Rollo found it hard to believe someone this skinny had ever conceived offspring.

"A boy, three, and a one-year-old girl."

"Why don't you let me see them?"

"Are you kidding? My mother wouldn't let you in the apartment."

"I'm not the type of guy you'd want to take home to Mom?"

She tapped his knee. "Come. I know where we can go."

It turned out to be a gutted six story apartment building on Tiebould Street. When they pulled up, Lucinda said, "Wait here. I'll come back."

"I might have gotten the fuck out of here by the time you return."

"It's your loss, not mine."

"From where I'm sitting, it appears to be one of the few losses I can be proud of."

She moved to kiss him. Rollo turned his head. There was no way her lips were going to touch his; he didn't want any communicable diseases.

Lucinda was gone for twenty minutes. He should have left, but, he had the bird in the hand. Suddenly, she reappeared on the sidewalk, breathing rapidly. "Come on, Tito. It's not my mother's apartment, but it'll do."

She coaxed Rollo out of the car, led him by the hand to the courtyard entrance. Glass and empty crack vials littered the steps. The stairway was partially covered by a hood of a car, which Lucinda and Rollo edged past. Suddenly, Rollo stopped. "Why would someone enter a building where the most likely inhabitants were vermin?" he mumbled. Lucinda held his hand tighter and started to caress his nuts. "Oh yes, that's why," he said. Lucinda laughed and continued leading the way down.

Rollo, looked down. "What am I doing? What have I done to deserve this?" The concrete courtyard was covered by mud, broken green, brown and clear glass - a new urban tundra - broken bricks and empty beer, wine, scotch, gin, vodka and whiskey bottles. In some spaces the refuse was piled so high it reached the first floor windows. A man who resembled the loser of every barroom brawl was lowering a white plastic pail from a second floor window. With him was a girl whose complexion was close to Rollo's. She had emperor plum eyes, an inch and a half thick natural and although skinny, was closer to normal than Lucinda. The man and the woman gave Rollo a long, hard stare. Rollo returned the favor. Lucinda broke the stalemate. She yelled, "Tito, this is Ralph. And this is my sister Maria."

"You got five dollars?" Maria yelled.

"What's this, the movies? You charge admission?" Rollo said.

"Does it look like I got any feature films to show you?"

When the pail reached the ground, Lucinda took what was inside and walked to a dark corner. Suddenly, everything was clear. Lucinda was a crack addict; Maria was a crack addict; Ralph was a crack addict. Everyone in this blight, except him was a crack addict. He was disgusted. The pigeon had led him to parasite breeding ground. And though it was stupidity to do what they were doing, he realized he was a worse fool for being there, especially after he had vowed to avoid chasing sleazy women.

He walked to where Lucinda had disappeared. Bricks littered the ground. A grayish dust lay over the mud. There was a strange sound as if wind were blowing between the bricks, but there was no wind in the summer heat. Rats scurried behind and beneath the bricks. In a corner of the darkened room, Lucinda and three other skinny girls were seated on a couch, smoking crack. Two dark skin men were sitting on broken chairs hoping to get leftovers from Lucinda and the other females. All around them the rats were making ear splitting squeals.

In high school and college he had read stories and seen films of concentration camps. Those people's captors had been exceedingly cruel, but seeing life in the crack house made him wonder who was worse off — people who had been enslaved by another group of people claiming racial or religious superiority who beat, maimed and killed their captives into submission, or people who of their own volition consumed a drug as merciless as any human captor.

Rollo staggered to the courtyard to escape the stench of smoke and urine. The sunshine and the cleaner air made him feel he was on another planet even though he had walked no more than fifteen feet. He was taking a deep breath when Lucinda reappeared. "You got a contact?"

"Let's hope not," said Rollo.

Lucinda pouted and stared as best as her semiglazed eyes allowed.

"What's the matter? A clear train of thought is too much for you to handle?"

"Not at all." Her hands reached toward his pelvis. She placed her right hand on his hip and her left went to the bottom of his midsection. She kept her left palm open as it covered his zipper. She began rubbing. Slowly, then with each passing moment, the friction grew.

Rollo had heard braggarts rant and rave about cocaine's aphrodisiac qualities, but he thought it was an old wives tale spread by semi-impotent bullshitters. He was very suspicious, but as inferior as she was to every girl he had been with, as inferior as she was to every girl he would ever have a desire to be with, a feeling was coming over him. As the friction increased, underneath his zipper became rigid. He had last copulated three days prior, an eternity for someone with his prowess.

"Let's go in the back" said Lucinda.

"I'm willing, but I'm not sure I want to take the risks." Lucinda rubbed harder, so hard her right hand gripped his hip for leverage. It had the desired effect.

She led him past the din and the darkness. Again he heard the rats stirring beneath the brick and the mortar. She led him to a corner of the building that received some sunlight from cracks in the wall adjacent to the street.

She kneeled in front of Rollo, unbuckled his belt, unbuttoned his jeans, pulled down his zipper, tugged his shorts and placed a condom on the mass of flesh and muscle she had trouble taking her eyes off of.

Rollo was accustomed to using condoms only when he was going to stick it in, but considering where he was and who she was, he wished Lucinda had a surgical tent instead.

She cupped his left cheek with her right hand. Her left hand gripped the shaft; her lips now had a steady target. Her aim wasn't affected by consuming drugs; neither was her technique.

The blood surged between his legs. He was in a building resembling one bombed by the Allies in World War II, had a crack whore kneeling before him attempting to satisfy him, and he wasn't dreaming. Was there a logical reason for this situation?

As Rollo tilted his head back, he felt Lucinda gently release his buttock. He opened his eyes and saw her right hand move toward the jeans on the ground. Then her hand was in his pocket. She was moving something toward her cut-off's pocket until his Avia tennis shoe, moving as if it had wings, struck her wrist so hard the currency flew through the air and the tennis shoe landed against her face.

Tears flew from Lucinda's eyes. Blood seeped out from her face. "I need the money!"

Rollo picked up his briefs and his jeans. "Cash isn't going to solve your problem."

"Fuck you."

"You couldn't even finish what you started here. And you know something? You're not going to get the opportunity to sleep with me, and you may not live long enough to sleep alone tonight."

"I'll live longer than you think. There are other guys who want me."

"Yeah that's why you're on the streets of Hunts Point ready to put out, because other guys *want* you."

Tears were streaming from your eyes.

"The truth does that, huh?" asked Rollo. He gripped her chin and turned her head to where he could see the scratches. He shook his head. He shouldn't have been violent; he had let emotion get the better of reason. She needed a tetanus shot. He picked up the five dollar bill and crumpled it into a ball, ready to toss it to her, but at the last second, his fingers gripped the cash tighter. If he gave her the money, she wouldn't use it for a shot. He placed the crumpled bill in his pocket and stepped over a pile of bricks. She was sobbing on her knees as he left. He found it odd nobody came to her aid. Dodging liquor bottles as if they were land mines, he ducked under the car hood, scampered up the littered steps and returned to the sidewalk wondering which were more dangerous - the four-legged rats he hadn't seen or the two-legged ones he had.

A black girl who had been on the couch with Lucinda was returning to the crack house. "What's up?"

"Getting out of here is what's up," said Rollo. "You better go see about your friend Lucinda."

"Who fuckin' cares about that stink ho?"

Rollo looked at the girl as if she preached blasphemy. "Isn't that your homegirl."

"You could've iced the bitch. Nobody would have been upset."

"Not even her sister?"

"She might have thanked you the most. Everytime Lucinda comes home deranged, she has to deal with it. It's taken its toll."

"But she's on crack, too." It felt bizarre to be more concerned about Lucinda than her sister and a friend.

"Remember you saw her sister handling the pail. She's not totally out there' yet."

"I see." A trapist monk's existence seemed saner.

"Where are you going?"

"Home."

"Let me go with you?"

Rollo shook his head.

She placed her hand on his wrist. "Look. I'm a sister. I'll be nice to you. I won't try to get over."

Rollo removed her hand. "Hey! Don't run no ethnic pride crap on me. Anyway, how do you know Lucinda tried to get over?"

She smiled. "I saw her take you to the corner. I know what goes on there. If she had done you right, you wouldn't be out here now."

The girl was astute; quite an accomplishment when he considered her condition. He looked her over. Her skin was toffee colored and she had a little more meat on her bones than Lucinda. She was being straight forward and not giving a phony rap; and his apartment needed straightening; she could clean his flat if she couldn't finish what Lucinda had started. Last he heard, monks did socialize. He touched her back with the palm of his hand, directed her toward the Puegot, and they were off.

It was still early morning and the Puegot was traveling in the opposite direction of what would become rush hour traffic. The highway's open space and the safety of his own car made the crackhouse seem unreal — except he knew there were many such crack houses throughout the entire New York Metropolis.

"What's your name?" Rollo asked.

"Tasha. It's short for Notasha."

Rollo smiled. "Your parents were looking at Rocky & Bullwinkle when you were born?"

"Yeah. My mother had me a week after my father was shot being mistook for someone else."

"I'm sorry."

"You didn't know. He lived as a vegetable for two and a half years before it was over."

"Your mother must have had a rough time raising you."

"Along with my two brothers and two sisters."

"Ooh brutal." Rollo wondered what was prompting him to think of Tasha as a nun. She had an unseemly upbringing, yet seemed sincere.

The Puegot pulled into Rollo's apartment complex. "Ooh, you can see the Palisades," Tasha said.

"I chose to live here. I didn't create the view," Rollo said, but his view of the massive, wooded cliffs sure beat the hell out of Hunts Point crackhouses. He showed her the indoor pool and the rec room.

"Damn. Wish I had my bathing suit. Can I skinny dip?"

"No!"

They went inside.

"This is pretty clean for a bachelor's crib."

Notasha thinking the flat clean brought a smile to Rollo's face, but his smile disappeared when he remembered what she was comparing it to. He showed her around, taking her into the kitchen first. She opened cabinet doors and the refrigerator. "Corn beef, Rice-a-Roni, onions. Look, you even got French bread! I'll cook us lunch," she said.

"Sure. Anytime you offer a bachelor food, especially having it cooked for you, you don't turn it down."

As they went back into the living room, Tasha gazed out the window. "You ever think of painting the cliffs?"

"I'm a song writer, not a painter."

"You wrote any songs about it?"

"I don't find it as inspirational as you."

Tasha frowned. "Where's your bathroom? Can I take a bath?"

"A shower," said Rollo. "I don't have a plug for the drain."

29

"Why don't you get one?"

"Why should I? This way every time a girl keeps me company, I can ask if we can take a shower together."

"I take it that was your way of asking me?"

"I don't like repeating myself."

"You can scratch my back."

"You can't scratch mine."

He did scratch her back. He was glad it was clean to begin with. When they were done, too tired for any physical exertion, Rollo opened the sofabed, they lay down and slept. When he awoke a few hours later, Rollo went straight to the phone, called Oasis and asked him to put his name on the late list so he could arrive at the ballpark one hour before the game instead of three. "What's making you late all of a sudden?"

"I have a dubious young lady keeping me company and I want to make the most of it."

"Yo Rollo. She has any girlfriends?"

"None you'd want to meet, Oasis." Another faithful husband, thought Rollo, hanging up.

He was putting on his bathing suit when Tasha awoke. "What are you doing?"

"What does it look like I'm doing?"

"You're going swimming now?"

"I got to get in my exercise."

"You got to go swimming for that?" She wiggled her hips suggestively.

"Swimming will make that more enjoyable."

"What am I going to do in the meantime?"

"Take some of my magazines. Sit down by the pool. If you don't socialize with my neighbors, you can read. You can read, can't you?"

"Of course. Why do you ask?"

"Now-a-days you can't be too sure. You that crackhouse's resident scholar?"

"I wouldn't go that far, but I'm no functional illiterate."

"Good. You ever heard the smarter you are the better lover you are?"

"Who told you that?"

"I heard it on a T.V. Quiz Game Show. Let's go," said Rollo.

Swimming had worked up his appetite. Being on crack and not having eaten a real meal lately also increased Tasha's cravings. She mixed together onions, Rice-A-Roni and corn beef hash in a skillet, buttered the French bread and toasted it. As the food cooked, Rollo fondled her breasts through the t-shirt he let her wear.

When the food was ready, they sat down to eat. Rollo ate slowly. It was delicious. She must have learned how to cook before going on crack. He looked at Tasha. "You're gobbling down your food as if it were going to spread wings and fly! How long has it been since you've eaten?"

"Four days," she said, in between gulps.

"You shouldn't be eating solid food then, much less devouring it. You're going to puke up corn beef hash and Rice-A-Roni on my carpet."

"If I do, I'll lap it up as fast as I ate it."

"You'd still leave crumbs. I'd have to call a carpet cleaning service."

"You're sick. You wouldn't call a doctor?"

"You might be beyond what remedies they can offer."

"You'd cast me off that easily?"

"You don't think you've already done that, smoking crack?" Rollo bit into a piece of French bread.

They stared at each other.

"Where'd you learn to cook like that?"

"My mother and an aunt taught me."

"Why don't you learn how to be a chef? Don't you think that's better than what you're doing now?"

"Too time consuming. Where am I going to get the money for that?"

"If you keep doing what you're doing now, how long are you going to have time to consume?"

Tasha chewed slower as she resumed eating. She hadn't put much food on her plate and over half of it remained on her plate when she pushed it aside.

"Satisfied already?" asked Rollo.

"You don't eat too much when you're like me," said Tasha.

"How much weight have you lost since you started doing crack?"

"I lost more than twenty-five pounds in the first six weeks. Since then I've leveled off."

"If only you could get a patent."

"What'd you say?"

"Nothing."

She watched Rollo finish eating. "You want what's left on my plate?" she asked. He shook his head. She got up and moved toward his garbage pail.

"Don't throw it out." Rollo said.

"You don't want it, right?"

"Wrap it in plastic. I'll give it to my neighbor for her dog."

"What if her dog becomes emaciated?"

"I'll tell her to take her dog for a walk by your crackhouse, have him go inside and have a feast. He'll have a choice of lean meat or bones and he won't be skinny anymore. He'll have performed a great public service, and then she can donate his body to science to study the effects of massive consumption of addictive drugs in a short time."

"Who's the real beast, you or your neighbor's canine?"

"Who deserves to be caged. You and your fellow crack addicts or my neighbor's Doberman?"

"It's a toss-up, huh?"

"I don't think so. The Doberman, if it's well trained, only attacks people looking to harm its owner. Crackhead men mug people, and the women'll fuck a skunk if it'll get them the next fix."

She took a deep breath and wrapped the leftovers, threw them inside the refrigerator, then she and Rollo went to the bedroom where she finished what Lucinda had started. When they were done, she asked, "Was I good?"

"Not bad. I've had better."

"Give me twenty dollars. I'll let you stick it in and I'll show you what I can really do."

"You crazy? I'm going to give you a Jackson head so you can

go kill yourself slowly? I ought to smack you upside the head. Knock some sense into that drug-ravaged brain."

"Forget I asked. Can I watch some tube?"

Rollo tossed her the remote control. "Go ahead. Pump some buttons."

"It's too late to catch any soaps. Cartoons are showing." Tasha stopped switching channels when she saw a Bugs Bunny cartoon. "Ooh, Bunny Hugged."

"Not this one," said Rollo.

"What's the matter? This is funny."

"They show it all the time at my job."

"Well can I look at it now?"

"No."

She grabbed what she wanted him to stick inside her and began stroking. "Pretty please, can I look at it?" She stroked faster.

"Yeah," said Rollo. "Go ahead. The longer you stay here, the longer before you return to that hellhole."

"You want me to move in?"

"The minute that cartoon is over, you put on your clothes. I'll drop you off on the way to work."

"Can I have your phone number?"

"No way, I'd be signing my own arrest warrant."

"Why do you say that?"

"The minute you're arrested or die from crack the cops are going to go through your personal effects. If they find my number, I might as well be history."

Tasha was stroking even faster than before.

"Just passing through, just passing through," said the Crusher as Bugs Bunny inflicted a blow to his adversary, causing a huge pump to grow on the Crusher's bald head.

33

CHAPTER IV

THE DAYS AFTER

Brad Brown was munching on a barbecue chicken wing when Rollo entered the rightfield commissary. Rollo considered Brad Brown a lucky man. Brad Brown had retired from bachelor life more than three seasons ago to marry the mother of his baby girl. They lived in Montclair, New Jersey, with a recent addition to their family - a baby boy. The additional bundle of joy compelled Brad Brown to work a fourth job to maintain his standard of living. Besides Yankee Stadium, he worked at Shea Stadium and Madison Square Garden as a security guard and was a lab technician at Roosevelt Hospital. Rollo sensed the family man wasn't elated working four jobs. As a bachelor he had been a 'party animal' and very popular with the ladies. Since Brad's marriage, Rollo had heard him complain about his social life being curtailed and his spouse always having her hands out, but Rollo figured there were advantages to his marriage. After all, he wasn't dealing with a Lucinda nor a Tasha, and though he might be working many late nights now, he did have someone to run home to.

Brad finished eating, threw the chicken bones in the garbage can, walked to the front of the commissary and looked at the assignments on Simeon's table. He banged his fist on the table. "Damn, what do I gotta do to get beer?"

"Kill a few people," said Oasis, who got the last beer spot.

"Don't tempt me."

"Relax. You can make money on hot dogs," Oasis patted Brad Brown on the back.

"Not as much as you'll make."

34

"Probably more than anybody besides me in the commissary," said Oasis.

"Why should you be excluded?"

"Because I got four kids to feed."

"I haven't kept pace with you there, but that doesn't entitle you to earn more," Brad Brown said.

"I know. We could both use more money. The question is where we going to get it?" Oasis asked.

Oasis made a hundred-fifty mile round trip to work at Yankee Stadium; was a top producer amongst vendors, but the income from two jobs didn't make ends meet. Married with four daughters, he often complained if it wasn't for the money he earned at the Stadium, he didn't know where his family would be. This despite being a State Correction Officer. He played every lotto and numbers game he could; he was waiting for the digits that would make his daughters childhood more fun than the poverty he was struggling to avoid. The odds of Kelso's business plan working were better than Oasis hitting the lottery, but still Oasis had doubts.

Even on days when Oasis sold the most beer trays, gas, tolls and the expense of raising four daughters made a C note or two disappear fast. He didn't know what he could legally do about it. He was tempted to do something illegal; he thought of the moral fortitude a correction officer was supposed to have and the example he was supposed to set for his daughters. He told himself Kelso's plan couldn't be too bitter if he was considering illegal activities.

Brad Brown smacked Oasis's bicep and smiled. Brad Brown knew how to earn extra income. He was too proficient at it. He had almost been fired twice for embezzling funds he was supposed to pay bankers. But his smile was short lived. Reality struck. "Kelso's plan better come off. This four jobs shit is whacked. Make more money and no time to enjoy it. There's got to be a better way." He went to get his frank bin as Rollo walked through the commissary door.

"How'd it go with the dubious young lady?" Oasis asked Rollo.

"I made the most of it."

"What do you think of Kelso's plan?" Oasis asked. He was more skeptical than Brad Brown.

35

"It has its merits. It has its faults," said Rollo. "As despised as he is, Kelso's a proven entrepreneur. He's already taken lemons and made lemonade."

"True. But whatever he's planning, it's drastically different from his real estate deals, his car dealership and limousine service."

"What's the big deal? If Kelso's proposal works, it'll make us wealthy."

"I could live with that. Even with this and a Correction Officer's salary, it isn't easy to finance my daughters' college fund," Oasis said.

"How can you have such doubts? If Kelso's plan works, you stand to benefit the most," said Rollo.

"If it backfires, I'll also get hurt the most."

Oasis had a burning desire to find the means to harness into ever-lasting prosperity - or at least affluence for him, his wife and his daughters.

He gave Uranso and Errol the most subway. He kicked back fourteen percent of his gross commission to Uranso and Errol. If they didn't get subway, they made up the beer trays slower, undercooked the hot dogs and the machines mysteriously broke down more frequently.

Maybe Rollo was right. He ought to take Kelso's plan seriously. Maybe it provided the opportunity to be more than an expensive wage slave.

She sat between her father and younger brother, in Section 22, Row D, Seat 5, looking like a red-skinned Mona Lisa. Her jet black hair, as lustrous as a silent, cascading waterfall, fell straight down to her waist. Her dark brown eyes and smile invited the kind of attention reserved for the original Mona Lisa. Heads seemed riveted to their shoulders at one hundred eighty degree angles as they looked at her while walking by.

She paid no attention. Keeping her eyes on batting practice — the flights, paths and trajectories of the batted balls and the players in tight knit pants chasing them - she turned and spoke to either her father or brother when she tired of watching.

As Rollo got closer, he could see her beauty was a gift beyond her years. Serious involvement with her could lead to being arrested, convicted and worse, as in inmates wanting to tear him apart. He thought of how good freedom was. To come and go as he pleased despite the recent undesirable outcomes with Lisbeth and Lucinda. And he knew he wouldn't find any potential soulmates to his liking in jail. The red-skinned Mona Lisa would have to wait for someone else to approach her - it wouldn't take long.

Rollo finished selling his first tray and returned to the commissary. Oasis came in behind him.

Brad Brown, Lenny Mo Dinner, Slow Dee and Rod Somer were already there. Uranso was munching beef jerky as he prepared a beer tray.

"You checked out that girl near the auxiliary scoreboard? The one with her father and brother?" Oasis asked Rollo as he put down his empty tray.

Rollo nodded.

"She's fine," said Oasis. "Eighteen or nineteen, wouldn't you say?"

"I'd look again if I was you," Rollo said.

After sealing the cups with plastic wrap, Uranso handed Oasis a full tray.

"I'm going to go rap to her."

"You're asking for trouble," said Rollo.

"You're going to tell my wife?"

"You're missing the point. Nobody has to tell your wife anything. You want to end up behind bars? Lose that correction officer job? Have those inmates you've been guarding sticking you up the ass? That girl is no eighteen or nineteen. She's jailbait."

"You kidding!"

"It's awfully hard to support a family behind bars."

"You really don't believe that girl is eighteen or nineteen?"

"Go on. Talk to her," said Rollo.

"Will you two shut up. How you expect me to check cards while you're making noise?" asked Simeon.

"Hey, they're screaming and yelling out there. What do you think this is, a library?" asked Rollo.

"Keep bugging me and you're going to think it's a soup kitchen line when it's time to check out."

Oasis picked up a beer tray but hesitated by the door. He loved his wife and had been faithful, so he was no longer skilled at picking up girls. "Is she Puerto Rican, Dominican or Panamian?"

"What difference does that make if you get her to spread her legs for you?"

"None. Still, it doesn't hurt to know."

"She looks Guyanese, Venezuelan or Caymanese."

"They have contract marriages in Guyana, right?"

"I'm not sure. Why, you ready to marry her already?"

"I just wanted to know. Perhaps you're right."

Rollo had done his commendable deed for the day. He was so proud of Oasis refraining from approaching the young girl, he decided he would.

"I'll ask her how old she is when I go back out," said Rollo, picking up a fresh tray.

When Rollo got back out to the row where the girl and her brother were, her father had left momentarily. He had to think fast. If her father returned, daddy wouldn't take too kindly to someone approaching his daughter. "I see you're here with your brother and father getting ready to enjoy the game."

The girl gave Rollo a look between a smile and skepticism.

"You enjoying yourself so far?"

The smile part of the look appeared to be gaining control. "Yes."

"You're older than your brother?"

She nodded.

"And how old are you?"

The smile left her face. "Why do you ask?"

He smiled, knelt down. "You see I'm selling beer. And though you don't look like the type, you might ask me for a beer."

She gave Rollo a look that, said - that's a good story. "Sixteen," she said.

"Thank you. You and your family enjoy the game." Rollo arose.

"Damn, Rollo! You cradlesnatcher!" Brad Brown yelled.

Rollo finished selling his tray and returned to the commissary with Brad Brown. Oasis was already inside. Rollo shook his head. "Sixteen, Oasis." He turned to Brad Brown. "Oasis thought she was eighteen or nineteen."

"Oasis, you crazy?"

Oasis lowered his head.

"What's come over you? You been looking at girls too long or what?" Brad Brown said.

"He's been looking at his own daughters too long," Rollo said.

"All right, that's it!" said Simeon. "Beer men stop selling. And you can't leave until I've checked everyone else out."

"You're going to punish us for expressing ourselves? You know damn well beer men are supposed to check out first! Your going to keep us here until peanut and pretzel guys check out?" asked Oasis.

"You darn right. You heard me."

"How'd a low life like you get this job?" Oasis yelled.

"Never you mind. You're looking up to me now - right?"

"I ain't gonna look at you at all for a while."

Oasis, Rollo and Brad Brown walked outside. The Detroit Tigers were winning two to one in the middle of the second inning.

Rollo grinned. "Oasis, if you're having trouble noticing jailbait, maybe you're making too snap a judgement about Kelso's plan."

"Fuck that. I'm down with Kelso's plan," said Brad Brown. "We just listened to that narrow minded fuck talk to us as if we were younger than that girl. We're men. And I'm sick and tired of letting things happen, I want to make it happen. I'm gonna go kick his ass!" Brad Brown turned toward the commissary.

"Don't do that," said Rollo. "Yes. Simeon is a narrow minded bastard. But what would going back there and firing him up accomplish. You'd get fired. He could press charges and even though you'd feel good kicking his ass, you'd be giving him the satisfaction of knowing what he does and how he acts controls you. That's just the kind of satisfaction a narrow minded bastard covets."

"Cool. Cool. I'll chill until Kelso's meeting." Brad Brown uncocked his fists and shook Rollo's hand.

"You guys are right. I'll attend Kelso's meeting and see what's going on," said Oasis. "If his proposal works as well as it's been hyped, that's the better way to kick Simeon's ass: make more money than he'll ever know what to do with and deprive him of it.

Besides, Kelso's gotten the renegade to loan us his club. If he can do that, there has to be something to whatever he's put together."

CHAPTER V

KELSO

It was the weekend following Simeon's outburst. Close to a score of the men were seated in the basement of the renegade's club. Kelso was seated at the bar, his leather attache case laid open on the forty feet long, two and a half feet wide bar. He grabbed a copy of his business proposal and started reading. Lenny Mo Dinner, Oasis, Brad Brown, Rod Somer and Andy Metzger, seated in chairs on the dance floor, took Kelso's hint and opened his business proposal while they waited for Copperblum, Rollo, Mordecai Kaplan, Iggy Biggy, Ben Feldstein, Errol, and Uranso to arrive.

Terence Kelso swore he had the answers to everyone's problems. Yet, there had only been one person who loved Kelso and whom he had genuinely loved: his father, Edgar Kelso.

Edgar Kelso had believed in the American notion of honesty and fair play, teamwork and respect for your fellow man. Belief in these notions led to his death. Two men came into his delicatessen, displayed .44 magnums, took fifteen hundred dollars out of the cash register and, as they were leaving, shot him. The wound was so severe he lost part of his shoulder socket. The limb resembled an inverted empty lobster shell, after the operation to repair it. The robbers were caught. Edgar Kelso's family thought justice would be done. They thought wrong. The case was thrown out of court on a legal technicality: the gun that wounded Edgar Kelso had been confiscated by the police without a search warrant. Edgar Kelso still believed in America.

Three years later Edgar Kelso suffered a hairline fracture of his right leg when it smashed through the wooden staircase of a Bronx apartment building he was considering purchasing. He sued the building's owner for medical expenses beyond what his insurance company would pay. He didn't collect anything. The arbitration board found the building owner wasn't at fault. The building had been inspected and met all specifications. The building inspector was found at fault for allowing the building to pass inspection in spite of substandard grade materials. Edgar sued the city, but the case dragged on so long, the statue of limitations expired leaving Edgar no legal recourse. Besides the hairline fracture there was internal bleeding. To prevent his right leg from being amputated there was $75,000 in out of pocket expenses. This for a man with a wife and two boys and a girl to provide for. Edgar Kelso still believed in America. Terence Kelso, now eleven years old, still loved his father, but the seed of doubt had been placed in his mind about the American way.

Four years after recuperating, Edgar Kelso invested in Pocono Mountain time shares. He didn't own the real estate outright. His contract with a Florida based real estate syndicate stated he could buy the property outright if he turned a $100,000 profit in nine months. Edgar's units turned a $75,000 profit in six months. He was well on his way to exceeding the contract stipulation, until the syndicate spread a rumor that whooping cough was being contracted in Kelso's time shares.

A local media blitz by radio, print and television journalists wiped out Edgar Kelso's customer base, and the syndicate sold the property to a casino conglomerate for far greater money than Edgar could raise.

Edgar suffered a massive heart attack. Summoned to his father's deathbed, Terence, now almost sixteen, looked at the tubes, needles and monitors helping him cling to life. His father resembled a withered Frankenstein, his body sapped of the vitality and robust cheerfulness Terence had seen him repeatedly display despite honesty and fair play jerking him around. With what little strength remained, Edgar summoned his children to his side, one by one. Terence was the last to approach. "Don't worry about me," his father said faintly. "You be honest, play by the book and look out for your mother."

Terence squeezed his father's arm.

Before daylight, he died.

After his father's funeral, Terence loved his father more than

41

ever. Yet, he thought him a fool to cling blindly to the notion of honesty, fair play and high minded American ideals as potent tools for an improved way of life. These notions had led to his father's death.

Well, if Edgar Kelso was a fool, his son wasn't. Young Kelso vowed he'd never work for anybody. If there was going to be any deceit, trickery or lies, he was going to be the perpetrator instead of the victim. Me first became a commitment. Whatever it took to succeed became a credo. Honesty and fair play meant as much to him as a desert does to a whale. He thought not only that the ends justified the means, but that there were no means. This philosophy served him well enough that he was able to buy his mother a retirement home in Naples, Florida, by the time he was twentyfour. His mother, on minimum subsistence most of her life, was grateful. She never questioned how Terence got the money to buy the home and send her four thousand dollars per month expense money.

Kelso, waiting for the stragglers, closed his attache case and sucked his teeth. Figuring out schemes and scams never fazed Kelso. It was his greatest attribute. It was what made people consider what he had to say before they hated him. His best scam to date had made certain schoolchildren and teenagers tolerate him and law enforcement officials want to hang him by his testicles. It was so simple and insidious that it was still generating a lucrative daily income two and a half years after its inception in spite of numerous legal battles to stop it.

Three years ago during Spring Break in a hotel room in Miami, he screwed a young co-ed he picked up on the beach. After they had orgasms and were relaxing, she opened her pocketbook and pulled out a plastic bag containing white powder, which she put on the tip of her index finger, and snorted into her nostril. "You want any?" she asked.

"You mean more of you or the white powder?" responded Kelso.

"The white powder."

Kelso took the bag, stuck in his index and middle fingers, put them under his nostrils and snorted. "This is the best I've ever had."

The co-ed smiled. "Me or the white powder?"

"What do you think I meant? Can you get me some to take to New York?"

"You can get it yourself, you silly idiot." She laughed and rubbed her back against the bed's headboard, keeping her eyes on Kelso.

"How would I do that?"

"Go to a drug store, buy some Niacin, some lactose and pungent complex Brewer Yeast. Take it home, mix the Niacin and lactose in equal portions, cut them with a quarter as much yeast, and you can have the same thing."

"Then we're not really getting high on this?" Kelso licked the substance off his fingertips.

"Of course not. This just shows getting high is as much psychological as physiological."

"So, this isn't what I thought it was?"

"That's right."

"How'd you learn to make it?"

"I'm a bio chemistry major. I got the Niacin and lactose from my classes. The brewers yeast I got from a health food store."

"How does this work?" Kelso reached into the plastic bag.

"Niacin is used to cut genuine coke and helps prevent pellagra. That eliminates the serious disturbance of the nervous system. The lactose when mixed with the brewer yeast gives it its powdery crystalline texture. It's enough to fool all but the most addicted coke fiends."

A strange look came over Kelso.

"Had you fooled, huh? I just snort it for the goof. To see how people react when they snort it."

Kelso looked at the co-ed. He felt a tranquil buzz, as if feathers were stimulating his skin. Then a mesmerizing electrical surge traveled to his brain. He felt like he was levitating. "Ooh, baby. You just gave me music for my ears."

He placed the bag on the co-ed's thigh, grabbed his underwear and jeans, put them on, grabbed his socks and sneakers, and with his free hand, ran his fingers through the co-ed's curly hair. "See you soon, honey."

"Can you give me cabfare?"

43

"Honey, your friends are still down on the beach? And they've got boyfriends who have cars?"

"Get lost! You won't be seeing me anytime soon," the co-ed screamed.

Kelso closed the door and moved toward the elevator. He might not have cemented a friendship, but money not used for cab-fare could go toward the purchase of the mixture's ingredients. He smiled.

As soon as he got back to New York, he went to a neighborhood pharmacy, bought Niacin, Lactose and pungent Complex Brewer's Yeast, took the ingredients home, mixed them as the co-ed had instructed and invited friends to his apartment to sample. The friends said they never felt better. They wanted more. Kelso smiled. He let his friends take home three ounces each. He let them continue thinking the mixture was what they thought it was. There were so many phone calls he seriously considered starting a 900 number: 1(900) T-A-S-T-E-I-T.

The next day he went to schoolyards throughout the Bronx and Upper Manhattan and gave schoolchildren samples. They liked it. If they wanted more, he asked an exorbitant price. When they couldn't pay him, he asked if they wanted to distribute. Almost all agreed. He told them they could keep fifty percent. They wouldn't have to bother their parents for spending money or work as peons in fast food restaurants. If they could get more than his price, the excess profit was theirs.

Kelso thought of himself as the drug world's Henry Ford. More appropriate would have been the drug world's Santa Claus. He was letting schoolchildren think they were big time drug pushers, when all they were were deceit mongers.

When arrests did occur, he secured a lawyer who proved the children were selling a non-narcotic, non-hazardous substance. Not one child was convicted. At first mad at having been duped, the disgruntled distributors spread the word about the imitation Cocaine. There was a slight decrease in sales while the distributors pondered whether to continue working for him, but it made no sense to forgo a higher weekly income than their parents - combined. When the trials ended, they returned to 'Uncle Kelso's Network', quelled the imitation cocaine

44

rumors by claiming their lawyer lied to the judge about the drug's ingredients, then they had a half price sale. Soon sales were back to normal.

When one distributor was killed by a crack addict for his money, Kelso hired Savage Service - vicious ruffians renowned for taking action first and asking questions, if any, much later. Savage Service found the murdering crack addict, put a sawed off double barrel shotgun in his mouth and pumped. Then they cut his heart out with a Saigon knife, gave it to their pit bull Romeo for lunch and threw the corpse in the Bronx River.

Kelso's distributors didn't encounter any further piracy attempts. However, as Crack and Ice became more popular, Kelso's profits waned. Thus the new scheme he was suggesting to his Yankee Stadium co-workers today. With his insatiable lust, Kelso was relieved he had thought of it and was determined to make it work.

At last, Rollo and Copperblum entered. Mordecai Kaplan, Iggy Biggy, Ben Feldstein, Errol, and Uranso, who had arrived almost an hour ago, gave them piercing dirty looks.

Kelso looked at the gathering before him. Everyone who had agreed to attend was. His beady brown eyes shifted from face to face. As he rose from the bar stool, his pale cheeks took on a scarlet hue. "Are there any questions regarding my proposal?"

"How are we going to pull this off?" Brad Brown called out, disregarding everyone with a hand raised, including Lenny Mo Dinner, who sat beside him.

"I'm glad you asked that," said Kelso. "We got everything we need at our disposal to make this work."

"How you figure?" Somer asked.

"There are farms near Oasis in Orange County, right? We can get the raw materials from there. We can get all the empty kegs we need from the ballpark. Once we've penetrated the market, we can use Iggy Biggy's six story apartment building for a storage bin and my house as a distribution point upstate."

Lenny Mo raised his hand.

"You have a question, Andy?" Kelso found it strange Andy Metzger, a schoolteacher who vended, hadn't spoken.

"No." Andy Metzger answered like a dominant wild animal demanding to be left alone.

"How'll we get people liking its taste?" Rollo asked.

"We'll tell them they're sampling a new beer, so there'll be no problem getting taste testers. And as long as it's cold and contains alcohol have you ever known anyone to complain about the taste of beer? Copperblum can process the rusults of the survey we'll conduct as a trial balloon."

"Who's going to be our brewery master, make the beer for us?" Copperblum asked.

"Uranso and Errol always make us lemonade and whatever else we need to pull us through a game. Why don't we let them make it?"

Heads nodded.

"You can get 190 proof grain alcohol, Uranso?"

"Positive vibration, wayo," said Uranso.

"Does that mean yes?" Kelso asked.

"It don't mean no, mon."

"Who's going to provide the other key ingredient?" Errol asked.

"Didn't I say Oasis lives near farms upstate?"

Errol nodded.

"And on farms usually you can find horses, right?"

"Yeah," said Errol.

"So we let Oasis go to the farms, speak to the farmers about providing us with what's needed from the horses, and once he gets it, he brings it down here for us."

"What makes you so sure farmers are going to give it to me? I'm not into conversing with Rednecks."

"Tell 'em you need it for your daughter's biology project in school. Farmers believe in civic unity and pride."

"What if I have a problem asking them, or just doing this whole damn thing period? What you're thinking of is mind boggling. It's scuzzy, trifling and disgusting. I don't know if I want to stoop so low just to make more money."

Kelso's scarlet hue became more noticeable. He pointed his index finger at Oasis: "Aren't you the one who constantly tells me, 'I want the best for my daughters: the best clothes, the best education, the quality of life', and all that other nice noble stuff. Well let me ask you a question pal. Are you going to be able to do the things you'd like to do for your daughters if you keep running around that ballpark like a jackrabbit, selling beer like your life depended on it? Can your family afford your being a 'Pillar of Morality'?" Kelso paused to let it sink in.

"Can I take someone with me?" Oasis asked. He didn't like the idea of approaching redneck farmers alone.

"Why not? Who amongst us wouldn't want to go for a nice ride in the country? And a very profitable one, at that."

"That remains to be seen, but speaking of profits, how are we going to divide those?" Errol asked.

Kelso put his palms together and rubbed. "Now we're talking real business. Everyone who's in and pulls his fair share is entitled to an equal share in the profits. Oasis, Iggy Biggy and myself'll get expense accounts since we'll be storing and transporting the merchandise."

"Ay mon. What about me? I'm going to be purchasing dee grain alcohol?" Uranso asked.

"You'll get reimbursed and anyone who incurs expenses will be reimbursed. As long as it's legit."

"This whole thing doesn't sound legit," said Mordecai Kaplan, a court officer who also vended.

"Remember, only in America. Now, are there any other questions?" Kelso's beady brown eyes scanned the assembly. "Great." Kelso said, "Now I figure we can be in production in two weeks. Oasis, Feldstein, Uranso, Errol, Somer and Copperblum, stick around. Everyone else can leave. And remember — not a word of this to management." Everyone got out of their seats.

When he thought they were gone, Kelso said, "Oasis, you go to the farmers with Rod Somer. The farmers won't be scared of seeing a Black man if there's a white one along. Uranso, Errol, your commissary'll process the brew and distribute it first. Copperblum, you put together a standard contract for everyone who's participating."

"Remember, I'm no expert at speaking to rednecks," said Oasis.

"Whatever you can't get across, I'm sure Somer'll relate quite well."

"It might take me longer dan two weeks to get my equipment installed, mon," said Uranso.

"You want to supplement your subway faster than that, don't you?" asked Kelso.

"Forget about supplementing subway. I woont to buy beachfront property in Jamaica."

"Then getting the equipment installed in two weeks should be no problem. In fact, I don't see why you can't do it in two days."

"Look Kelso. I just can't bring equipment in so everybody see. Have to be discreet, mon."

"Should I put a lot of legalese in the contract?" asked Copperblum.

"Make it simple enough for Lenny Mo to understand," said Kelso. "Any more questions?"

Lenny Mo Dinner raised his hand.

"How're you going to handle the renegade?" Rod Somer asked.

"We're using his club, aren't we? If he's making money here, this could be an excellent spot to taste consumer response beyond the Stadium."

"Where is he now?" Iggy Biggy asked.

"Maybe Beezer's seeing a mother of one of his children," said Kelso. "Leave him to me. I know how to handle him."

"Are you sure? I don't want him going off, acting wild and belligerent. He'll end up telling someone who shouldn't know," said Mordecai Kaplan.

"Relax. You don't know Beezer as well as I do." Kelso said.

"Forget the renegade," said Ben Feldstein. "He may be wild, but he knows a good business deal when he sees one. He's making money with this hole in the wall. The more pressing question is what're you going to do about Simeon?"

"Yeah, Simeon'd rat on us in a second," said Rod Somer. "He's bound to sense something fishy going down. He'd love to nail us."

"Yeah, him and that sneaky college kid of his," said Rollo.

"What's to keep him from finding out?" Copperblum asked.

"We're not going to move into his commissary immediately. When we do, we'll know at least two things: whether our creation has captured market share in the seats covering third base and leftfield.

And, how to keep our secret from Simeon," Kelso replied.

"Let's take care of the former before we start worrying about the latter," said Brad Brown.

Lenny Mo Dinner was frantically waving his hands.

The renegade's club emptied.

Rollo and Copperblum walked toward Copperblum's Nissan Stanza lugging their copies of Kelso's business proposal. "Is he off his rocker or does he think we're as mad as he is?" Copperblum shook the proposal as if he were holding a dangerous reptile.

"He's not off his rocker. His proposal can work," said Rollo.

"You agree with him?"

"Heaven forbid, but if you tell people something in a certain way, they'll believe it, no matter how incredible it sounds. Remember what Hitler and Goebbels did in Nazi Germany? What Orson Welles did with 'The War of the Worlds'?"

Copperblum nodded.

"Well then, in light of that, does Kelso's plan seem ludicrous?"

"Well, I do see it taking place everyday in more sophisticated forms. Sodas that rot your teeth become elixirs when endorsed by rock stars and athletes. Fast food commercials shown as music videos turn junk food into gourmet cuisine. Whatever's on t.v. is accepted as gospel."

"What we're planning to sell is as American as that stuff food conglomerates and mass media hype, right?"

"I don't think patriotism has anything to do with this."

Rollo smiled. "We're just as capitalistic as everyone else using more sophisticated methods."

"I agree," said Copperblum. "And we're as entitled to the pursuit of happiness as anyone else; so unfortunately, as much as I despise Kelso, as much as you despise Kelso, as much as everyone he gave this paper to despises Kelso, what he proposes can make us wealthy."

"See. He isn't mad and neither are we."

As Kelso left the meeting, Lenny Mo Dinner followed him across the street to Yankee Stadium. As they neared the leftfield gate, Lenny Mo patted Kelso on the back. "Hey, hey, Kelso you know I love your plan. You can count me in no matter what. Just tell me what you want me to do and I'll do it, kid. But I got to ask - you saw my hand raised. Why didn't you call on me?"

Kelso took his long arm and embraced Lenny Mo Dinner. "Do you think I or anyone else wanted to hear what you had to say?" Lenny Mo Dinner's mouth dropped open. "Shut up and stop making a fool of yourself. When the time comes I'll tell you what we have in store for you, Lenny."

"Why can't I be an immediate help? I told you I want in right now. I want to attend fantasy baseball camps with Willie Mays."

"One reason is you're being a nuisance. Another is you kiss too much ass for me to cut you in from day one. Ass kissers don't deserve money until their tongues are completely brown. And I only give 'em enough to clean their tongues. Besides, I have a funny feeling Willie Mays will be waiting whenever you get to a fantasy baseball camp."

They showed their I.D.'s to the Burn's Security Guard.

"Hey. Is that any way to speak to me? You know how I feel about you. You know I always say what's on my mind."

The guard waved them through the steel door.

"When was the last time you were straight forward honest with someone?"

Lenny Mo took off his glasses, wiped them clean on his handkerchief.

"What's the matter Lenny, cat got your tongue? See Lenny. All it'd take is someone belittling you. You'd take it personally. Then in order to feel important you'd say, 'Oh yeah. Well I'm in business with Kelso and we're making beer with bla, bla, bla'. The whole plan, months and months of preparation, would be flushed down the toilet. All because you want in from day one, square one."

"I oughtta ....," Lenny Mo made a fist with his right hand and drew his arm back.

Kelso tapped Lenny Mo's fist. "Now, now, Lenny. Is that anyway to treat someone whose plan you love? At least you're being honest now." He directed Lenny Mo's arm to a nonhostile position. "Lenny, look. Why don't you go to the locker room, change and go watch management's underlings make out the sheets, like you always do. Better still, why don't you go drive your cab? And I'll go change

and find someone I want to go over things with. And when I'm ready
to set you loose, I'll holler for you. Okay?"

"I'm very disappointed in you."

"Lenny, your mother was disappointed when she had you. Your
wife was disappointed after she married you. Practically everyone's
disappointed after they know you. Most people experience disap-
pointment throughout their life, but yours is one colossal disappoint-
ment. Now get lost." Kelso moved past Lenny Mo.

Lenny Mo stood still and watched him go to the locker room.
He still had not moved when Copperblum walked by.

"You auditioning to be one of those cigar store Indian statues
or what?" Copperblum asked.

"Ha, ha, ha. Kelso said my life is a colossal mistake."

"Well, Lenny, if he could find a word describing enormity that
goes beyond colossal, he'd be even more accurate," said Copperblum.

"I don't have to take that from you."

"Then don't. But your like a wind blown flag: you blow
whichever way the wind blows." Lenny back pedaled two steps. "I
see your moving now. It'll be harder when they come get you."

"When who come gets me?"

"The guys in the white coats. They're going to put you in
Cooperstown, Lenny."

"I think I belong in Cooperstown. Look at all I've done for vending. I played stickball with Willie Mays!"

"You'll get to Cooperstown Lenny," Copperblum tapped him on
the shoulder. "If there's a sanitarium up there, you'll fit in just fine."

Lenny Mo pushed Copperblum's hand away and went to the
locker room. He took off his civilian clothes and put on his vending
uniform. For someone approaching fifty he had the physique of a
thirty-five year old who exercised everyday. People were often surprised by his strength and athleticism. Once he sold ninety trays of
beer during one doubleheader. But as much brawn as he had been
blessed with, he was equally cursed by a lack of intelligence. He did
have a brain. He rarely used it effectively; constantly begging approval
from others.

He closed his locker, locked it, sat down, put on crew socks and
his sneakers, then went to management's office where the assignment

sheets were being prepared, telling each vendor which commissary he would work that day. The office was a combination of a fortress, a lounge for those invited and workstations.

Lenny Mo sat down in the reception area, picked up a copy of PEOPLE magazine lying on the side table and turned its pages while he waited for the vendors' supervisor to finish the assignment sheets. The supervisor noticed him. "Come here, Lenny Mo."

Lenny Mo jumped up as if he were a child seeing his first Christmas toys.

"You want to make call?" asked the supervisor.

"You know I'm always willing to make call."

"You save me the trouble of telling the vendors which commissary they're working out of and what product they're selling."

Today, before performing his daily ritual, Lenny Mo noticed something on the sheets he didn't like. He had rated beer all right, but not in the commissary of his choice. "Why didn't I get behind the plate in the field?" he asked the supervisor.

"You didn't rate it, Lenny Mo."

"But I've been here thirty-six years."

"Chill out. Lenny Mo. You want to sell ice cream or peanuts instead?"

Lenny Mo kept quiet. Then performed his daily ritual. Several union vendors he approached asked, "Still making call, Lenny Mo?"

"I don't mind."

The vendors chuckled or shuck their head. Thirty-six years of vending and he couldn't rate his first choice.

CHAPTER VI

EVELYN GIZZARI

She possessed the beauty of an irresistible seductress and used it strategically to educe its maximum effect. Her figure wasn't quite hourglass, but her legs were taut and supple, the waist as narrow as a baby's, and her breasts though not large were full of vim and did nothing to discourage a man considering looking her way. When she wore high heels and swayed and wiggled, getting what she wanted from the opposite sex was simple.

Her name was Evelyn Gizzari. She was mulatto: half Morroccan, half Palestinian. Since she was in the United States and had to get along with people she loathed, she used her stage name of Didra Diaz to conceal her identity. She pretended to be Argentinian, acted Latin, and reverted to Spanish whenever she wanted to express herself freely. So convincing was she that there had been offers by male admirers to accompany her to Argentina to meet her family, to which she politely refused.

She had had three older brothers: Akbar, Punjab and Romodan who organized P.U.F.F.H.(Palestinians United For a Free Homeland) in Morocco when she was a child. It was a peaceful organization comprised mostly of college students, professionals and business people. They held rallies, raised funds, sent petitions to influential politicians and used other non-violent means to achieve their goal of a free Palestinian Homeland.

The organization was infiltrated by a radical element who thought her brothers' methods were too passive and counterproductive. The radical element resorted to intimidation and acts of terrorism. Evelyn's brothers tried to distance themselves from the extremists, but to no avail - a majority of P.U.F.F.H. wanted swift, immediate action and results. The extremists ignited bombs at Western European and American oil refineries and offices sympathetic to Israel.

The C.I.A. and MOSSAD soon became very interested in P.U.F.F.H. The intelligence organizations' action was swift and immediate. At a meeting between Evelyn's brothers and the P.U.F.F.H. extremist leaders held in a deserted Tangier nightclub, a pipebomb exploded sending everyone inside to meet Allah.

Evelyn was only eight years old when her brothers were murdered; from that moment on, she was no longer sure God existed. If he did, why did he allow her brothers to die? She left her native Morocco at the age of sixteen, dancing in topless bars to make a living, drinking alcoholic beverages and sleeping with what she would have considered infidels before her brothers' death, but she didn't sleep with men who worked for oil companies. Nor did she sleep with men who were reluctant to part with a dollar. When she mingled at the bar between dance sets, if she discovered the man talking to her worked for an oil company or was cheap, she was gone. She just left and danced unemotionally until she found something or someone who could change her expression.

One night the person who changed her expression was Rollo Boyce. A man seated next to Rollo didn't give her a tip, after she gave him her undivided attention for three minutes. Rollo noticed the morbidity where minutes ago there had been near rapture. He dug into his jeans pocket, pulled out two dollars, placed them in Evelyn's palm and said, "What happened? You look like you just saw your worst nightmare come to life."

"I've already lived through my worst nightmare. Unfortunately it was no dream," she said.

"I'd like to hear about it. But obviously you're not in the most conducive position for a meaningful discussion. Join me for a drink when you're done?"

Evelyn nodded and resumed her enticing swaying for an additional twenty minutes.

Beverly's Bustout & Breakthrough, where Evelyn danced, had air conditioning, but she was perspiring when she sat beside Rollo.

He put his index finger on her shoulder and then licked it.

"This is high in sodium. As pretty as you are, I expected it to be sweet."

She ran her fingers through her hair. "Do you always start touching girls when they get next to you?"

He put his palm on her thigh and gently rubbed. "Only when they're as pretty as you. Besides, you wouldn't want me having you think I'm gay, right?"

She placed her hand over his. "Why would you invite me over here if you went that way?"

"Maybe you're fooling me. Maybe I'm convinced you're a chick with a dick."

Evelyn drew back her hand. Rollo grabbed her wrist before she could deliver a blow. "I was only kidding," he said, kissing her hand.

"Don't kid with me like that." She yanked her hand from his grasp. "What made you say something that absurd?"

"I wanted to make sure I captured your attention. That is different from the typical line you hear, right?"

Evelyn's brown doe eyes got wider. "You didn't have to say that. You look good. I'd notice you without you trying to impress me."

"Really?" Rollo smiled. "Then why don't we have lunch tomorrow. Somewhere where we don't have to yell to hear each other?"

"I can't," said Evelyn.

"Why not?"

"I wake up too late for lunch. Let's have dinner?"

"I can't," said Rollo.

"Why not?"

"I work nights."

Evelyn shook her head. "Perhaps it wasn't meant for us to be together."

"I have an idea," said Rollo. He placed his other hand on her thigh and sent both hands exploring. "Let's have a power breakfast?"

"A what?" She crossed her legs. "Honey, by the way what's your name?"

"Rollo."

"Mine is Didra." She extended her hand. Rollo shook it, kissed it and let it go.

"That's not a good name for you. Too homely," said Rollo. "You mind if I call you Didi?"

55

"No, no problem. Anyway Rollo, when I have breakfast, I'm finishing the night."

"What's your real name?"

"Do I have to tell you now?"

"If we're going to meet at a restaurant and you arrive first, I don't think you'll remember to tell the hostess, 'Didi's here,' if I ask for you."

"Evelyn's my real name."

"Great. You want to go to a christening also?"

"We can wait awhile before going to a christening."

Rollo smiled. "I guess I am being presumptuous asking you for a second date right away. So is the day after tomorrow good for breakfast?"

"Where at?" Evelyn asked.

"The Rubicon Diner, that's nice."

"What time?"

"Five A.M., good?"

"Perfect."

"Looking forward to seeing you."

"I'm glad you realized we should make sure we like each other before planning a second date. It does make sense."

"A lot of sense." Rollo's voice was conciliatory. He shouldn't have been anxious. He hoped he hadn't scared her out of the first date.

"Looking forward to having a nice meal." She smiled.

It sounded reassuring.

"I got to get ready for my next set. If your here when I'm done, I'll come back. While I'm gone maybe you should talk to my friend, Severina. Be nice to her. She doesn't have it easy." Severina was standing nearby at the bar. Evelyn motioned her over.

Rollo looked at Severina. She was mulatto also and they bore a slight resemblance, but she was a couple of inches taller than Evelyn. They told men who wanted to indulge in sister fantasies they were sisters. Her breasts swelled like grapefruits. Her waist, though flat, didn't show any muscle definition and her legs, though attractive, had traces of cellulite. She was attractive, but he didn't see any reason to give up rapping to Evelyn. "You'd trust me with a girl this gorgeous?"

"Oh, I think I can." Evelyn said confidently.

"Well, I doubt I'll be here when you come back. And you don't have to worry about me running off with Severina. It's past my bed-time."

"If I had known that, I would have helped tuck you in," said Evelyn.

"My loss." He watched Evelyn walk to the dressing room, then turned toward Severina. "Hi, my name is Rollo. Sit down." He pointed to Evelyn's seat. "So why does Evelyn think she can trust me with you?"

"Could be because I'm not going to be working much longer. I just had a baby. I'm giving up dancing to be a fulltime mom."

Now the swelling breasts, the wee stomach bulge and the traces of cellulite made sense. "You got enough money to be a fulltime mom?"

"I'll be living at a Counselors of Unwed Mothers residence. I won't need too much money. My daughter's father might help, but I'm not depending on it."

"Is he owning up to his fatherly responsibilities?"

"On a very inconsistent basis. Thank God for the residence."

"What's so great about staying there?"

"I'll learn to be self sufficient. I can learn household mainte-nance skills, improve my cooking. When you have a lot of money tossed your way, it's easy to forget that doing simple things can give a lot of satisfaction."

"How many months were you before you stopped dancing?"

"Three months. I could've danced till maybe my fifth month. It really didn't become too noticeable till then, but I didn't want to take a chance. Imperfections get cemented in the minds of the men who come here. Then it takes a long time to erase it." Severina looked at her watch. "Oh, I gotta go dance."

Rollo playfully tapped her wrist. "It was nice meeting you. And tell Evelyn I said, 'goodnight'."

"It really is past your bedtime?"

"If you get some leisure time while being a fulltime mom, why don't you join Evelyn and I'll let you both help tuck me in. Then you'll know for sure."

Severina smiled, got up, mussed Rollo's hair and left.

Rollo took a sip of his Fuzzy Navel and examined Beverly's. The bar was as structurally impressive as some of the women who danced there. There were giant screen televisions tuned to sports events for the men who were tired of watching dancers; the chairs were vinyl-covered and comfortable. Brass adorned the bar and defined the border of the seating gallery. It gave a touch of the turn of the century to an ultra modern facility. It was a pleasant place to unwind.

By having worked in his late father's pub, he had learned to be very careful in dealing with the people one met in bars. People drinking alcohol could behave in peculiar ways. Even if they didn't drink, many people who frequented bars were charlatans out to impress those around them. He would be careful in getting better acquainted with Evelyn; more careful than he had been when getting to know Lisbeth and Lucinda.

CHAPTER VII

IGGY BIGGY

Iggy Biggy's daughter had recently presented him with his first grandchild. There was going to be a christening at his apartment building near the Cross Bronx Expressway's Third Avenue exit. Everyone he considered a friend at the ballpark was invited.

Iggy Biggy usually pumped beer in the commissary where Rollo, Lenny Mo Dinner, Oasis and Brad Brown worked. Having done it a long time, he was indifferent to the job. Often he was more concerned with the apartment he had to fix at his building; the girl he was trying to sleep with; who would he get reefer from; and how long it would be before the seventh inning ended and he could leave. But since the birth of his grandchild, there was a twinkle in his eyes and he pumped beer with such consummate skill that vendors could enter the commissary, grab a tray and get out in one swift motion. Their sales increased. His subway increased. The twinkle in his eyes became a gleam.

There was an escalation of the warmth, radiance and congeniality Iggy could always spread when he set his mind to it. He began to play disco music on his boom box so loud the pulsating rhythm drowned fans cheers. Beer vendors waiting for a tray, started dancing, the commissary was turning into 'Disco 14'. Simeon usually worked in a different commissary than Iggy, so his loud music didn't cause problems.

The increased subway these days made Iggy willing to stay past the seventh inning. When beer sales were brisk, the vendors always wanted to sell past the seventh inning, but management wouldn't allow it. Drunk fans got too rowdy. And when the Yankees were in the pennant race, the Stadium became a combat zone.

"This seventh inning, two hours after the game starts, whichever comes first rule sucks," said Iggy Biggy.

"It's all relative," said Oasis, sipping the beer he had poured himself.

"To what?" Rollo asked.

"To what the powers that be want."

"Can you put that in laymen's terms."

"It means we're screwed," Oasis said.

"You couldn't say that in the first place?" Iggy Biggy asked. "Traveling through three counties to get here saps your brain?"

"No and no." Oasis took another sip of beer. "Still, you got to remember, on an animal night like the Silver Shields game, when we sell enough beer to start a flood, you want to be out of here well before the seventh inning, when the fans start behaving like zoo animals seeing breakfast approach."

The night of the Silver Shields game, police and firemen packed the stadium as all proceeds went to the Police and Firemen's Widow and Orphan Fund. It was always the biggest 'animal' event of the year in Yankee Stadium.

"That reminds me," said Iggy Biggy. "You guys gonna come Saturday to the Christening? Bring your family,Oasis."

"If I come."

"What's to keep you from coming?"

"Distance I have to travel. Prior commitment to in-laws. I'll do what I can." Oasis put down the beer cup, signed his card and left.

"I'll check it out, Iggy. It's solid," said Rollo.

The day of the christening Rollo arose around noontime. The sky was overcast. As shower water pelted his skin, it dawned on him if he and Evelyn had gone to the christening and discovered they weren't compatible, they could have ruined a festive occasion. It made him feel better about going solo. He didn't want to ruin a friend's solemn jubilee.

When Rollo came out of the shower, he put on powder, deodorant and cologne but still felt sticky. Summer had arrived in May. He put on a white cotton tank top, bikini undershorts, gray cotton walking shorts and thongs to keep the stickiness to a minimum. After combing his hair, he vacated his flat and drove the Puegot to a nearby supermarket. Iggy Biggy had asked everyone to bring something. Rollo was certain there'd be chicken at the celebration. Somebody would bring beer, and since he considered beer the swill of the masses, he bought instead two dozen bottles of wine cooler. He put them in the Peugot's trunk and resumed the journey to the Cross Bronx Expressway's Third Avenue exit.

Driving on the Bronx River Parkway, then the Sheridan Expressway, Rollo noticed the Bronx's topography change. As he moved southward, attractive one, two and three family homes in working class neighborhoods disappeared and gave way to gritty factories, empty warehouses and attempted revitalization around the Third Avenue exit.

Iggy Biggy's building was well kept. No garbage, debris or glass was strewn across its sidewalks. No graffiti on walls. It was a stark contrast to the crackhouse about two miles away he had entered with Lucinda.

Rollo got out of the Puegot, took the wine coolers out of the trunk, and went inside. The interior was as clean as a hospital. Tiled floors sparkled. The elevator was not only clean, it didn't reek of urine. What a difference it made when people cared about where they lived, thought Rollo. Still, it was a tough neighborhood and couldn't have been easy. There had been an ugly rumor around the ballpark that Iggy Biggy had wasted someone. Rollo knew he could be violent, too, but he pondered what made him only kick Lucinda while Iggy Biggy may have ended someone else's life. Was it really that easy to weave violence in and out of your life?

He rang Iggy Biggy's doorbell. A woman with gray hair who bore a slight resemblance to Iggy Biggy answered the door and introduced herself as his mother. "Iggy's making a few stops. He'll be back soon. Guests are downstairs in the backyard," she said, cradling a baby and pointing to the kitchen.

Rollo carried the coolers into the small, compact room. Chicken was frying on the stove. Bowls of potato salad, macaroni salad and coleslaw stood on top of the dishwasher. Rollo was tempted to dig in but restrained himself, opened the refrigerator and put the coolers inside.

Then with a Black Cherry cooler in hand, Rollo walked downstairs to the community room, where neatly arranged paper cloth covered tables and chairs awaited the guests. As he stepped into the backyard, Rollo was amazed at the number of children running around, laughing, posing, pulling innocent pranks. Chicken, hot dogs and hamburgers were cooking on two barbecue pits. Nearby stood a buffet table with salads, potato chips, nacho chips and plates, utensils and paper cups. Rollo introduced himself to the adults preparing the food. Then he took a plate and prepared a sampler. Upon taking the first bite, he was glad he had held his appetite in check until he arrived. It was difficult confining himself to one plate, but he knew more food was on the way.

He looked across the sizable backyard. The lawn was as wide as a two lane highway and long enough for a little league game. The fences surrounding the backyard were cast iron, ten feet high, curved at the top facing the street and entwined with barbed wire on the side adjacent to a two-family home. Having seen the nearby crackhouse inhabitants, Rollo knew why it was necessary.

There were no girls who made him look twice, but having met Evelyn, he was not disappointed. Maybe it was best Evelyn didn't come. What would she think of a guy who took her someplace protected by barbed wire for a date?

A psychedelic plastic ball landed near him. He picked it up and carried it toward the children who were playing unorganized volleyball. The players were no more than twelve years old, more boys than girls. The boys were on one side of the make shift net, the girls the other. Rollo got on the girls side to help even the odds. He had a few practice serves and volleys to loosen his muscles and assess the talent he was playing with. The boys were very aggressive and often more concerned with hitting the ball hard rather than where opponents weren't. The girls were more focused. They'd hit the ball where opponents weren't or toward Rollo, who'd hit it toward inbounds empty space.

A van pulled up on the other side of the cast iron fence. The door opened and out popped Iggy Biggy. The children ran toward the van.

Iggy Biggy motioned for Rollo and two other men, unlocked the iron gate, then opened the van's side door. There were two paraplegics inside, Iggy's ex-Marine buddies who had served with him in

Vietnam. Rollo, Iggy Biggy and two other men unloaded the ice, beer and charcoal while the electric stair lowered the men's wheelchairs. When everyone who belonged inside was, Iggy Biggy locked the gate. Now that Iggy Biggy had provided replenishments, the cooking was going full throttle. One of Iggy Biggy's friends in dreadlocks set up a stereo. Music filled the air. Rollo went upstairs and brought down the wine coolers. Then he took a seat and waited for the food simmering on the barbecue pit. He wondered if Iggy Biggy would use profits from Kelso's business project - if it worked - to provide for his grandchild.

While Rollo waited, Iggy Biggy brought out a baby basket. Inside was a three week old baby. Iggy was beaming with pride. Rollo arose, walked to the basket and looked at the baby. He was cute; he had big dark eyes, long straight raven hair and a reddish yellow complexion. Rollo asked, "Your daughter named him yet?"

"No," said Iggy Biggy.

"What's she waiting for?"

"I imagine a name she feels suitable."

"She'll think of something. Nobody else from the ballpark came?"

"Brad Brown, Oasis and Copperblum said they'd come, but aren't here yet."

"This is a nice building you got here."

"Yeah, but I'm working 24/7 to keep crackheads out. I don't know what the deal is now that there's a baby to protect. My daughter's scared. I hope Kelso's plan works."

"If it does, you can move or turn this into a fortress," said Rollo.

Iggy patted Rollo's shoulder. "Help yourself to the food."

When the food was ready, Iggy Biggy had the children form a line so everyone could be served without chaos. Rollo fixed himself a heaping plate, sat down and enjoyed the fare.

When they were done eating the children wanted to play more volleyball and other games. Rollo led those who wanted to play volleyball. A women led some of the girls in Simon Says. No game lasted too long. Soon there were dance contests, dodge ball games and catches. Everyone was having so much fun that Iggy Biggy went upstairs, got his Camcorder and taped everything, until it rained and everyone moved inside for the unofficial Christening.

First, the women walked by, whispering phrases wishing peace and prosperity to the baby, Iggy Biggy and his daughter. When the ladies were through, Iggy Biggy moved toward the baby basket, picked up his grandchild and said, "This is all because I love you." He put his beaming face close to the baby's and rubbed his skin. The baby cried.

He passed the baby around so every adult in the community room could hold it. When it was Rollo's turn, he looked at him, remembering Psalms 8:2.: "Out of the mouths of babes and sucklings ..."

As he left Iggy's building, night had fallen, and it was misting. Although the fences around Iggy Biggy's building were necessary, Rollo realized the community's faith and hope were also crucial in the effort to prevail against the forces of destruction beseiging it. It was disgraceful Iggy's plan to improve security hinged on Kelso's business project. Rollo felt a man shouldn't have to depend on shady business ventures to protect his loved ones.

As the Puegot pulled onto the Expressway, Rollo thought of Evelyn. If she was all he hoped for, one day they might be giving a christening also.

CHAPTER VIII

THE RUBICON CAFE

Rollo drove the Puegot into the Rubicon Cafe parking lot. It was early morning, but the only space he found was far from the door. He was glad he'd suggested the Rubicon for their rendezvous. Fine girls came there unattached with more than food on their minds. If this encounter did not turn out better than his previous two, maybe he'd find another female to chance rejection with.

Calling the Rubicon a cafe was like referring to St. Patrick's Cathedral as a place of worship. Varnished oak beams spanned the ceiling. Ceiling fans turned lazily above. Windows extended from the ceiling to the sparkling silver glitter table tops while turquoise leather upholstery covered the booths and plush, matching carpet, the floor. What a waste to have only breakfast here, Rollo thought. That is, if Evelyn kept the date.

A red haired waitress wearing a neat uniform approached. Rollo ordered herbal tea to calm his nerves. When the waitress brought it to him, he sat there sipping it and looked out the window at the faint red-streaked sky of the coming dawn.

Between what he had gone through with Lisbeth and Lucinda and what he was about to enter into with Kelso and his fellow vendors, he wondered whether life was unraveling or coming into sharper focus. He was worried about Kelso's scheme. He didn't know what would happen if it was uncovered, yet it they were successful, the money would mean he could vend less and devote more time to songwriting. Rollo was aware Kelso had a shady background and valued money more than anything else. Rollo had dealt with similar entrepreneurs in the music business and had learned as long as the bottom

65

line showed profits, the shrewd ones let the people producing the profits alone. He didn't anticipate Kelso deviating from this pattern. At least he wouldn't have a domineering boss peering over his shoulder.

The new-found money would also mean he'd have more time to spend on women. His recent experiences had him thinking what type of women. If he has serious about his songwriting career, girls like Lucinda and Tasha had to be cast aside. He enjoyed bachelorhood, but either he was moving toward achieving his goals or he wasn't. Sleazy women might serve a purpose, but they weren't best for the path he had chosen. He vowed, even if he and Evelyn weren't to be, there would be no more sleazy females. He finished the tea, and looked out the window as a black Dodge Charger pulled into the parking lot.

In Evelyn he sensed a sincerity that was totally lacking in Lisbeth and Lucinda. Rollo had grown up in an environment where misinterpreting people could spell the difference between life and death. In the harsh inner city an ill advised stare, a misunderstood smile or an incomprehensible stare could be fatal. Of course women had fooled him before. It was possible he was incorrect about Evelyn, but he doubted it.

Rollo saw the lady behind the cash register point toward the dining room, and Evelyn entered, smiling. Rollo got up and held the seat for her to sit down. She looked different. Not wearing a revealing outfit, or having stage lights directing attention to parts of her body, she no longer resembled a sultry vixen on the cover of an erotic magazine. She seemed personable, alluring, like a girl he'd approach at a mall.

"You been waiting a long time?"

"I've been kept waiting longer."

"I'm glad you're here."

"Why?"

She shrugged. "I'm not being stood up."

Rollo found this inconceivable and placed his palms under the table to keep from hitting himself in the face. "What kind of a moron would stand you up?"

"Hey, it happens to the best of us."

It was comforting to know he wasn't the only one having bizarre outcomes with the opposite sex. "Thank God I'm not stupid," he said.

"Hopefully, that'll be your sentiment by the time we leave."

"When we leave, maybe we'll be sentimentally attached."

"I could live with that."

"Great!" Rollo placed his hand over Evelyn's.

The waitress came. Evelyn ordered apple cobbler, Rollo, carrot cake and a second cup of tea.

"Why am I so lucky?" Rollo asked.

"You mean why am I here with you instead of with one of the many who hit on me?"

"That's one way of putting it."

"Instincts aren't always right, but I see in you something - in a man - I haven't seen in a while."

"And that's?"

"Generosity, compassion and understanding."

"In the scant moments you've known me, I've radiated those qualities?"

"You aren't tight with money. I hate penny pinchers. Also, you seem emotionally stable, not like you're not running a game on me."

In between bites they told each other details of their lives. Rollo told her of his earlier success in songwriting, about vending since attending junior high school and his hopes to make it big in songwriting once again. Evelyn told him about her life in Africa and the Middle East, about being raised according to the tenets of Islam, and about the murder of her brothers. She ate the last bit of her apple cobbler. Rollo finished his tea. "Their murder was so devastating," she said. "I converted to agnosticism and I hate men who work for oil companies."

"Do you really find it beneficial hating people because of something that happened years ago by a few people who felt they were doing their patriotic duty?"

"It serves its purpose."

"How could you hate a group of people for what a few individuals had done?" Rollo found it abhorrent. "What do you hope to accomplish if you maintain this attitude?

"Vigilance for my brothers!"

67

"What do you find enjoyable besides avoiding male oilers and pennypinchers?" he asked, seeing she was resolute.

"Going to comedy clubs. Shopping in the village, hanging out in Sports bars and camping."

"You like sports?"

"Not really. I only go to sports bars with pool tables."

"You like to shoot pool?"

"Only in sports bars."

"Why?"

"When I take a tough shot, it's exhilarating having so many men look at me bend over."

"You win most of the games you play?"

"I win my share. I'm not going to make anybody forget Minnesota Fats."

"You want to shoot a game or two with me?"

"I only play girls."

"That's sexist."

"It's practical. You beat some of these men in sports bars and it's as if you take away their manhood. They got to spend the rest of the night proving themselves, redeeming their honor."

He understood. He hoped he didn't go to such extremes, but he remembered as a kid, he didn't like losing to girls at ping pong. "Why don't we go camping?"

"I don't know you well enough."

"How are you ever going to get to know me well enough?"

"Come shop with me in the village next Saturday?"

Rollo reached into his jeans pocket, took out his wallet and removed his Yankee schedule. The date Evelyn suggested, the Yankees were on the road. "No problem."

"Can Severina come also?"

"I'm not big on shopping in the village. Why don't you let me take you to a baseball game? Severina can bring her baby, too."

"I've never been to one."

"That's more of a reason you should go."

"Your going to take me to where you work?"

"I met you where you work."

"Let me know which game you want to go to." She removed

her hand. "Thanks for inviting me here for breakfast."

"You're welcome, but you don't have to thank me."

"Yes I do. A lot of guys wouldn't take me here."

"Where would they take you?"

"Most want to get to the bottom line fast. So if we don't go some-place where we can do that, I'm taken to seedy, macho restaurants, where I keep my eyes on everything except the guy who brought me."

"As a precaution?"

"Yeah."

"If seeing each other becomes a habit, I know places better than this where those thoughts won't enter your mind."

"So do I."

CHAPTER IX

ROD SOMER

Rod Somer and Oasis were in Oasis's Topaz, driving upstate for the key ingredient in Kelso's beer. Considering what he would be asking for, Oasis felt it best to have a white man along. He wasn't sure if Rod Somer was the best man for the job, but when he considered the alternatives: going alone or taking someone who'd definitely rub the redneck farmers the wrong way, he decided Somer would suffice.

In his heart Rod Somer not only wanted to take care of his wife's medical expenses, he wanted to take care of everyone - he wanted to make the world a better place to live, to make it right. Two obstacles prevented him: his personality and his looks. He constantly talked. If he talked while he slept, then he never kept quiet. What with his buckteeth and pimples, looking at him tested peoples' patience. In spite of the mockery caused by his appearance and stuttering, Rod Somer treated everyone as if he were his friend. Rod always spoke what was on his mind, even if it wasn't popular, so most people didn't like him, let alone call him a friend.

He was on the plus side of thirty and thinking beyond jobs and making ends meet. He wanted to wake in the morning and go to work because he wanted to and not because he had to. He had tried many things: independent network marketing, real estate sales, flea market selling and promoting a rock group. None had produced the wealth he longed for, but he hadn't given up. He was searching for the next avenue to prosperity. Hence, Kelso's business plan. He hoped it worked immediately. He was entering the third year of his marriage, and it was teetering between bliss and doom. His wife suffered from Cerebral Palsy. Taking care of her with this affliction tested the mar-

70

riage's survival. With all his heart he truly loved her, but the cost of caring for her was exorbitant. At Yankee Stadium he earned money at exponential rates, but after he was done with his wife's medical expenses, they were barely getting by.

"We got much longer to go, Stacey?"

"About twenty minutes," said Oasis.

"Good," said Rod. "I gotta-gotta stretch my legs or they might fa-fall off."

"Can't be that bad. What do you think of Kelso's plan?"

"I've been in crazier schemes."

"Did any of 'em work?"

"All but one ended up flat on its-its conceiver's face."

"The one that got over bear any semblance to Kelso's?" Oasis surveyed the lush mountains near the road.

"No. We sold designer warm-up suits we got at Customs auctions for slightly below retail. Everyone thought they were getting a bargain."

"Yeah. That's mild compared to Kelso's plan."

"Still, I figure our chances are better than fifty-fifty. Remember we're dealing with a product the public can't get enough of. I worked games when people would have given their first born for a beer."

"And a second mortgage on their homes for the next round." Oasis smiled.

"Imagine what those we didn't reach would've paid. That's-that's the key. With Kelso's beer we'll be able to serve more customers. And as wild as its recipe is, how much worse can it b-be than what we serve now? A game doesn't go by without complaints."

Oasis frowned. "Yeah, that stuff'll never win any taste test."

"We might be on our way to becoming independently wealthy."

"Even if we aren't, it'll make a difference in how we live." Oasis eased his eyes from the lush mountains. If he didn't live through the next thirty miles, differences wouldn't matter.

The Topaz maneuvered a hair pin turn. As the vehicle came out of a wooded area, Oasis and Somer saw a red and white barn, a cornfield and some brown and white animals grazing in a field. Oasis slowed down. "This could be a possibility. Look over there." He pointed.

71

"Yeah," said Somer. "Looks like a prairie state, not New York, but thems not horses. We need h-horses, remember?"

"I know the difference between cows and horses. But where cows graze, can horses be far behind?" Oasis slowed the Topaz to ten miles per hour. "Hey, hey. What'd I tell you!" Oasis pointed to horses prancing behind the barn.

"Let's go!" Somer punched Oasis's thigh.

The Topaz pulled into the farm. 'Mckeesport Acres' a sign proclaimed. Oasis parked next to a Dodge Pick-up. He and Rod Somer got out and walked towards the barn. Behind a barbed wire fence, cows, horses and mules watched the men approach. As the vendors neared the barn door, a tall, grey haired man came outside. His walked expressed a deliberate stoicism. He stuck his right hand out toward Oasis and Rod Somer, "Elmo McKeesport IV," he said. "How can I be o' service to you?"

"Sir. My name is Stacey Oasis and this is Rod Somer." They shook hands.

"Pleased to meet you," said Elmo.

"Sir," said Oasis. "We need the by-product of your horses."

"I beg your pardon?"

"What, uh-uh comes out of their-their genitals," said Somer.

"I don't breed horses, son."

"We know this isn't a stud farm, Sir. He means their waste. We need their waste."

"Manure? You men own a nursery? Frankly, you men want cow manure. More nutrients than what horses give. Don't exactly know why, but I think it's got to do with ..."

"Ah, ah, Mr., Mr. ..."

"Call me Elmo, son."

"Yes, Elmo, well it's not exactly manure we're interested in. It's the other stuff."

"The other stuff?" The farmer looked dumbfounded.

"Excuse me in advance for offending you, Sir, but it's horse piss we're after."

The farmer's eyes narrowed. "What for?"

"My daughter. She's a really bright kid, Elmo. She's working on this school project called, 'the Beneficial Aspects of Equine Urine'."

"My brother's vice president of a fertilizer company. His company buys manure from me for next to nothing, but he never asks for piss."

"You want me to pay you?" Oasis asked.

"Your daughter's in high school or grade school?"

"Next year she starts high school."

"I don't think it's fair to charge for something she's going to use." Elmo gingerly tapped Oasis's shoulder. It was the first time he had seen a Black in person outside of the politicians, athletes and entertainers he constantly saw on television. Oasis didn't seem like one of the belligerent ones. "I didn't know Blacks study science."

"How do you think Blacks become astronauts and doctors?" Oasis gave Elmo a warm, friendly smile.

"I see your point. I'll be glad to help your daughter, son."

"Thanks. You don't know how much it means to her. She's done a lot of research. She's trying to see if horse piss can be an alternative fuel in automobiles."

"That's real ambitious. If she can work that out, she'll have no problem winning a Westinghouse Science Scholarship."

"And you-you'll be one of her benefactors," said Somer. "Of course, it's going to take an awful lot of raw material."

"You come back and get more anytime. Me and my horses would be proud to oblige. You two hop in my pick-up, and I'll drive you over to the stalls. You just got to promise I'll be the first to know if it works. Boy, that would sure save me money if it did."

Oasis and Rod Somer smiled.

Rod went back to the Topaz and pulled out two twenty gallon steel milk cartons out of the trunk.

"You need that much?" Elmo asked.

"Remember we're talking alternative fuel source," said Oasis.

"In the experimental phase of any science project, you need a high quantity of all the materials you're te-testing," Rod Somer added.

Elmo nodded. "Come to think of it, my brother needs a lot when his fertilizer company develops a new product."

Rod put the milk cartons in Elmo's pick-up truck and got up on the bed also. He'd let Elmo and Oasis have elbow room in the cab.

Elmo drove more than half a mile before the truck came to a slow stop. Elmo and Oasis got out; Rod hopped off the back.

"You go in there and do what you gotta do. I got to make sure the new barbed wire's holding up. I'll be back soon," Elmo said.

Oasis and Rod took the milk containers to the stalls. Elmo had three plow horses, two mules, five old thoroughbreds, one Arabian stallion and four Palominos. Twelve were in their stalls. Oasis chose the Palomino in the far left stall. It looked the healthiest. He thought it might relieve itself first. He placed the container under the Palomino very carefully. He didn't want the beast kicking him because he was placing something near its testicles.

Rod Somer took a look at the mule in the near right stall. It was huge. He might be slow to relieve himself, but when he did go, it would be a river.

"Do you think Kelso'll notice the difference between horse piss and mule piss?" Oasis asked.

"What-what's he going to do? Taste it and say, 'This is mule piss. Take it back and get horse piss'? Besides a mule is half horse anyway," said Rod Somer.

Somer looked at Oasis. He did not belabor the point.

Somer placed his container under the mule. He was careful also. The waiting began.

The animals ate hay.

The mule relieved himself first. Rod picked up the milk container.

Four quarts. It didn't smell as disgusting as he expected. He placed the container under the plow horse in the next stall. Just then, he heard the Palomino making use of the other container. It took the horses close to ninety minutes to fill the containers.

On the drive back to the Topaz Elmo asked, "You get your fill of that horse piss, son?"

"Those containers are so filled moving 'em is an upperbody workout," said Oasis.

"Good," said Elmo. "I'm glad I can help our youth in a worthy endeavor." He stuck out his right. They shook hands.

Elmo helped load the containers into the Topaz's trunk and waved as Oasis and Rod drove off.

When they were several miles from Elmo's farm, Oasis and Somer yelled, "We're on our way." They exchanged the best high five they could in the cramped Topaz.

"We did it! Man! Can you picture people going for beer made of this?"

"Why not? You know what gives the meat you eat its-its taste?" Rod Somer asked. "When the animal is killed urine passes through its blood system. That which isn't removed in preparing the meat for sale belongs to the customer, except when it's Kosher; even then, there's traces."

"How do you know that?"

"One of my uncles is a butcher."

"Perhaps Kelso has a winner."

Rod Somer smiled. His expression resembled the kind a father gives his teenage son when the kid grasps an important lesson in maturing to manhood.

"His beer'll sell!"

"There's not too much doubt in my mind."

Oasis floored the gas pedal, and as the Topaz hummed along, the two men fell silent. Oasis was helping his daughters pick out which Ivy League colleges they'd go to, while Rod Somer was emptying a suit case full of cash on his wife's doctor's reception desk. "There's plenty more where that came from," he was saying when Oasis called out and pointed to skyscraper tops just visible in the distance. They burst into song, singing at the top of their lungs.

"If I can make it there,
I can make it anywhere.
It's up to you.
New York, New York."

They were going to find out the truth of that statement.

CHAPTER X

SLOW DEE

Uranso took the lid off the metal container and sniffed. "Dis brew's going to turn out fine. I woonted to use dee stout recipe of my grandmama, but I use her ale recipe instead, since we gotta move fast. Errol, bring dee bottled whaatah."

"Won't tap water do?" Errol asked.

"No! With what we're putting in already, it'd be ripping off dee consumer. Now help me haul out dee things hidden in dee back room!"

It took Uranso and the other men half-an-hour to haul out the equipment and set it up. Uranso used a multi-gallon stainless steel soup pot, a food grade container bucket, six gallon carboys, plastic tubing with a one inch blow-by, a bubbler, a siphon hose and spigot, copper tubing, a thermometer, funnels, pots and pans, a small postal scale and a notebook to record the results. It took him four hours to mix the ingredients. When he was through, he leaned over the bubbling pot and sniffed.

"Dis smells familiar. Help me get dis in dee fridge." He covered the barrel containing his creation. Errol, Rod Somer and Oasis helped him roll it into the refrigerator, and Uranso shut the door.

"I'll let it age for two and a half weeks; then there'll be a taste test."

"We're not taste testers!" Errol, Rod Somer, Mordecai Kaplan and Oasis said in unison.

Two weeks had passed. As fast as it takes a Palomino to fill a drum. The day of the test, the men were standing around arguing over who should taste the beer first.

76

"I got an idea, mon," said Uranso. "Let's look over dee cards when dey arrive and have one of dee younger vendors, eager to drink anything alcoholic, taste dee beer." Their heads nodded simultaneously.

The cards arrived at 6:15 P.M., an hour and twenty minutes before the scheduled game. They looked at the cards. There were plenty of young vendors to choose from. They chose one not so young but perfect for the job.

His name was Delvin Beckinport, commonly referred to as Slow Dee. Close to thirty years old, he behaved as though he was barely out of diapers. He had never had a steady relationship with a girl. The prostitutes with whom he spent time treated him like guano. His best clothes were jeans, t-shirts and motorcycle boots. As sparse as his wardrobe was, it was an improvement on himself. He cut his hair in a Caesar. He was a freckle face; getting a look at his eyes was a task because he wore coke bottle thick lenses. He'd tell jokes abandoned by most children after sixth grade. He'd ask someone to slap him 'five'. When the person obliged, he'd quickly move his palm and form a zero using his thumb and index finger in front of his eye and say, 'Cheerios'. He was still looking for his first full time job.

Although he bragged of the L.S.D. trips he had taken, Slow Dee was the epitome of drugs keeping one from being all they could be.

"Come here, Slow Dee." Errol said, when he walked into the commissary. "You're just the man we wanted to see."

"Hi guys. Slow Dee soon to go out. What's up, Errol?"

"It's hot and humid today."

"You know it." Slow Dee pulled a handkerchief from his back pocket and wiped his brow.

"Looks like you could go for a cold beer."

"You gonna gi' me some, man?"

Errol shrugged. "Perhaps."

"If you don't gi' me beer, I won't give you subway."

"You don't give me subway, and you're going to be even more stupid looking than you are now."

"If I'm stupid lookin', why do you want me drinking beer?"

"We don't want you wilting in the heat," said Rod Somer.

"You need plenty of fluids when it's hot and humid," said Errol.

"I can drink water," said Slow Dee.

77

"You want that warm seltzery agua stuff?" Errol pointed at the sink.

"I can put ice in it and let the seltzer evaporate."

"Why go to all that trouble?" Errol placed his hand on Slow Dee's sloping shoulder, "Have some beer. Yo Uranso, hook up Slow Dee."

Uranso smiled and went into the refrigerator with a beer cup. He came out with the cup filled and gave it to Slow Dee. Slow Dee brought it to his lips.

Everybody looked away.

Slow Dee took a sip.

"Should be nice and cold. It's been in the fridge long enough," said Oasis.

Slow Dee took another sip. "Tastes stronger than what I'm accustomed to. Almost like malt liquor. Nothing beats good ol' window pane acid for me, though."

"Is it too strong for you?" asked Rod Somer.

"Not at all. Look I'm not complainin'. I appreciate your hospitality."

Errol, Rod, Mordecai and Uranso covered their mouths with their hands.

Slow Dee threw his head back and took a long drink. "I'll put this back in the fridge and get the rest as I need it."

"Give it to me, mon. I'll put it away for you." Uranso snatched the cup out of Slow Dee's hand.

"You're going to have to hook us up with serious subway now we let you sip brew, right?" Errol said.

"Don't worry about it," said Slow Dee. "That stuff sure hits the spot on a night like this. The fans'll be blessing you before the night's over." Slow Dee put on his soda price badge and walked out.

"Remember, Slow Dee, you want more. You ask me or Uranso." Errol closed the commissary door and slipped to the floor and with his back against the door. Just then the organ started up. Oasis, Mordecai and Rod Somer laughed so hard they fell to the floor and rolled back and forth. Uranso banged his head on the checker's desk. "He liked it! He actually liked it!" they cried.

"Too bad we don't start selling it till next week," said Errol when

78

the merriment had ended.

"Look at the bright side. We need to build inventory and get broader consumer opinion," said Rod Somer.

"I guess we do need more opinions than Slow Dee's. Most of the vendors, even the young ones, aren't as gullible as Slow Dee," said Oasis. "If one fan really gets a good sniff of the product, the whole venture could collapse like a house of cards. Everyone could lose his job, face arrest. It'd be the end of my career as a Corrections Officer."

"Don't worry, Stacey. It don't stink so bad. The fans will sample it," Errol said. Someone was banging on the commissary door. Errol got up, peeked out. Kelso and Rollo pushed open the door. Errol told Kelso and Rollo what happened. Kelso grinned. "Don't worry. We'll get whatever consumer opinions we need by next week."

"How?" asked Errol.

"Now you see why I'm the brains of this operation," Kelso said. "Has everyone forgotten about the survey I said we'd conduct?"

"Doesn't anyone remember him mentioning it at Beezer's?" Rollo asked.

"You expect us to remember everything discussed at the renegade's club? How's this survey going to work?" asked Rod Somer.

"Simple. We approach fans right after batting practice. The fans'll be glad to participate when we give them our survey along with the All Star Game ballots."

"What-what's to stop them from saying thanks for the ballot, now get lost," Somer asked.

"They get to taste the beer as part of the survey."

"But that'll eat into profits." Rollo said.

"I've already counted the samples as part of the cost of doing business," said Kelso.

"You're quite a man."

"It helps when you want to make money as much as I do."

"When are we starting this survey?" asked Errol.

"Let's see. We're going to begin selling beer on the eighteenth, when the Yanks play the Royals, right?"

"Yeah," said Oasis.

"Starting tomorrow, we'll send twenty people out - ten in the lower deck, five each in the Loge and the Upper - to survey ten fans apiece. By the eighteenth we should have a response from at least a thousand fans."

"That's a nice round number," said Rollo.

"What questions are you going to ask?" asked Errol.

Kelso smiled. "The survey'll have twelve questions, including: How many Yankee games do you attend each season? Do you buy refreshments here? Do you drink beer? What qualities do you want in the beer(s) you drink? Do you have a designated driver for the trip home?"

"Is this going to be like a GALLUP poll?" asked Oasis.

"We're not looking to identify trends. We want one simple question answered: 'Will people be willing to pay for our beer?'"

"If they are willing to pay for it, how they going to ask for it? We don't have a name," said Rod Somer.

It was the one thing Kelso had not thought of. He puffed his cheeks, let the air slowly seep out of his mouth, and suddenly grinned. "I got it - Kehlmeyer! That conveys a strong fatherland image. Beer marketeers usually have a macho pitch. Strength will be ours." He banged his left fist into his right palm.

Errol ran his fingers through his wavy hair. "Slow Dee did say ours was more potent than Busch."

"See, this is just the tip of the iceberg. Once we're kicking ass here and we expand, we can have a sexy pitch, a leisure pitch, a comic pitch, a nature pitch and an adventure pitch just like the other breweries. We can even have a Kehlmeyer Light." Kelso was steadily turning red. He arose from his seat and waved his arms in a menacing and exultant manner, like a gorilla preparing to beat his chest. Rollo and Errol pushed him back into his seat. "Jesus, Kelso! You want Simeon to hear?"

"Sorry guys," said Kelso.

"As long as we make money, you don't have to apologize," said Errol.

80

CHAPTER XI

HOW TO CONDUCT A SURVEY
AND INFLUENCE PEOPLE

Rollo was reading his copy of the survey in the right field commissary when Lenny Mo Dinner entered carrying his. He didn't look happy.

"What's the matter?" Rollo asked.

"I'm scared," said Lenny Mo.

"Of what?" Rollo placed the survey on the soda rack.

"Asking fans to respond to the survey."

"You want to make the money we're going to make?"

"Sure."

"There's a price to pay for making it work."

"I'm going to be out there selling the product when it's ready."

"Yeah, you are. But that's Step E and this survey is Step C. If we go out of sequence, we could be in big trouble."

"I don't wanna ask fans questions."

"What exactly are you scared of?"

"The fans might be suspicious."

Rollo laughed. "You don't think they're suspicious already? This isn't exactly gourmet cuisine we serve."

"They're accustomed to what we serve."

"Right. And just like they can get accustomed to Kelso's beer, you can get accustomed to doing the survey, and we can get accustomed to earning a lot more money, but first you gotta get accustomed to overcoming fear."

"You make it sound easy."

"Not easy - doable. The fans weren't always accustomed to ballpark hot dogs, cold pretzels, cardboard pizza and watered down beer with black specs in it. They saw other people try them. They sampled them. It was a developed habit, not some intuitive instinct.

"The cab you drive - the one you claim you'll drive to any neighborhood at any time? Were you accustomed to going anywhere when you started? You probably were shittin' bricks the first time someone asked you to drive to East New York or the South Bronx, right?"

"There wasn't as much violence when I began hacking."

"As it became more vicious, being the man you claim you are, you kept taking fares to and from those neighborhoods...."

"Okay, okay, let's do it." Lenny Mo took a deep breath.

They grabbed their survey sheets and left the commissary. Rollo let Lenny Mo walk in front.

"Lenny, I'll watch you do a survey. If you have trouble, I'll help. Now do it!"

Lenny Mo approached a fan. It seemed to go off without a hitch. As he approached another fan, Lenny Mo gave Rollo the thumbs up.

So much for fear thought Rollo. It was time for him to find a fan.

A raucous group of men dressed in jeans, t-shirts and sneakers were taking the seats directly below him in the first row next to the field. Rollo approached the one seated next to the aisle and tapped on the shoulder. The man turned. "Did you get your All Star Game Ballot yet?"

"No," said the man.

"Here's one for you." Rollo handed him the ballot along with the survey.

"What's this other paper?"

"A survey of a new brand of beer being test marketed at Yankee Stadium. If you answer the questions, you get a free cup of beer.

The fan looked at the survey. He pulled a pen out of his pants pocket. "You said we get free beer if we do the survey?"

"Yeah."

"Then just don't stand there. Give some to my friends." He pointed to the men seated beside him. They practically ripped the surveys out of Rollo's hands.

While they answered the ballot, Rollo asked the man his name. "Phillip."

"You a big baseball fan or you here 'cause your friends are?"

"I love baseball. I tried out with the Mets when I got out of high school."

"What you doing here then?"

"I'm a Yankee fan. Besides, I didn't impress the scouts at the tryout."

"Why didn't you keep trying?"

"It wasn't worth it."

"With the money they pay these guys, how can you say that?"

"I couldn't picture myself going through the minors in backwoods, hick towns, being away from friends and family."

"How do you earn a living now?"

"I'm in sales."

"If this beer goes over big, you could have a new job opportunity. The company'll probably need sales and marketing people."

"That'd be great." Phillip handed his completed survey - along with his friends' - to Rollo. "I could get real excited about beer sales."

"I'll be back with your beers before the first inning is over." Rollo and Phillip shook hands.

As Rollo walked toward the commissary, Lenny Mo Dinner caught up to him. "This wasn't as hard as I thought."

"What did I tell you? Now maybe you can learn how to earn a living doing something besides vending and hacking. Let's go see how the fans answered the questions."

Uranso, Errol, and Rod Somer were already in the left field commissary and going through their surveys. "Listen to this!" Errol said. "Best beer I've tasted at the Stadium."

"That isn't saying too much," said Oasis.

Rollo held up his surveys. "Listen to this: 'Has the qualities I look for in a beer.' 'Willing to pay premium price for it.' 'Glad I tried it.'"

"Hey, mon. I'm going to get dat beach front bungalow in Ocho Rios!" Uranso gave Errol a high five.

"And I can open that art deco restaurant," said Errol, hugging Uranso.

"My daughters aren't going to need scholarships. I'm going to take care of it all by my lonesome." Oasis wanted to breakdance, but the commissary was too small. He swung his fist above his head.

"I'll-I'll have enough money for my wife's medical bills," said Somer, patting Oasis on the back.

Oasis shook his head. "I don't know."

"'Would be glad to serve to my guests in my home,' doesn't win you over?" Somer asked.

"How do we know the guy doesn't serve his guests from bottles with skulls and crossbones?" Oasis asked.

"Shut up with your God damn negativity!" Errol yelled. "Everyday, people buy designer jeans, wigs and toupees made from horses' tails, dolls and teddy bears to stick in their cars. They don't need these things, yet enough sell to make certain people rich. Hell, the chances of Kehlmeyer working are better than hitting the lotto. As long as you can create the right image for any product or service, you can get over."

"Do you honestly think the *right* image can be created for Kehlmeyer?" It dawned on Oasis he *might* be overly pessimistic.

"Sure mon," said Uranso. "Don't you watch any t'ievin, lyin t.v. progroms with your darghters?"

Oasis nodded.

"Well that's where this survey comes in," said Errol. "It helps us find an image consumers identify with. Once we find the right image, Kehlmeyer can be as big as even the most popular beers."

"Yeah mon! You'll make more money dan you ever cood runnin' round dis stadium in a lifetime."

"All right!" Oasis pointed to his surveys. "But how do we use these?"

"Simple. We find a way to apply mass psychology. What do you call it?" Errol snapped his fingers. "A NICHE. Once a niche is established and the quality of the beer remains consistent, there shouldn't be any major problems. Kehlmeyer's ingredients may not be approved by the Food & Drug Administration, but no one's complained about its taste."

"An usin horse urin's bizarre, mon. Who know if it crime. No one got sick off it and dey no proof anyone will. Tink bout dat when you and dee odders expand Kehlmeyer into Simeon commissary." Uranso dug into a plate of Red Snapper spiced with hot peppers he'd brought from home.

So far Kelso's brewery venture had encountered little difficulty. Farmers generously granted access to their horses; the fans found Uranso's recipe delicious; and the survey had succeeded beyond their wildest dreams. What had started out as nothing more than an idea in Kelso's mind was ready to expand. Tangible goals were becoming vivid. Pessimism and doubt were left behind. Lenny Mo Dinner was calling travel agents about openings in Fantasy Baseball camps. Oasis was looking at BARRON'S Guide to American Colleges and Universities. Uranso was calling real estate agents who handled Caribbean property. And Somer was looking into better medical care for his wife. They actually smiled when they saw each other, and bitched less about who got the best beer spots.

But with the Silver Shields game approaching, they were about to risk everything. They were going to distribute beer from the right-field commissary. If it worked, then the lower deck, the bleachers and the loge's rightfield would be theirs. Only one man made the risk dangerous. One man who could have had a share of the enterprise, a share in the excitement of starting something from scratch. Most of all, he could have shared in the profits. But he didn't get a chance, because Kelso and his cohorts knew he would never participate. That was why they discussed Simeon the checker during the initial meeting at the renegade's club. Not doing so would have been the venture's suicide.

Simeon so despised the vendors earning more money in less time than he worked that he stayed up nights thinking of ways to torture the men. Simeon relished rain delays. He took great delight in making the vendors stay out in the rain. If they didn't, they weren't allowed to sign their cards until the following day. He coveted tied games in late innings. Every vendor would be forced to sell his product until the tie was broken, except the beer vendors. At checkout time he insisted the vendors form neat lines in front of his desk or else he would not sign them out. If a vendor leaned over his desk to see his card, Simeon threatened him with suspension. He lived to make the vendors' lives regrettable. If he found out about Kehlmeyer he would lead management straight to the kegs.

Kelso's plan to get the beer in and out of the rightfield commissary without Simeon seeing it was simple. "Iggy, you bring Kehlmeyer to Simeon's commissary in regular beer kegs and attach them to the freezer cables and couplings attached to the regular beer. If Simeon gets thirsty, don't serve him Kehlmeyer. Remember, Simeon's been to Munich several times for the Oktoberfest, probably's tasted every beer ever made. You tell everyone to look out for Simeon wanting to drink beer. If the plan fails - Kehlmeyer's through." Kelso looked at Iggy Biggy, seeking recognition he understood.

Iggy Biggy punched Kelso's shoulder and nodded.

It was an early evening in June. Kelso, Brad Brown, Oasis, Rollo and Lenny Mo were assigned to vending beer out of the rightfield commissary. Fans started arriving. Using his massive arms and sturdy legs, Iggy Biggy pushed a cart containing eight full kegs of beer into Simeon's commissary.

Simeon was behind his desk, puffing on a Parliament.

Iggy Biggy came out of the refrigerator, took the full kegs off the cart one-by-one, carried them into the refrigerator and fastened them to attachments. He returned outside, went to the beer machine, pressed the tap down. The beer flowed as if from a waterfall.

Outside in the seats it was sweltering. The crowd sweated profusely, as if they were in a mass wet t-shirt contest. The beer vendors always looked forward to this most 'animal' night - the Silver Shields game - but it came with greater responsibility: since transactions were occurring so rapidly, vendors had to watch out for fans attempting to heist beer. Not everyone in attendance was a silver shield.

A half an hour before the game began, Simeon yelled, "Everyone else is out. Beer vendors get going!" The beer vendors vanished before Simeon finished speaking. The temperature was eighty degrees with high humidity. From the first sale on the first tray onward, the fans wanted to swim in beer.

The increased sales had the beer vendors brimming with excitement. They weren't just running back to the commissary, they were galloping. Fans in the stadium corridors thought they were seeing a track meet, as the beer vendors went by in a blur.

"You beer guys have already sold at least ten trays apiece. You've made as much money as I'm going to make the whole damn game!" screamed Simeon before the national anthem.

By the fourth inning, the beer vendors had sold twenty-five beer trays apiece. And if supply and the machines could keep pace, they were going to sell a lot more. The Yankees, behind clutch hitting, excellent pitching, and inept fielding by the opposition, were pounding their opponents into submission. The organist was playing so often the Stadium sounded like a church revival. The fans were getting emotional. They wanted beer to quench their thirst and to sharpen their faculties for the rout.

"This is unbelievable. I might do thirty trays tonight," said Brad Brown to Lenny Mo Dinner when he returned to the commissary and got in line for another tray.

"Me too," said Lenny Mo.

Simeon was seething.

"What're you guys here to do, socialize or sell beer?"

Brad Brown smiled. "Tonight, you should be glad we're doing both. You might miss checking a tray or two if we don't slow down."

"If I have to recount, you know you'll be here a lot longer than you planned."

"As much as we're making tonight, we're willing to stay a little later." Brad Brown shrugged.

"Let's see if you say that at check-out time."

"Aw, you're too good of a checker to make a mistake. I know you've marked us for these trays we're taking." Brad Brown smiled again and left. Lenny Mo Dinner followed him.

Simeon marked their cards. The heat, the humidity, the frustration and the constant turning of the neck, to see whose card he was marking, made Simeon thirsty by the sixth inning.

He walked from behind the desk toward the beer machine, picked up a cup, placed it under one of the beer machine's taps and turned the lever as Iggy Biggy walked in. Iggy Biggy's eyes grew as large as tangerines. The beer flowed into Simeon's cup.

As Simeon brought the cup to his lips, the commissary's phone rang. The banker, a tall lanky collegian recruited for the summer, answered. "Simeon the call's for you." Simeon put his cup down, returned to his desk and picked up the phone as Oasis, Lenny Mo and Andy Metzger returned with their empty trays.

While conversing, Simeon gawked at his filled cup as if he were experiencing a mirage: within his sight, out of his grasp; taste tangible, yet inaccessible. Iggy Biggy, Oasis, Lenny Mo and Andy Metzger stared at him. Never taking his eyes off of the cup, Simeon's face contorted, and he did heel raises, silently imploring the person to hang up. The sweltering heat, the stifling humidity, the impending completion of cards on which he'd write sums for men who earned in two-and-a-half hours more than an impoverished third world family's annual income transmogrified the beer from swill to an ambrosia he could not abstain from.

Finally, he hung up, walked over, grabbed the cup, returned to his desk and placed it on the desk top. Iggy Biggy and Oasis shrugged at each other in helplessness.

A loud ovation. The organ boomed, signaling a Yankee hit a home run. Simeon turned his head toward the commissary doorway. There was something different about the cheer. "It sounds as if a triumphant general's being greeted. If it gets louder heaven may part," said Simeon, gesturing at Torin, the banker, to keep an eye on the cards, and going out.

Oasis lost no time. He signaled to Iggy, got a fresh tray, went to the banker, told him he was going out.

"That's twenty-nine," said the banker.

"No it's not. That's only twenty-eight."

"You'll have to go over that with Simeon."

"Can't you get anything right?" Oasis asked.

While they were arguing, Iggy Biggy stopped pumping beer, moved to Simeon's desk, grabbed the checker's beer, took it to the sink and emptied it. Breathing a sigh of relief, Iggy Biggy refilled the cup with Busch and placed it on Simeon's desk in the exact spot. On the way back to the beer tap, he flicked his index finger at Oasis's hip.

Feeling it, Oasis said, "Perhaps twenty-nine is right."

"You can still go over it with Simeon if you want?"

Oasis ran out of the commissary. He had helped maintain the secrecy of the enterprise, but in less than three minutes he had fallen at least two trays behind his competitors. He wanted to keep pace, if not finish on top, as a matter of pride and for his daughters. Prep schools and Ivy League college tuition showed no signs of becoming less expensive.

As Oasis passed Simeon, he turned to watch Oasis accelerate and shook his head in awe. "Why aren't you a professional athlete?" he yelled.

Upon reentering the commissary, Simeon reached for his beer cup. "You should have seen it. The replay showed the centerfielder hit a home run that missed being the first fair ball hit out of Yankee Stadium by less than a foot. It struck the top level of concrete surrounding the left field escalators. A little more to the right and it might have gone past Babe Ruth Plaza on 161st street. The fans are going wild.

"At last I can quench my thirst," he said. Before he could grip the cup, Kelso lumbered into the commissary, swinging his empty beer tray as if it were a yo-yo. It hit Simeon's desk. The cup fell and the beer spilled.

"You crazy idiot. Can't you be careful?" Simeon said.

Kelso noticed Iggy Biggy shaking his head and realized he had made a grave mistake.

Simeon grabbed his cup, walked to the beer tap, pushed the lever down, filled his cup with Kehlmeyer, put the cup to his lips and drank half the cup before stopping. Iggy Biggy's mouth opened as wide as a wash basin. Kelso closed his eyes.

Simeon raised the half filled cup toward the ceiling. "This is good. It don't taste like the regular beer. Some new stuff snuck in here on us or what?"

"You guessed it. A new brand's being test marketed here at Yankee Stadium. The fans, they like it too," said Kelso.

"Why didn't anyone tell me?"

Simeon returned to his desk, with the beer cup and resumed checking.

Rollo, Kelso, Lenny Mo Dinner and Brad Brown gave each other high fives.

"What are you up to, over there?" Simeon asked.

"We just feel awesome selling so much beer," said Brad Brown. And he and the other beer vendors sped outside.

Kelso went outside with another beer tray. The noise had barely subsided since the home run. The fans yelled the center-fielder's nickname. "Steady! Steady! STEADY!" The noise was so loud, fans had to order by hand gestures rather than spoken requests. "Five here." We'll take three." "Seven for me and my buddies." Almost every male who opened a wallet had either a police or a fire-man's badge. Consuming beer as if it were their final request. "Make that siiix. I haaad enough," said a man next to the one requesting seven.

Kelso heard a fan yell, "Ahhh, I've seen balls hit farther."

Kelso heard a commotion and turned around.

Two men were going at it. As fans noticed the altercation, all rightfield fans rose and looked, like a boxing crowd viewing the final flurry.

Kelso walked away before the Burn's Security Guard's tram-pled him, trying to stop the fight.

As Kelso moved to another aisle, a Stadium's Burns Security Guard yelled, "cut the foul language or your outta here," to a group screaming: "Fuck the umpires."

As Kelso walked toward other customers, he placed his beer tray down and served a fan, dodging a left cross intended for a fan behind him. He thought of complaining, but the Burns Guards were already inundated trying to contain hooliganism. A blur was spreading throughout Kelso's brain. Sending him toward a blank abyss. Law and order seemed a myth. Besides their Silver Shields, what was the dif-ference between inebriated police and firemen and criminals? It could be said this was their way of unwinding from a high pressure job. Any day could be their last - they were honoring fallen colleagues who had made this self evident. But it didn't entitle them to primi-tive behavior.

He wondered if he could ever feel safe. He wasn't going to depend on others for safety - not after seeing the line between cop and criminal become obscure, not when he remembered the justice sys-tem treated his father like a marionette, not when he could easily be a victim of law enforcer or law breaker. No, the only way Terence

90

Kelso would achieve a sense of security was by making sure Kehlmeyer successful.

As he left the aisle, he gingerly navigated the last few steps to avoid vomit. In less than a minute and a half he had sold the entire beer tray and already had reservations for the next two. A huge smile crossed his face.

"That's it. Shut the beer off," Simeon yelled.

"I'm glad you did that. It's really wild out there," said Kelso. Though he had told the truth, Simeon's command made Kelso's desire to see Kehlmeyer succeed keener. It was trifling having to take orders from someone as spiteful as Simeon.

CHAPTER XII

CHATTING PROGRESS

Three weeks after Silver Shields night, Iggy Biggy, Oasis, Brad Brown and Andy Metzger were seated in the Stadium Bowling Lanes, describing what happened when Simeon drank Kehlmeyer.

Kelso moved toward the gathering. He had chosen the bowling lanes to discuss Kehlmeyer's progress. The bowling alley was sparkling clean and due to a lack of business, quiet. The volume of foot stomping laughter increased as stragglers arrived and heard of Simeon tasting Kehlmeyer.

"All right. Calm down," said Kelso. "Since every game isn't 'animal,' is it reasonable to say we'll sell twenty kegs per game?"

"Very reasonable. Maybe conservative," said Copperblum.

"It's better to be conservative. We don't want supply exceeding demand yet. Based on an average of twenty kegs per event, and five hundred dollars per keg, we're talking a gross profit of ...."

"That's $10,000 per game," said Brad Brown. A bowling ball struck a pin in a nearby lane.

"I don't know the exact number. Copperblum can give us the exact figure later. But let's use fifteen. Ten thousand divided by fifteen we're talking roughly six hundred sixty-six dollars per man per game. Correct?" Kelso said.

"Yeah." They spoke as one.

"Are we ready to expand?" Kelso asked.

"What do you mean, expand?" Rod Somer asked.

"Moving beyond the ballpark."

"Where beyond the ballpark?" asked Errol.

"What's wrong with wherever beer's sold?"

"You crazy, mon," said Uranso.

"Major corporations do the same thing. Establish a core market. Dominate it. Then expand."

"One tiny thing," said Rollo. "We're not a major corporation."

"We *can be*," said Kelso, sounding like a paternalistic land baron talking to his serfs.

"Lenny Mo Dinner *can be* President of the United States. Do you see either the Democrats or the Republicans coming to get the fuckin' idiot?" said Brad Brown.

"Leave Lenny alone."

Lenny Mo Dinner gave Kelso the grateful look of a distressed maiden seeing her hero.

"If we depend on the Stadium as our sole market, how long is it going to take to be discovered? How long before another beer's introduced that customers prefer? How long before we reach the saturation point and nobody wants Kehlmeyer anymore?" A ball slammed into the pins two alleys over. Kelso didn't think they could hear him, still, he lowered his voice. "Before Kehlmeyer can become a household word, we must crawl. From the ballpark we expand over the next six weeks into the Bronx and Manhattan."

Heads nodded. Everyone was paying closer attention. They hadn't realized there were so many pitfalls.

"Remember we were going to use Iggy Biggy's building as a distribution center. Can you still do it, Iggy?"

"You got it," said Iggy.

"Great! From there, we make our move."

"How much profit are we talking?" Errol asked.

"We got to see how many kegs we move. Which restaurants, bars and clubs we can get into. Until then I can't tell you anything."

"How many kegs we moving out of the renegade's club?" Ben Feldstein asked.

"Last I checked, six to eight per month," Kelso said.

"You sure Beezer's really trying to push Kehlmeyer?"

"Don't worry about him, Metzger. With all those mouths to feed, he wants to make money, too. I'll set up another meeting about a month from now to chart our progress. See what problems we're encountering. You can pick-up your current share of the profits from

Copperblum. If there're no other questions, that's it."

Everyone began to leave.

Kelso went to see about a free drink.

The editors of SUCCESS magazine weren't looking to place Beezer on their cover, but neither would Kelso embody their idea of an ideal businessman. Placing them in partnership was like mixing soil and water: the resulting mud wasn't something to step into; yet, from it came flowers and vegetables.

Kelso wanted to see if hanging posters in local bars would boost Kehlmeyer sales. To initiate the campaign, he chose the after-hour clubs of Beezer the renegade.

How Beezer came to own bars was proof that in America anything was possible. James Bezel, a.k.a. Beezer the renegade, resembled a brown mango, who never wore proper fitting pants nor underwear, triple XL being hard to find. Still, somehow the opposite sex found him attractive. He had fathered five children out of wedlock.

After graduating from Dewitt Clinton High School, he attempted selling vacuum cleaners but quit after a while - five months seemed more than enough - and launched his renegade career selling genuine crack when the drug first hit the streets. Being amongst the first enabled him to turn a quick, massive profit. Then, he got smart. He decided to get out of the business and plowed his crack profits into discreet after-hour clubs. Located in the basements of buildings used by the government to relocate homeless families, his clubs were tolerated by the police because they were a magnet for drug runners. As long as there was no indiscriminate violence, Beezer's clubs eazed the taxpayer's burden. As long as the riff raff were hanging out in Beezer's clubs, they were spending less time perpetrating crime. The clubs' flourishing amid squalor contributed to Beezer's renegade legend.

The next day after the meeting at the bowling alley, Kelso went to Beezer's club near the intersection of One hundred sixty-fifth street and Walton Avenue. Inside was dark and dingy. A sixty watt light bulb hung from the ceiling. Beezer was sitting at a bar forty feet long and two and a half feet wide. Beezer motioned for Kelso to join him.

They wanted to discuss their business and get out of each other's sight. They disliked each other because while in high school, they both tried to rig the student government elections for themselves, but they were willing to put animosity aside to earn money.

"Where're these posters?" Beezer asked.

Kelso pulled the lid off a yard long cardboard cylinder and pulled out three posters and flattened them against the table.

"That looks hip," said Beezer. "None of you funky white folks are in it."

Kelso took in a deep breath. The nerve of Beezer to call anyone funky. "What if I used monkeys in the poster instead of either black or white folks?"

"I'd tell you to take the poster to the zoo and see how it'd boost Kehlmeyer sales amongst the animals. Where's a poster with some whities? I know you didn't make 'em all with people like me in 'em."

You got that right, thought Kelso. He separated the outer poster from the middle one, flattened it on the table.

Beezer's eyes glowed with admiration. A smile that matched the width of his waist came over his face at the bikini clad blonde supposedly holding a lipstick-smeared mug of Kehlmeyer. The blonde was giving a suggestive smile. Beezer said, "That's a fine white babe. How come I never see you with any like that?"

"How come I never see you with the mothers of your children?"

"I'm busy earning money to take care of 'em."

"That's no excuse. Oasis brings his family to the ballpark once in a while, and he probably doesn't make as much money as you. Bring them to the ballpark. That won't put too big a strain on your child support."

Beezer was ashamed to admit that none of his children's mothers wanted to be seen with him in public. "Let me hang this poster and the first one you showed me on the wall?"

"It'll take you, what, about three weeks to get a fair idea what impact they're having on Kehlmeyer sales?"

"That sounds right," said Beezer. "I'll let you know three weeks from today. One more question though. Was that babe in the poster sipping Kehlmeyer?"

"You think I'd let a girl that gorgeous drink horse piss? That's sparkling Apple Cider."

"You're a real All American guy Kelso. And I'm glad to be in business with you." Beezer and Kelso shook hands. While shaking hands, Beezer put his left hand over their right's.

Kelso smiled. "Nothing's too good for us former Clinton homeboys."

CHAPTER XIII

THE INCREDIBLE HUNK

Four days later Feldstein was waddling down the ramp behind the bullpen when Kelso spotted him. Feldstein was hard to miss. His sheer bulk made him a magnet for curious eyes. He stood five feet four - both ways - and was known to his co-workers at Yankee Stadium as the Incredible Hunk.

"Hi, Ben. You working Chippendales tonight?" Kelso yelled.

A vendor nearby laughed.

"Yeah, I'll be there tonight. All the babes are going to be lusting after my bod."

"Great, glad to hear it. Let me be the first to congratulate you. I knew you could do it." Kelso stuck out his hand.

Ben Feldstein stopped smiling. "You could care less if I work at Chippendales. You don't care if I work period. Now what has you acting all complimentary when I know damn well you don't care about anything besides yourself?"

"Now that you mention it, there's something I been meaning to ask you." Kelso put his left arm around as much of Ben Feldstein's shoulders as he could.

Ben pushed Kelso's arms off.

"After you, sir." Kelso bowed.

Ben Feldstein waddled past and into the locker room. "Okay, Kelso what you been meaning to ask?"

"You still a renting supervisor with the Housing Authority?"

"Over at Forest Projects."

"Can you get us a one-bedroom apartment?"

"What do you mean us?" Ben opened his locker.

"You're in with our brewery operation?"

"What does Kehlmeyer have to do with a one bedroom apartment in the projects?"

"The difference between stagnation and expansion, standing still and going forward, moving backwards or moving ahead. Can your fat ass relate to that?"

Ben slammed his locker shut. "A lot better than you think. Exactly what do you need the apartment for?"

"Storage space."

"There's not enough between your place and Iggy Biggy's?"

"When we were a mom and pop operation, yes. Now that we're a thriving enterprise, no."

"Why don't you lease a warehouse?"

"Because I want more profits to pass on to my partners and plow back into the business."

Ben shook his head. "There's an eighteen month waiting list to get into my buildings."

"You're a supervisor. You got pull."

Ben shrugged. "I'm a civil servant. I got to deal with bureaucratic red tape."

"What would it take to get around the red tape?" Kelso rubbed his fingers through his glistening hair.

"Come up with a destitute family rejected by every welfare hotel in the city, and I can get you a one-bedroom apartment."

"Once I find this 'model family,' how long before they get in?"

"They gotta go before a Housing Authority Review Board."

"What does this review board base decisions on?"

"I don't know. I don't attend the hearings. I just send people to 'em."

"Typical dedicated civil servant."

"Look, Kelso, I process enough families to start a small nation."

"That's why you're working with us - to get out of that grind; to make some real money instead of just getting by. To experience the difference between earning a living and living life the way you want it to be."

"I know. I know. Don't push me, Kelso." Ben picked up a pile of paperwork he had to complete by the following morning. Feldstein had only become a part of Kelso's venture in an attempt to raise his standard of living. He had reservations about risking his civil service job to satisfy Kelso's greed, but the more he thought about it, the more viable the risk became. He reasoned the city's munificence when it came to hiring employees could end at any time. There could be lay-offs and he could be amongst them. Then he'd be just another New Yorker beating the pavement, looking for work.

"Look, Feldstein. You don't want to be a paper shuffler the rest of your life, do you? Listen. I'll have a family ready in three days. You gonna' be able to hook me ... us up?"

"I'll do my best. I'll find out what actually happens at the hearings."

"Good, you womanizer you." Kelso gripped Feldstein's fleshy love handles and shook them.

Ben put his arms between his hips and Kelso's arms, raised them, broke Kelso's grip and waddled away.

The day after his conversation with Kelso, Ben Feldstein attended his first Housing Authority Review Board in six years and learned the board was facing a reverse discrimination case unless more white families were put in the projects.

When Ben Feldstein told Kelso of the reverse discrimination suit, Kelso viewed it as a twist of fate. If he did find a poor family whose skin color matched his, their misfortune would be his opportunity. He would go before the Housing Authority Review Board, champion their cause, right a wrong, and get the space to expand his brewery business.

The same day Kelso spread the word among his white powder distributors to find a white family to pose as his poverty stricken inner city inhabitants. He figured he'd have a family by lunchtime. It didn't work out that way. The families weren't destitute enough. They drove cars. Not Cadillacs or Mercedes Benz, but six and seven year old Fords and Chevys pushing 100,000 miles. They didn't have vacation homes in exotic locations, but several did have time shares in the Poconos. The first day ended without a family. The second day came and it looked as if Kelso'd still be seeking a family on the third day, late in the afternoon, one of his twelve-year-old distributors, a boy named Junito in

Spanish Harlem, told Kelso he had something interesting.

"What are we waiting for? Let's see 'em," Kelso said.

"Hail a cab," Junito demanded.

"Can't we take the subway?"

"You want to get there fast, or you wanna fight the rush hour crowd, bro?"

Kelso hailed a cab. When they got inside, Junito told the cab driver to go to the Seventy-first Street exit of the East River Drive. When they arrived, Kelso paid the fare. He didn't give a tip. Junito led Kelso to the crosswalk a few blocks north. They crossed the crosswalk and were on the pedestrian side of the East River Drive. Junito hopped over the iron fence separating land from water. "Jump to it, bro. You eager to find this family or what?"

"Where we going?"

"You'll see," said Junito. He led Kelso to a dry, ten foot sewage pipe, bent down and yelled, "Yo Pete! You in there?"

A blond youngster, grime on his face, came out. "Junito. What's up?"

"Your old man inside?"

"Yeah, drinking Thunderbird."

"Mother in there?"

"Nah, she's out with my little sisters trying to scrounge up gap."

"Get your old man out here," Kelso said. As badly as he needed a family, he was not going inside a sewage pipe. Pete disappeared inside the pipe and soon came back with a man as tall as Kelso who would have a problem being seen if he turned sideways. When he got about five feet from Kelso and Junito, the stench of Thunderbird overwhelmed them. Kelso took a step back. "Can you have your family ready to go to the Bronx tomorrow? We're gonna get you some housing," Kelso said.

"I don't see why not."

"Good. We'll pick you up at 10:30 A.M. tomorrow."

"We'll be ready."

Kelso nodded and started walking. Pete and Junito did a soul brothers handshake. Junito reached into his pocket, pulled out a ten dollar bill, placed it in Pete's hand, then broke into a slow trot, hopped over the fence and caught up with Kelso.

"Where did you find them?" Kelso asked.

"Pete was in front of a McDonald's I ate at yesterday. He looked starving, so I bought him a burger and fries. While we ate, he told me his father's story."

"I'm all ears," said Kelso.

Junito told Kelso that Pete's father, a former bank vice president was arrested and convicted for embezzling just after the 1987 Stock Market Crash. Legal fees for the court case and appeals devastated the man's fortune. From prince to pauper in nine months, he was too proud to beg, to ask for help. A bottle of Thunderbird and other cheap spirits became his closest friends, a sewage pipe, his family's only refuge from the elements.

The day of the hearing came. Pete, his father, mother and sisters were dressed in jeans, casual shirts and blouses, stood in the lobby of Bronx Family Court. Junito, Kelso and Ben Feldstein were dressed in suits and looked at the family as much as they looked at them. Surprised to see each other in clothes they weren't accustomed to, everyone felt they were adequately prepared and they entered the Hearing Room.

"This man." Kelso pointed to Pete's father. "Gave his all for his family and his employer. He worked on Wall Street to get his taste of the American dream and look what it's led to - rats for his innocent children's neighbors?"

By the time Kelso was through, those members of the review board - two Blacks, two Hispanics, an Asian, an Italian and a Serbo-Croation - who weren't crying were examining papers to make sure admittance of Pete's family was expedited. They approved a three bedroom apartment in a project right off the F.D.R. drive on the Lower East Side of Manhattan, a site Kelso wasn't entirely pleased with because of its distance from Yankee Stadium, but it had more spacious rooms, elevators that broke down less frequently, easier access to major traffic arteries and a similar quantity of violent crimes as in the Bronx.

Kelso, Pete's family, Junito and Ben Feldstein left the hearing and walked to a nearby subway, where Kelso put tokens into the turnstile and told Pete's father, "I'm sorry you have to find this out now, but you and your family are going to live in a two bedroom flat on Coney Island."

"What happened to the Lower East Side?"

"It's been set aside for something else."

"What about my family?" asked Pete's father.

"You're out of the sewer."

"What if I don't want to go to Coney Island?"

"You wanna experience a dwelling space lower than sewage pipes?"

"What's that supposed to mean?"

"Move your family into Coney Island, enjoy the Amusement Park, the Aquarium, take 'em to Nathan's and forget about the Lower East Side. You'll visit there once a month. Ben'll tell you the date."

Kelso watched Pete and his family get on the D. As the train left the station, Kelso turned around and put his hands on Ben's shoulders. "I did it! I did it!"

"You mean *we* did it."

"Whatever," Kelso said. "Isn't it great to be around a man of vision! By force of will, now I've got a distribution center with easy access to the five boroughs and New Jersey. Wherever beer's drunk, Kehlmeyer's going to be a choice. And one day it will be *the choice!*"

"Get your hands off me, you insensitive chameleon." Feldstein took a deep breath, held in his gut, and squeezed through the turnstile.

Alouiscious sat in the bleachers, looking at four telephone numbers. He'd tell everyone they were 'woomen's' phone numbers. The high Summer sunshine caused his large brown eyes to squint.

Kelso's hand appeared on Alouiscious's right shoulder. "Alouiscious, my man. How are you?"

Alouiscious studied Kelso's face. "What's up?"

Kelso explained what had transpired with his beer venture so far and what role Alouiscious could have in its expansion. How he would help Kelso raise funds.

After hearing Kelso out, Alouiscious removed Kelso's hand. "How can you ask me to do such a thing? Money actually means that much to you?"

Kelso's eyes got wider. "But Alouiscious, this is the opportunity of a lifetime."

"I've heard that before. In fact, I've heard it so much, I feel like a third generation cat."

"Well, this is the opportunity that'll change you from scavenging alley cat - needing all those lives - to a proud lion - the king of beasts." Kelso patted Alouiscious's back.

"If I do what you ask I'll be a beast not a king. Besides, what would the woomens think of me if I did something like that?"

Kelso interlocked his fingers, as if he were about to pray. "Forget about what the women would think. You ever heard the saying: 'He who has the gold rules.'?"

"Yeah, I heard it," said Alouiscious. "You ever read in the Bible: 'Do not lay up for yourself treasures on Earth; but lay up for yourself treasures in Heaven.'?"

Kelso arched his eyebrows. "Which Bible passage is that?"

"Matthew 6:19-20."

Kelso shrugged. "I don't remember it."

"When was the last time you read anything in the Bible?" asked Alouiscious.

"The last time I read the Bible, I was in summer vacation Bible day camp."

Alouiscious nodded. "I had a funny feeling the truth was something like that."

"What difference does it make? People who read the Bible aren't necessarily any better than I am."

"I've considered that possibility," said Alouiscious. "People who merely read the holy Scriptures can be just as wretched as you. People who read the scriptures, then put them into action, those people, in my opinion are - at least - better than you. No matter how much more money you have.

"Anyway, the only place I'll be if I did what yc   ʔnt is behind bars, numbers across my chest. And that's if I'm luck   ʔ "

Kelso got up and began walking away. He tur
"Alouiscious, this isn't heaven we're in. You're r
think you are. If you change your mind let me k
down the steps and into the rampway.

Alouiscious looked at him disappear. Alo

103

more money he'd probably be gathering women's phone numbers' instead of men's. Despite being broke, his parents had instilled in him a deep appreciation of virtue. He might never be wealthy, but at least he would go to his grave saying he had never asked another human being to drink beer containing horse urine.

CHAPTER XIV

MARSHAL IGGY BIGGY

Iggy Biggy was in his apartment setting up a still in the spare bedroom. Uranso had given him the Kehlmeyer recipe, so he could make the beer and distribute it to local bars and clubs. The beer was growing in popularity locally and by the end of the baseball season, Kelso was planning to take it national. Iggy knew Kelso was already working on a logo for bottles and cans and speaking to advertising firms about commercials.

As Iggy connected a plastic tube to a barrel, he heard screams. He went to the window and looked out. A crackhead was trying to grab his grandson out of his stroller. In a flash Iggy was out of his apartment, down the stairs and out of the door. He pushed the addict off his daughter and grandchild and got them safely into the building. The crackhead took off.

It took Iggy Biggy a quarter block to catch him. When he did, Iggy threw a tremendous overhand haymaker that hit the crack addict flush on the face. As if he had been struck by an artillery shell, the addict crumpled to the pavement. Iggy Biggy picked up the unconscious figure, threw him over his shoulder, went back to his building and dumped him into the elevator. He pushed the basement button. The elevator went straight there. He dragged the addict in front of a tool closet, took a set of keys from his pants pocket, opened the closet, took out electrical masking tape, half inch thick rope and a six foot long, four feet wide, four feet deep Sports equipment bag from the Stadium. Iggy checked the addict's pulse. He still had one. Iggy took the addict's handkerchief, shaped it into a ball and stuck it in his mouth. He placed masking tape over the mouth, around the addict's face, jerked his arms behind his back and tied the rope around his wrists, ankles and thighs. Iggy bought the ankles almost two feet behind the wrists at a hundred eighty degree angle. He connected the ankles to the wrists using nearly a yard of rope.

After making sure all the knots were tight, he opened the equipment bag, pushed the addict inside and zipped it shut. As he did so, his eyes fell on the five pound sledgehammer he used to crack the sidewalk. He shook his head. It wasn't necessary. He shut the closet, picked up the equipment bag, turned off the basement lights and summoned the elevator. When the elevator arrived, he put the dufflebag in front of it as a doorjamb, then went to the incinerator, opened its outer door, took a book of matches out of his pants pocket, lit a match and tossed it in. A fresh, unsavory aroma arose. He closed the incinerator doors, ran back to the elevator, kicked the duffle bag inside and pressed the button for the top floor.

The elevator stopped on the fourth. A young girl got on. She pressed the button for the fifth floor, looked at Iggy Biggy and down at the equipment bag. "What's wiggling inside that bag?" she asked.

"I got a pet python. If you be nice, I'll let you see it."

"No thank you," said the girl. "I'm small enough to be its next meal."

The elevator stopped at the fifth floor. The girl got off.

"Next time walk one flight, please," Iggy said.

The girl stuck her tongue out and ran away.

The elevator door shut. Iggy Biggy breathed a sigh of relief. The elevator ascended one more floor and Iggy got off, dragging the equipment bag behind him. He pulled the bag up the flight of stairs leading to the roof, then carried it to the grated triangular fence covering the incinerator shaft. He pulled the pyramid off and looked down. Far below amber flames licked the dark, rising smoke. He picked up the duffel bag and tossed it in. He heard a dull thud. Thicker smoke rose. He replaced the grated pyramid fence and returned to the roof's staircase wiping his hands. Having previously turned a Caucasian into ashes, now he had done the same to a member of his own race.

Now I can tell my daughter and my grandchild I believe in equal opportunity, he thought as he walked down the staircase.

Soon the word spread how Iggy Biggy took care of the crack addict who tried to kidnap his grandchild. Since people in his neighborhood didn't mingle with the police, the word didn't spread to New York's Finest, but whenever people saw a known crackhead or pusher, they started talking loudly about what happened to addicts trying to kidnap a neighborhood child.

"From smoking dust to being dust. All in a matter of minutes. Check it out," was the most frequently used quote.

The crackhead would finish what he came to do very quickly and leave the neighborhood immediately. It would be a long time before he returned - if ever. Fewer crack vials lay on the streets, the number of shootings diminished and neighborhood inhabitants became less hesitant about walking the streets.

Iggy Biggy was treated as a conquering hero. Everyone was inviting him over for dinner. Everytime he walked in a store, if he didn't get what he wanted for free, he got a substantial discount - and he didn't have to ask. All the older ladies were introducing him to their unwed daughters and to daughters they felt had lousy husbands. More girls were putting out for him than he had time for, what with his duties as building superintendent, Yankee Stadium porter, Kelso business partner and grandparent. Iggy Biggy contemplated early retirement and never setting foot outside of his neighborhood again. Reason prevailed. He knew the orgy of bliss wouldn't last forever. And he'd get tired of doing all the neighborhood girls anyway. He took solace in knowing he had slowed the spread of a menace.

CHAPTER XV

KELSO THE FUND RAISER

Later that afternoon Kelso was driving through a Bronx neighborhood to pick-up white powder money from his young sales force. Kelso was excited. He couldn't wait to pit Kehlmeyer against nationally advertised beers.

He was so proud of how Kehlmeyer was evolving, he paid little attention he was in the slums. At each red light his mint condition '64 Pontiac GTO, worth more now than when he bought it, stopped. Kelso would close his eyes a few seconds, envisioning how a national television campaign would impact Kehlmeyer scales. Then he'd open his eyes, continue moving and look at the beer ad billboards on brick walls. The ones showing predatory animals striking an aggressive pose; scantily clad women positioned so alluring he couldn't help but get the subliminal message: drink this beverage and you'll seduce me - all night long; and beer bottles and cans placed at angles making them resemble erect phallic symbols. He shook his head. "If this is the best my competition can do - I can't do no worse," he said to himself.

Granted Kehlmeyer would have more to overcome: maintaining the key ingredient's secrecy and processing enough of it to go nationwide. Also, funding a national advertising campaign was going to be tough.

He had read in ADVERTISING WEEKLY it cost $20,000,000 for a nationally televised campaign. Legal fees and accounting costs - this was way beyond the skills and scope of Copperblum - would push the final bill over $22,500,000. He could get some of the money via his own assets; however, like many wealthy people, he preferred

108

using other people's money. There was one hitch: his personality made it difficult for anyone to consider loaning him a dime much less twenty million dollars. He'd have to find another way to get it.

He slowed down. There was a vision of urban splendor amidst harrowing ruin ahead. A brownstone standing three stories high, the ground surrounding it spotless. He wondered who the landlord was to pull off such a coup. When he saw the building's address, he slammed on the GTO's brakes. He owned the spotless brownstone! On the varnished wooden beam over the door were the words: "Counselors of Unwed Mothers Residence."

An idea hit his brain like a beacon invading total darkness. He had heard about C.U.M. Unwed mothers, teenagers barely past puberty, hardcore welfare mothers living together, trying to break the habit. The mothers had made admirable strides to improve the quality of their lives. With the help of a local nun, they had started their own nursery. They convinced friends and relatives who were carpenters, electricians and plumbers to come to the home and teach their skills so they could fend for themselves. The nun was so proud of the improvements, she obtained two night school teachers for the girls, most of whom had never finished junior high school. "Sorry sister. But all good things must come to an end," vowed Kelso.

A crackhead was running around in circles in the middle of the busy street. The GTO was one of several cars that stopped short to avoid hitting the drug addict. Drivers waved fists at the addict. One yelled, "Hey asshole! Get on the sidewalk." No one got out of his car to help the crackhead. But when the crackhead got near his GTO, Kelso opened the door, grabbed the addict's elbow and pulled him inside.

"What's happening, blood?" Kelso reached past his passenger and shut the door.

"I wuz runnin' the Marathon," said the addict.

"Were you winning?"

"No one wuz keeping up with me."

"Would you like to be in the Olympics? They're being held a couple of blocks from here."

"What event am I going to be in?"

"You're such a marathoner, you've earned the right to carry the torch."

The addict gave Kelso a bewildered look.

Kelso drove to a convenience store, parked, whispered into the addict's ear, reached into his pants pocket, pulled out his wallet, took out a crisp one hundred dollar bill and slipped it into the addict's right palm. "There's a Grant waiting for you if you finish the job," he said.

The crackhead went inside, purchased a pint of rubbing alcohol, and returned to the GTO. It sped toward the brownstone. The crackhead drank orange juice and swallowed aspirin he'd purchased to try to calm his nerves. Kelso let the crackhead out two blocks from the brownstone. It was almost dusk. People were either having dinner, watching television or blasting stereos - the street was empty. The crackhead picked up an empty glass bottle and went into the weedy lot next to the brownstone. He kneeled behind a thick bush, opened the rubbing alcohol and poured its contents into the bottle. He then took a soiled handkerchief out of his back pocket, twisted it into a long bandanna and slipped it inside, leaving four inches out. The addict pulled out a cigarette lighter, flicked it. An amber flame stood a half inch high. He struck the flame to the handkerchief. It didn't catch. He tried again and watched as the flame consumed the handkerchief and engulfed the alcohol, turning it into a blue meteorite of glass, fire and gas. He threw the bottle at the brownstone's basement window. Instantly, flames roared up. The fire was so swift, the people inside panicked. Gasping and choking, some of the women made it to the doors, but billowing flames made them scamper back. Some tossed their babies out the windows. Three were caught. Two were on their way to a more peaceful world. The mothers could toss no more. The building collapsed. The flames and gases emitted a hot wind. Friends and neighbors ran for the safety of the other side of the street. The only water to be found was the tears in onlookers' eyes as they gasped in horror.

The crack addict was on top of a nearby roof, clapping and smiling, thinking of the additional fifty dollars he'd receive. He didn't know the fatalities would be fortunate to be buried in a Potter's Field. He didn't know if the infants who survived would be adopted or remain orphans. He didn't know how many women and children he'd killed. Crack made it so he didn't care.

At a prearranged rendezvous site, a school playground a few blocks away, Kelso sat in the GTO, looking at his home owner's insurance policy. He realized he couldn't continue burning buildings until he raised twenty million dollars, not without getting caught, but this fire would secure the seed capital necessary to start the national campaign. As far as he was concerned, the women and children who died were pawns he had put out of misery. Their lives weren't going to change history, his already had, and with the $275,000 insurance settlement, there would be further glory.

The crackhead came.

"You were good. You win an honorary gold medal." Kelso gave him the fifty dollar bill.

"You want to help me celebrate?"

"I'd rather you do that yourself."

"At least drive me to my house."

"You have a house?"

"My crackhouse."

"Oh! No problem. Nooo problem."

Kelso drove him to a crackhouse where he purchased enough vials to fill a small popcorn bucket, and smoked several vials before returning to the GTO, where he smoked more crack. Kelso drove him to a different intersection and let him out. This intersection, at Southern Boulevard and Westchester avenue, was far busier than the previous one. "Okay, blood. Continue the marathon tradition," said Kelso, as the crackhead left the GTO.

Somehow he was still able to run circles and avoid cars, but he couldn't dodge an onrushing Metropolitan Transit Authority Bronx #42 bus, whose driver slammed on the brake so hard that passengers suffered whiplash and broken bones. They would live to tell of their harrowing experience. The crackhead wouldn't. The only person who could tell of Kelso's role in the brownstone fire was another statistic.

The following day the headlines screamed: "C.U.M. burned," and "Babies Fry, Fly and Die." The more prestigious Times stooped to using: "Unwed Mothers United with Soot and Ashes," on the front page of the Metropolitan Section. The articles suggested the fire was the locals way of having a macabre form of fun, letting off tension or releasing frustration. Little note was made of the mothers' efforts to improve their plight, or of the positive impact the home had had on the community. The crackhead's collision with the bus didn't even rate a line.

CHAPTER XVI

RUNS, HITS AND ERRORS

They were exhausted and fulfilled. They had reason to be. During the night they shared imtimacy. She was the best Rollo had had since he broke up with the swing club girl years ago. Evelyn was in rapture. At last she had someone who made running home, after dancing and getting horny on stage, a pleasure. It wasn't their first mating; they had no intention of making it their last; so far it had been their best.

They hugged and congratulated each other. Evelyn asked, "You want something to drink?"

"Any kind of juice?"

"I have oranges and a squeezer. I'll make you some fresh squeezed." She took the blanket off and got up.

Rollo grabbed her waist. "No relax. I'll make it. You deserve a rest. I feel like running ten kilometers." Rollo posed like a runner in stride, grinned at Evelyn and walked to the kitchen.

It was barely bigger than a closet. Thank God she lived alone. Rollo had had his fill of competing for party space with women's siblings, parents and roommates. He opened the refrigerator. It was filled with fruit and vegetables. He saw very little meat, which could've meant she had less cholesterol clogging her arteries. He took four navel oranges, cut them in half and squeezed them. The juice filled two glasses. Rollo found a tray in the cupboard, put the glasses on and returned to the bedroom.

Evelyn had turned on the radio to WBLS's hourly news. It was giving details of a fatal fire. "A three alarm fire has demolished a C.U.M. residence home in the South Bronx. The fire appears to have had a suspicious origin," the announcer was saying.

"Damn, who'd want to torch a place like that?" Evelyn said.

"Have you forgot where we are? People pursue danger for simple, idiotic reasons."

"But a home for unwed mothers?"

"They could have been as pure as the driven snow. It still could have happened."

"I know."

"The newscaster said the fire at 845 Tarenton Avenue seemed suspicious."

"Oh shit! That's where Severina and her baby live."

"I'll go downstairs and get a newspaper. Maybe it's a mistake." Rollo grabbed his jeans, put on his sneakers without tying the laces, went to the candystore on the corner and grabbed a NEW YORK TIMES.

By the time he returned, Evelyn had put on a 'Loose Lips, Sink Ships,' black and white mini dress and was rinsing the juice glasses. He sat down on the love seat in the living room and opened the Metropolitan Section. The Police and Fire Department had no witnesses, but area residents had seen a well-known neighborhood crack addict nearby as the building went up.

"There's no mention of survivors. In the name of Allah, Severina! And if it wasn't arson, then what was it?" asked Evelyn.

"Maybe providence."

"Why would the supreme being treat its subjects in such a way? Especially Severina, who wanted to get into the 'straight' scene?"

"Maybe there's a lesson to be learned or a triumph hidden in the ashes and ruin."

"Oh come on," Evelyn flicked the page off her thigh. "We're dealing with reality. What good is any analogy, metaphor crap going to do for Severina and her daughter? Is that the thanks she gets for giving up topless dancing?"

Rollo turned toward her. "Nothing. You're right. Analogies and metaphors are for those whose hearts are still ticking. The best that can be done for them is a decent burial and finding out how the fire started. It must be great to be at peace. You never hear any of those folks complaining."

"Do you want to be at peace?"

Rollo kissed Evelyn's full lips, then wiped tears from her eyes. "I'll wait till the time comes. There's a few things I'd like to accomplish before my name's on a tombstone, if I can afford one."

"Such as?"

"Write more hit songs. Do something for those not as fortunate as myself. Leave a legacy I can be proud of - if and when I have children." Rollo looked at his watch. "And I'd like to get to the baseball game on time."

Evelyn kissed Rollo's lips. "Don't worry, we'll get there on time. Who's going to be the mother of your children?"

"She's out there somewhere. Why do you ask? You want me to make you with child?"

Evelyn placed her right thigh over Rollo's. "One day, maybe, but not today." She moved the rest of her body onto Rollo's lap. "Look at what's probably happened to Severina and her baby. They sure as hell didn't have a primrose path. Neither did my brothers. Her palms covered her face. "Why would I want to bring a child into such an unforgiving world?"

Rollo rubbed her back.

"I may have been too young to help my brothers, but if I ever get my hands on the scumbag who offed Severina and her baby, he's breathed his last breath."

It was a mid Summer matinee game. Yankee Stadium reverberated with the sounds of children yelling and screaming. Coupled with music - whether sung or from the organ - a cheerful atmosphere swept through the arena.

Rollo and Evelyn arrived as batting practice finished and sat near home plate in box seats facing toward third base. Evelyn watched for a few minutes and chuckled. After being in the United States for seven years, she still did not understand the natives' fascination with grown men hitting a little ball with a wooden club. She considered baseball a prime example of western decadence: the money spent on players' salaries, club ownership, television rights and player endorsements was appalling. Starving mouths could be fed; clothes could cover the near naked and homes could be made for the homeless with all that money.

On the other hand, then these Americans would do nothing but go to amusement parks, watch television and perhaps spend more time with their wives and girlfriends: let the Americans have their childish game, she thought. She did like one facet of baseball: looking at players running back and forth. Their buns provided more excitement than five teams separated from first place by two games with ten to go.

The crowd stood for the singing of the national anthem. When it was over, Rollo and Evelyn hugged. Through the first three innings each team had one hit. Rollo didn't like pitchers' duels. He found this one even less enjoyable because Evelyn kept up a steady stream of questions. "Why does the catcher squat when catching the ball?"

"So the pitcher can throw strikes," said Rollo.

"Why is the second baseman sometimes positioned closer to the first baseman than second base?"

"He thinks the batter'll hit the ball there."

"Why is the guy positioned between second and third base called a shortstop when he isn't short and never stops?"

"That position was named more than a century ago. It's worked so far. Why change it?"

"It's still a mystery how you Americans can love this game. But, come to think of it, it's popular in other countries. Even banana republics. Peoples' tastes can be so strange!"

"Remember how you earn a living, dancing ninety seven percent naked and having men toss you money," said Rollo.

"What I do is provide men with something they want - something they've wanted since prehistoric times and will continue to want, whereas baseball is a relative newcomer."

The visitors were rallying in the fifth inning: they had runners on second and third with no one out. Their clean up and fifth hitters were coming to bat.

The Yankee pitcher - a young lefthander with an overpowering fastball and a wicked slider - bore down. He went to a full count on the cleanup hitter. He threw a wicked slider. The cleanup hitter fouled it off. He threw another wicked slider. The cleanup hitter barely got a piece of it. The pitcher threw a rising fastball. The cleanup hitter tipped it; it went into the catcher's mitt - and popped out. The pitcher

116

flicked his glove against his left thigh and looked in for the sign. He got it. He reared backed and the pitch flew toward the plate.

"Rollo, why does the ...."

"Save it! Would you?"

The batter swung. He missed. The catcher tried to catch it. He missed. The ball went to the backstop. The runner on third base scored. The other runner advanced to third base.

The pitcher took matters into what he had greater control of. He struck the fifth batter out on three pitches: a fastball on the outside corner, a fastball on the lower inside corner and a high hard one straight down the middle.

Rollo caressed Evelyn's thigh and whispered into her ear, "Sorry, I was abrupt."

"You probably won't take any more novices to baseball games."

"Better you're a novice at baseball than certain other things," Rollo grinned.

In between half innings, Rollo and Evelyn saw a vendor nearby. "Who's ready for Cousin Blumski?" Copperblum was yelling.

"If I were going to buy a beer I would," said Rollo.

Copperblum turned, saw Rollo and Evelyn. He went silent. He had seen beautiful women at Yankee Stadium before. None before had stopped him in his tracks and put him at a loss for words. "What's the matter? You seen a phantom triple play," Rollo said.

"Something like that," Copperblum said.

He offered them free conventional beers. Rollo and Evelyn declined.

"Can I come back when I check out?"

"I can't promise you we'll be here, but why not?"

Evelyn pinched Rollo's arms. "I have business to attend to after the game, sorry, some other time."

Copperblum turned to serve a fan. He gave the fan two conventional and two Kehlmeyers. When he was done he nodded toward Rollo. Rollo, who had his right arm around Evelyn's shoulders, acknowledged the nod with a thumbs up. Copperblum scurried back to his commissary.

They were in the midst of thirty thousand other onlookers but felt alone. Rollo held Evelyn tighter. In earnest she tried to get a bet-

117

ter understanding of baseball by carefully observing the game and not asking questions.

The Yankees threatened in their half of the fifth, the sixth and seventh innings but didn't score. The Yankee pitcher struggled but kept the game a one run affair. Rollo and Evelyn stood with the fans when something dramatic occurred. Between Rollo's hugs, standing and the cheering, being the giver as well as the receiver of genuine appreciation grew in importance. She had experienced similar cheers working as a dancer. Experiencing it at a ballpark showed her the contrast: in Betsy's when she heard cheers she knew they were usually for selfish reasons - a man wanting to stick his cock inside her and/or have her lips sucking his cock - and rarely out of genuine appreciation. Cheering for the baseball players - who weren't expected to do anything extra after hearing the applause - demonstrated cheers could be given out of genuine appreciation instead of pure cynicism. Her discovery put her in a generous mood.

When they sat down after the seventh inning stretch, she put her left leg over Rollo's right. They hugged. She moved her arm around his neck and pulled his head close to hers. She turned toward him and nibbled his ear lobe, soaking it with a mellowing warmth. He put his right arm around her waist and caressed her hips. She placed her tongue on the skin covering his ear's gristle and gave it a bath. Rollo blushed. He had participated in exhibitionist scenes before - never in front of 30,000 potential onlookers. Doing it with someone he cared about and who cared about him made him want 75,000 onlookers and a television audience.

Evelyn stopped nibbling. They held each others hands and intertwined their legs during the bottom of the seventh. The Yankees loaded the bases with no outs and failed to score. It was their last scoring threat. They hit the ball hard in the eighth and ninth innings, but right at someone and lost the game one to nothing. Rollo and Evelyn's game was in the early innings; there were going to be no losers, no shutouts and no no-hitters. They went to Rollo's apartment to practice sliding.

The following night Rollo was back to work. He was seated on the floor in front of the police station in the passageway near management's office, had finished eating a pomegranate and was wrapping the pits in a napkin when Copperblum approached. "What you eating?"

"A Chinese apple," said Rollo.

"Is that as sweet as that girl, I saw you with yesterday?"

"She's fine. How do you know she's sweet?"

"Fine girls are given the benefit of the doubt. No doubt she's amongst the finest I've seen."

Rollo stood up, walked toward a trash container and tossed the napkin inside. "What were you expecting - a slouch, a bow wow, a P.A. momma or some other two-legged, below grade mammal."

"Forgive me, but what's a P.A. momma?"

"A public assistance momma, a welfare mother. You know, the ones twenty-two or twenty-three who already have seven kids from five or six guys, so they look like they're in their late thirties or early forties"

"You don't want to be seen with them. After seeing Evelyn, I wish my vision was better than twenty/twenty. She give you any spread yet?"

"If she has I'm not gonna tell you."

"Then why aren't you wholeheartedly agreeing with me?"

"I don't know if I have a whole heart." Rollo placed his hands over his heart.

"Wiseguy. A lucky one but a wiseguy."

Copperblum shook his head, patted Rollo on the back as Mordaci Kaplan entered the passageway, the New York Times tucked in his armpit. "Can we look at your Times?" Copperblum asked.

"Sure," said Kaplan.

Copperblum and Rollo read an article about the C.U.M. residence burning. The article recapped what was previously known and gave new information: arson had been confirmed. A local pharmacist stated that he had sold rubbing alcohol to a man who was seen on the block where the fire occurred. He was later found dead, run over by a bus. The dead man was linked to the blaze by threads in his pants pocket. It was the same material as the alcohol bottle's fuse. The police were at an impasse: they had no motives. Not even the dead man's name. No I.D. was found on him.

"845 Tarenton Avenue. 845 Tarenton Avenue! 845 Tarenton

Avenue!! Oh my God!" The Times slipped out of Copperblum's fingers.

"What's the matter? You know that building?" Rollo asked.

"Fill out a card for me the next three days.

"Why?"

"Because I'm going to be too busy to fill one out."

CHAPTER XVII

KELSO'S TRIAL

Kelso's brainchild was having a financial impact. It didn't make him popular, but men who had always had difficulty paying bills were now seeing their greatest dreams come true. Oasis had banked a year's tuition for an Ivy League college. His oldest daughter was already packing. Lenny Mo Dinner had paid to attend two winter Baseball fantasy camps: one with the 1961 Yankees, the other with the 1962 San Fransisco Giants. Ben Feldstein had saved enough money to produce his rap video: "I'm a Hunk." Uranso put his Kehlmeyer profits down on a beach house in Jamaica. His wife's medical expenses no longer crushed Rod Somer. And Rollo was able to work less and devote more time to Evelyn and songwriting. All the men praised Kelso. They saw him now for the genius he was. Little by little they were beginning to feel they were wrong about Kelso. He had done more for them than any friend they'd ever had.

Two weeks after the C.U.M. brownstone fire, the vendors and porters were gathered in the commissary before the Yankees and the Minnesota Twins game. Brad Brown was eating Chicken with broccoli and sharing with Iggy Biggy. Andy Metzger was hovering over the hot dog bins, anxious to start vending - hot dogs could go 'animal' also. Kelso was sitting on a keg in the corner reading THE WALL STREET JOURNAL. Almost everybody involved with Kehlmeyer was present. They were in Simeon's commissary, but Simeon wasn't present: he had been moved temporarily to the Loge commissary to observe if any stealing of inventory was taking place. The substitute checker had not yet arrived.

The door banged shut. "Where's Kelso?" Copperblum asked, excited.

Iggy Biggy pointed to the corner.

Copperblum ran over and grabbed the newspaper out of Kelso's hands. "You're the worst! You had that brownstone torched!"

"Yeah, so what? Those women and children weren't going to amount to anything anyway."

"I don't care if they were deaf, dumb, blind and crazy. Who are you to judge what a life amounts to?"

Everyone stopped what they were doing and moved near Copperblum and Kelso.

"What's happening, Copperblum?" Somer asked.

"I'm not sure exactly how he did it, but Kelso had his building torched for money."

"Where dee proof, mon?" Uranso asked.

"Remember, Rollo, when we were reading the paper, and I said 845 Tarenton Avenue sounded familiar? So I put two and two together, went down to City hall and examined the tax assessors records, and who do I find was the owner, none other than our beloved Kelso."

Kelso picked up his WALL STREET JOURNAL. "You like the money we're making?"

"Yeah."

"And you'd be happier with more money?"

"Not at that price," said Copperblum.

"What kind of venture capitalist are you?"

"Obviously not the kind you are. How can you equate what you did with venture capitalism?"

"I'm only trying to make this work," said Kelso. "We can be big. Bigger than G.M. and Exxon. But it takes money to make money. With the insurance money, we can expand nationally - go global." There was a far away look in his eyes.

"You're overreacting. You mean nobody's ever died at a rock concert sponsored by a beer company? What about defense contractors who try to convince you their products are video games instead of tools of destruction? Forget that, where's the positive self expectation?"

"If I told you where yours is, you wouldn't think it was so positive," said Copperblum. "Since yours is somewhere where the sun don't shine."

"You're just jealous you don't have my creative genius."

"That's why you're here, like you were when you were a teenager, vending?"

"I still vend because I like coming to the ballpark without having to pay to get in."

The people watching moved closer to Copperblum and Kelso.

Copperblum closed his hands into fists. "Don't bullshit us. You came here for the money, you'll always be here for the money and had that building torched for money."

"So what. In America money rules."

"No. Influential people - some, who make their money count - rule. You've gone overboard - money is all you live for."

Kelso smirked. "Money has saved many a drowning man."

"If I were you, I wouldn't count on any life preservers being thrown my way," Rollo said.

Kelso's face turned a searing red. "If I drown, I'm not going to be alone. Remember, we're all in this together." Kelso threw down his paper and left.

"Are you absolutely sure Kelso masterminded the brownstone fire?" Rollo asked.

Copperblum sat on the metal stool behind the checker's desk. "As an accountant I've made a few friends in the insurance industry. I asked these friends questions. One told me his company had to make a six figure payoff on an apartment house fire in the Bronx. A rare occurrence since many companies aren't too keen on signing Bronx residents to home insurance.

"Anyway this friend finds the address of the house for which the claim'll be paid. It's the same as the one given in the Times article the day after the fire. I go there. I look around. I ask questions. A young girl looking through her window, told me she saw someone peculiar speaking to a local crackhead, the day of the fire.

"I asked her what made this 'someone' so peculiar? She described someone who could be Kelso.

"To be sure I went back to my friend at the insurance company and asked him to get the name of the person the check for the apartment house fire was made out to. After uncovering a few aliases and 'dummy' corporations, he finally found Kelso.

"The company is doing an investigation into the validity of the claim. They don't have enough yet for evidence that'll stand up in court, and I couldn't give them too much 'info' without it making us look like culprits also, so ...."

"If Kelso's here next season we could be in big trouble. Once law enforcement and regulatory agencies are onto him, it won't be too long before they're onto us," said Rollo.

"If that happens there's no *could be*. We'll be in far deeper trouble and he'll have the bucks to hire the best attorneys," said Copperblum.

"Come to think of it, he doesn't have to be here next season and we could still be in big trouble," said Rollo.

"Hearsay, rumors we can handle - if he's not around."

"I have a gut feeling we'd be breathing a lot easier and sleeping a lot better if he weren't around."

"That's very reassuring considering your background."

"In baseball, if your team has a winning percentage above .500 it's considered good, but in the game we're playing ..."

"Right, sometimes good just isn't enough."

"By the start of next season we'll know what's good enough."

An eerie silence swept through the commissary. How could they atone for the deaths caused by Kelso's obsession? They had become his partners in order to earn more money and improve their lives. But what had started out as a lark, had turned ugly.

"I knew it would come to this," said Rod Somer.

"We all did," said Rollo. "We hoped and prayed it wouldn't, but sometimes hope isn't fulfilled and prayers aren't answered."

"You mean that cocksucker's going to get over on us again," said Brad Brown. "Do we really need him and Kehlmeyer anymore to be successful?"

"I don't think so," said Rod Somer, "but, how are we going to rid ourselves of him?"

"Yeah. What's our strategy?" asked Oasis.

"Let Iggy Biggy beat him senseless," said Copperblum.

"I can shoot him," said Mordecai Kaplan, his eyes glowing like iron in a smelting oven.

124

"Let's get the fans to stampede him, rip him limb from limb!" Rod Somer said.

"Guys, as effective as those suggestions are, we gotta be more subtle," said Rollo. "Any of those methods - if used - implicate us."

They proceeded to discuss schemes to take care of Kelso. Finally, someone mentioned a name from the past that inspired respect and fear: James Rivinello, a former vendor.

If it was a dull baseball game the day he worked, James Rivinello would manufacture thrills. Once he set a fan on fire. Another day he stabbed a man with his meat fork when the fan cheered for the opposing team. When a fan cheated him for a hot dog, he tripped him with his hot dog bin and broke the guy's leg. Another fan, feeling Rivinello was discourteous, literally kicked his butt. Rivinello responded by lifting the hot dog bin over his head and konking it on the fan's head. It took four uniformed security guards to prevent a riot.

Shortly after the near riot Rivinello found out he had passed the New York City Fire Department Fireman's test and was being called for the physical. "Has anyone heard from Rivinello since he joined the fire department?" Rod Somer asked.

"If we could find him, I'm sure he'd be willing to take care of Kelso." Errol said.

"Forget it. He's probably happy dousing flames, destroying buildings and watching people fry. Besides, do we want to change one monster for another who might haunt us?" reasoned Copperblum.

"Yeah, mon, Kelso milquetoast compared to dee Rivinello," Uranso said and took a large bite of a spiced beef patty.

"How can you shove that down your throat at a time like this?" Andy Metzger asked.

"Gentlemen, please! We got to take this to the next level. Everybody keep thinking of how to remove Kelso. Since tomorrow's an off day, we'll meet in twenty-four hours at the bowling lanes to see if we've come up with something both effective and discreet," said Rollo.

Everyone indicated agreement and went outside to serve the fans.

The game was over. The Yankees had beaten the Minnesota Twins, 10-3. Kehlmyer's sales enabled the vendors' pockets to swell, but they left despondent. Nobody could stomach dead kids being their source of wealth. Their gravy days were over. Rollo found a pay phone and called Evelyn. "Can you meet me at Mickey Mantle's?"

"What for?"

"Something deep's come up and I want to be with you for solace."

"I can't spend too much time there. I work a day shift tomorrow and need rest. Get there as soon as you can."

CHAPTER XVIII

MICKEY MANTLE'S

It took Evelyn less than twenty minutes to shower, dress, and get a cab to Mickey Mantle's. It was a beautiful evening despite the smog, when she looked up she could see several notable constellations. Nature's beauty made her thankful she could see it. She wondered if Severina and her baby were looking down at her.

Mickey Mantle's was crowded. Rollo hadn't arrived, but she didn't have to wait to be seated. She asked for a secluded table, far from the televisions showing the ESPN game between the Chicago Cubs and the Pittsburgh Pirates. Despite how appealing Evelyn looked, all eyes were focused on the baseball game. She was being ignored and enjoying it. She couldn't remember the last time that happened.

Two innings of the Cubs-Pirates game passed before Rollo stood before her. "Fighting midtown Manhattan traffic kept me busy. Hope you had fun while you were waiting."

"I did. I looked at these artworks." She pointed to various sports paintings, drawings and photographs adorning the walls.

"That's good. One work of art admiring several others."

She gave him a warm smile, slipped off her sandal and gently stuck her bare foot in his groin. "What's so deep? You look like you got the world on your shoulders."

Rollo grabbed Evelyn's foot. "I found out who's responsible for Severina's death."

"Who?" Evelyn's knee hit the table.

"Terence Kelso."

"That guy who makes beer out of weird ingredients?"

"Yeah."

127

"He ain't gonna be making beer much longer! He isn't going to be doing anything much longer!"

"What do you mean?"

"I'm going to kill him. You need me to write it on your forehead?"

"Wait a second. He had your best friend killed, so that makes you his executioner?"

"What do you suggest?"

"I don't like him being around either, but I don't want you to kill him."

"Then who's going to mete out justice?"

"There has to be another way."

"While you're busy concocting another way, I can get it done."

"I understand she was your best friend, but does that make it a Jihad? What happens if you're caught?"

"I can make it look like he was trying to kill me. Self defense."

"That sounds weak. Here comes our waiter. You want anything?"

"No food. A carafe of white wine."

Rollo ordered crabcakes. The waiter left.

Rollo's face contorted. "You're pretty adamant about taking him out?"

"The MOSSAD was pretty adamant about my brothers! This Kelso seemed pretty adamant about Severina and her baby dying."

"He didn't know they were in the brownstone."

"What good is that doing Severina now? Look, this is something I *have* to do. How could I live with myself if I didn't seek revenge for Severina. You don't understand. We're from different worlds. But if you want us to stay together, you're going to have to give me space and not interfere, no matter how much you hate it. If you can't do that, we're through. No matter how much sorrow I'd feel if I left you." Evelyn's eyes filled with tears.

A deafening crescendo enveloped the restaurant as Andre Dawson hit a three-run homer that gave the Cubs an insurmountable lead.

Rollo looked at Evelyn, then her empty glass. "How are you going to take care of him?"

128

"Leave that to me," Evelyn said when the roar subsided. "The fewer people who know, the fewer intrusions I'll have to deal with."

The waiter brought their food and wine.

Rollo raised his wine glass. "To the sexiest executioner the world has ever seen."

"You figured out how you going to ice him yet?" Rollo asked when they were at his apartment.

"I have a few ideas," said Evelyn, settling into his leather recliner.

"Such as?"

"Don't you like surprises?"

"There's more than enough surprises with you as it is." He placed his hand on her leg.

"What's that supposed to mean?" She removed his hand from her thigh and held it.

"Pleasant surprises."

She placed the palm back on her thigh. "Let this be another one."

"For every pleasant one, there are far more miserable ones."

"Well!" She twisted her legs away from the stool.

"I didn't mean you. I meant in general."

She placed her hand on his shoulder and rubbed it. "Honey, that's part of life."

"But I don't want this to turn out a misery."

"Neither do I. Remember who you're dealing with. I know how to make it work for me."

"How do you do that?"

"Like getting rid of Kelso, I make it fun."

Rollo took Evelyn's hand from his shoulder and placed it between his hands. "You plan on getting rid of me?"

She forced his right hand away from his left hand and directed it toward her crotch. "You and I have a different kind of fun."

He rubbed the area where his right hand rested; his fingers seeking the warm moist flesh beneath her satin panties. With his left hand he lowered her panties. "That's very reassuring."

She spread her legs enough to assist his exploratory efforts and Rollo tossed her panties. "You thought I was using you?"

129

His middle finger found what it was looking for. "Well, when you said making get rid of Kelso fun ...." She swayed her pelvis forward, allowing his finger to go deeper inside. "Wouldn't it be rather foolish to tell you what's in store for Kelso? I do like being with you."

His middle finger returned to the furriness above her snatch, then went back inside along with his index finger. "People sometimes do foolish things, think foolish thoughts. Look at what was running through my mind moments ago."

She swayed her pelvis with greater commitment. "What about now?"

"You think I'm doing or thinking foolishness." He plunged the fingers as far as they could go.

She secured her arms at the base of the leather seat's rear and raised her calfs on top of his shoulders. "Isn't what we're doing sometimes referred to as fooling around?"

"This isn't one of those times." He stood up, removing his fingers and cupped her butt with his left hand. With his right hand he opened his zipper and pulled out what could a lot more for her than two fingers.

A look of anticipation spread over her face. She arched her hips toward the ceiling, as the tip of Rollo's blood-engorged mass touched her pubic hair. With his right thumb and forefinger, he parted the pink sea he was about to enter. It was like a hot knife slicing into butter. Her moistness heightened his passion; his stiffness turned her womanly desire into frenzy. It went on until they were no longer thinking about time, locale, sports bars, occupations, restaurants, socio-economic conditions and Kelso's undoing.

At last their bodies lay still, sweaty on the plush carpet. They lay side by side, looking into each other's eyes. "Was that anything like the swing clubs?" Evelyn asked.

"Slightly. I'm surprised you've never been to one."

"Swinging my hips on stage is as far as I'll go."

"That's one less experience you'll be able to explain to your children."

"How are you going to feel when your children find out?" She slid her satin panties up her legs.

He touched the panties and rubbed them. "Similar to how I feel now - proud of what I did and ...."

"Ready to brag about it to anyone willing to listen."

"No. Willing to impart knowledge to those wanting to know how to handle a situation they might find themselves in."

"You make it sound majestic - as if it were valiant and noble. Do you believe those girls who fucked you there were in love?" She sat upright.

"Not with me, with what we were doing."

"And you kept right on busting your nuts."

"I didn't go there to jerk-off or go home with blue balls."

"Nor to catch disease."

"If it worries you, why are you with me? You know people who make active use of their bodies, tend to take better care of them."

"I understand that. But was the risk worth the reward?"

"You said you like being with me, correct?"

"And you attribute that to your experience in sex playgrounds?"

"The entire past can be a reference point - something to learn from."

"What lesson made you give up the notion of marrying a girl you met in there?"

"The Scriptures. It was futile to make vows to someone who reminded me of the Pharisees, the priests Jesus told his disciples to be aware of when they entered the temple in Jerusalem: "Do as they say. Don't do as they do.""

She put on a tan t-shirt. "Aren't you being sacrilegious?"

"Is there any doubts regarding lessons now?" Rollo put on his see through nylon bikini undershorts.

"At least not about where you meet potential spouses. Anyway, how could you and those other guys make a deal with Kelso, know-ing what kind of person he is?" She stood up and slid her slippers onto her feet.

"The same way you can accept money from guys you don't know from Adam and smile in their faces, concerned strictly with how they'll fatten your purse."

She put on white cotton walking shorts. "I understand your rea-soning. However, there is a difference: the guys who give me money are generous."

Rollo let out a faint laugh. "A few maybe, but do you honestly believe they aren't there seeking a quick fuck, a sexier rape victim?"

"Those type of men exist. If they come in Betsy's, I do my best to avoid them, but they're not doing what they do for money. They're acting out their hatred for women - denying their own self-hatred."

"As much as he acts like it, I think Kelso is the way he is for something besides money."

"Such as?" She picked up her maroon lizard skin belt.

"If I knew I'd be a clinical psychologist instead of a song writer."

"Were you really a songwriter?"

"Go look." He pointed toward the five milk crates containing record albums. "And find the Cliches: 'Love Will Save The World' L.P. and read its backcover. If finding the album isn't enough proof I'll write you a song while you look."

Evelyn began looking through the milk crates. She found jazz, club, soft rock, hard rock, swing/ big band, classical and opera albums. Some from artists who were recording before she was born; others by people she had never heard of. Toward the end of the fourth milk crate she found: 'Love Will Save the World.' She read the credits. Four of the five songs on side A were written by a Rolland A. Boyce and two of the five on Side B. Songs that brought tears of joy to her eyes when she still was a teenager. Severina had loved this album too. She carried the album toward Rollo and tapped his head with it. "I'm impressed."

"Thank you," said Rollo.

"What does A stand for?" She pointed toward the initial between his first and last names.

"Ahsante."

"Why'd your mother give you that middle name?"

"I don't know. When you meet her, you can ask her."

Evelyn threw the album onto the couch, knelt before Rollo, and smothered his lips with hers, her tongue thrusting for the opening between his lips.

Rollo gently stroked her hair. It wasn't much different from when he was at the height of his success, he thought. He moved his face away from hers. "All this because you know a songwriter?"

"I never did it with someone from the music industry."

132

"I've been with a few wild women; none from a terrorist environment. Guess this is something new for both of us," Rollo said and reached for the paper on the carpet by his left hip, picked it up and handed it to her.

Evelyn looked at it. It was the song he had written while she looked for the album. One verse read:

"You got me on top of the world, thinking of no other girl.
How'd you do it?
There's got to be something to it.
If you leave me you'll break my heart.
Please, please tell me we'll never part."

"You really feel that way about me?"

"I write what I feel. That has a lot to do with successful song-writing, poetry, prose; any kind of writing - even the comics."

She stood up. "The least I can do for you is cook you a decent meal."

"Let's go out."

"No. Let me cook you something." She stroked his cheek. "How about sauteed salmon and asparagus. I'll have it ready by 6:30."

"All right. I'll be back by then. I have some stops to make. You okay?"

"Yeah, I'm just remembering Severina. She liked your music, too."

"Don't be sad."

"There's no getting around it. Not until one Terence Kelso's erased."

CHAPTER XIX

THE FOREST AND THE TREES

The meal was delicious. The best Rollo had eaten that summer. As they sipped Canai White, Evelyn suddenly asked, "When are you going to introduce me to Kelso?"

"What's the rush?"

"After you introduce us, I'll see you only one more time until he's out of the picture."

Rollo choked. His wine glass struck the oak dining table and shattered.

"I thought you'd handle it better than that." Evelyn got up to fetch a towel.

"You thought wrong. You tell me after you meet that money-worshipping swine, I only get to see you once until you're through? You expected me to take it like a trooper?"

Evelyn ran her bare fingers over the damp spot on his jeans, then rubbed it with a towel. "Why don't you act like a man instead of a child?"

"I am acting like a man. A man deeply concerned about a woman he's in love with."

She sat on his lap. "If you mean that, realize I'm asking you to bear with me on this one for a higher form of love. I was a Muslim, remember? And if I strictly adhered to its principles - where there are more commands than requests - I wouldn't ask you to bear with me, I'd tell you."

"If you strictly adhered to its principles, you'd be covered with black from head to toe, and you wouldn't be earning a living the way

134

you do." He placed his arms around her waist. He held her tighter. "Put it this way, if you do kill him, much as I don't want you to, you're a genius. My friends and I have been trying to think of ways to off him since we found out it was Kelso who torched the building. The methods we thought of were far too crude, too obvious."

She kissed his nose. "I'll make the time we spend together before you introduce me to Kelso memorable."

Rollo looked into her eyes. "You should've said that in the first place."

She ran her fingers through his hair. "I may not physically be with you, but don't we have a certain amount of spiritual unity?"

Rollo nodded.

"Well then." Evelyn gave Rollo a deep stare.

He held her tighter, his palms caressing her hips and kissed her lips.

"Where do you want to meet him: the ballpark, Betsy's, a restaurant? You want me to give him your phone number?"

"Bring him to Betsy's. By looking at him from the stage, I can get an idea about how to deal with him."

"How soon do you want to be introduced after sizing him up?"

"Right after I come off stage and change. You hang around a few minutes then, adios."

"How long is your scheme going to take?"

"If there are no complications, six weeks."

"Six weeks! What am I supposed to do for sixweeks after our unforgettable evening together?"

She massaged his shoulders. "You'll think of something. I was going to surprise you, but everytime I remind you we won't be together, it seems as if you're mortally wounded, so we'll hang for a weekend instead of an evening."

Rollo held her hand tightly. "That'll make it harder to think of something."

"You want to have a cup of coffee, find me a cab and be on your way?"

"No." He held her hand tighter.

"Who is it?" Copperblum answered his phone.

135

"Rollo. Looks like we'll soon be rid of Kelso."

"How?"

"Remember Evelyn? The girl with me at the day game. She hates him more than us."

"What? She doesn't exactly look like she strikes fear in the heart of men."

"She's obsessed with getting it done. Tell the others. I'm going to be busy for a few days."

"Cool."

"One more thing. She isn't doing this for money, but she doesn't have the best of jobs. So for doing it, I think she should get a half share in Kehlmeyer profits we've accumulated and a second half if she's successful."

"Sounds reasonable. I tell you what. Rather than haggling with those other clowns, I'll put up my share to take care of it. I'll just get a few more clients for my C.P.A. business to take up the slack. Besides, it'll feel good knowing my Kehlmeyer profits aren't being wasted."

"Check you out in a few days."

Kelso was seated at the California Oak desk in the paneled study of his Yorktown Heights home. Behind the desk were book lined shelves and an oil canvas painting of a gray thoroughbred named: "Dalmation."

Kelso was drinking a martini and reading Kehlmeyer's Brewery Inc.'s prospectus, turning pages as if it were a best seller. He was happy and confident. On the first of October, twenty million shares of Kehlmeyer Brewery Inc. would begin to trade on the NASDAQ National Market. His broker was ecstatic about the finder's fee he'd receive for bringing Kehlmeyer public. But Kelso was still worried about how to keep Tilletson, Dodge & Wilkie from finding out about the horse piss.

He took a sip of martini and held it in his mouth. Suddenly, he had an idea. If Tilletson, Dodge & Wilkie wanted to know what the key ingredient was, he'd stage an elaborate tasting, let their employees compare Kehlmeyer to its competitors. If a beer connoisseur like Simeon could fall in love with Kehlmeyer's taste, why wouldn't

Wall Street executives? If they liked it, they'd feel more confident about the public offering. Nobody had ever questioned Colonel Sanders what the eleven herbs and spices were in his chicken. Why should they question him about Kehlmeyer's key ingredient?

Next, his thoughts moved to his plan to build a production facility on an industrial park near Iggy Biggy's. If he could put a brewery there, he could provide more jobs.

Kelso gulped what was left of his martini and poured a double refill.

He was beginning to see himself as a brewery mogul. He dreamed of consolidating all his interests into the making of beer. The bogus cocaine couldn't match Kehlmeyer Brewery Inc. in profit potential, but he had become sentimentally attached and didn't want the children selling it to have to switch to the genuine article. Still, he was astute at identifying popular trends in their embryonic stages and saw the potential in Kehlmeyer for what it was. With Kehlmeyer Brewery Inc.'s public offering on the horizon he wanted an effective ad campaign. The thought of adding $100,000,000 to his coffers made him giddy.

He lifted the martini. "A billion is better than a hundred mil," he said, then sipped. As the liquor went down his throat, he realized how much he longed for someone with whom to share his excitement. He had no one with whom to share even a toast. He was on the verge of achieving financial success beyond his wildest dreams; yet, for all his business acumen and commercial prowess, Kelso knew something was missing. He might continue lying to everyone about how companionship wasn't as important as earning the next dollar, but he couldn't lie to himself. He longed for the physical encounters that made men and women smile. He wanted to eliminate his wretched loneliness.

Kelso's phone rang. He picked it up.

"Hi Kelso. You interested in meeting my girlfriend's sister?" Rollo asked.

CHAPTER XX

READY AND AIMING CUPID'S BOW

Thursday night was the unofficial start of Labor Day and Betsy's Bustout & Breakthrough had a massive throng without resorting to promotional gimmicks such as porno queens, or female wrestlers rolling in hot mineral oil. Anybody with a reasonable amount of disposable income and a yearning to get out of town already had. So Betsy's was crowded, but with men living paycheck to paycheck, tourists on a fixed budget and connoisseurs of various government assistance programs as their sole incomes.

From what Rollo had told her, Evelyn didn't envision Kelso spending more freely than the rest of the assemblage; however, he probably would be the wealthiest male to enter the club. To Evelyn, that could pose a problem. If by chance the other girls found out about Kelso's affluence, they would feast on him like piranhas on a cow's carcass.

On the other hand, if Kelso didn't feel he had to impress her coworkers with his financial status, Evelyn could take her time and approach him after a set. The only other thing that concerned her was whether Kelso was so infatuated with blondes that he didn't look at brunettes or redheads. If he was, the whole plan could abort. Evelyn left the dressing room hoping for the best.

Rollo pulled in front of Betsy's and parked between a yellow Corvette and a burgundy LTD.

"What kind of joint is this?" asked Kelso, suspicious.

"My girlfriend's sister is a topless dancer," said Rollo.

"What?! Is she a whore? On Drugs? A lesbian?"

138

"Calm down, man. Her sister is an Argentinian I'm dating who's a lab technician in Montefiore Hospital's Serology Unit. She encouraged her sister to come to the U.S., but once she got here, she discovered she'd need more than youth and beauty to survive. Perhaps you can show her the ropes. Be her mentor. She wants to quit dancing and pursue a more socially acceptable means of subsistence."

Kelso and Rollo sat at a table behind the bar. Rollo pointed at the stage. Kelso nodded approval. A petite young barmaid with a Mediterranean complexion and straight, long raven hair approached. "Hi, what can I get you?"

"How about a round of, 'Sex on the Beach'?" Rollo asked.

The waitress's grin became as wide as an African Wild Dog's in front of a fresh elephant carcass. Her bosom heaved beneath her black and white polka dot blouse. "You were referring to the drink, right?"

"And if I wasn't?"

"This isn't the beach."

"Orchard Beach is less than twenty minutes away."

"In the dark there's no telling what'll get you in the sand."

"In daylight there's no telling how many people would watch, and you don't look like an exhibitionist. What are you drinking? I'll buy you one."

"White wine spritzer, but I'll drink with you later. Right now I gotta serve more customers. So, two 'Sex on the Beach'?"

Rollo looked at Kelso and nodded. No use asking Kelso anything right now.

Kelso was looking at the dancers as if he were a non-believer witnessing a miracle. From the days when his marriage was turning sour, he had wanted to go to a swing club. When his divorce was finalized, he was as eager as a bee wanting to enter its hive, but by then, the fear of AIDS had whipped people into hysteria. Although the popular swing clubs were now history, seeing the dancers gave him the old feeling. Sex wasn't allowed on premises in topless bars, but in Betsy's, he had the feeling no one would object if his imagination ran wild. He tapped Rollo's shoulder. "In spite of what I think of topless dancers, I'm glad you brought me here."

Evelyn's set was finished. She stepped off of the stage. In distant seats she saw Rollo and a man matching Kelso's description. She provocatively bent forward, flexed her butt cheeks as she snuggled her pink lace mini dress over her skin. She curved her legs so that more thigh and calf showed and picked up her purse.

Moans from the men around the bar.

"Ee-ha!"

"Eppa!"

"Esa loca!"

"Ooh sweetheart, I wish something beside that mini dress was gripping your butt," one of the men yelled.

She said something to the barmaid by the cash register, but the music blasting through the BOSE speakers was so loud, they resorted to sign language. Rollo waited until she looked across the crowded room and waved.

Evelyn maneuvered past the crowd. As she got near their table, Rollo extended his arm to help her up the platform and beneath the rail separating tables from the bar.

Once Evelyn was securely on the platform, Rollo continued holding her hand and kissed her on the cheek. She smiled and looked at Kelso. Seeing him wasn't the intestine-heaving experience she was expecting. He wasn't the most handsome man she had ever seen, but she had seen worse. His skin was pale. A square jaw led to fleshy cheeks and his eyes seemed mysterious. There was flab on his torso - he wouldn't be mistaken for a male model or a body builder - but he wasn't fat.

Rollo let go of her hand. "Didra, this is Terence." He looked at Kelso and mouthed, "Terence, Didra."

"Rollo was very modest in describing you," Kelso yelled.

"You're not what I envisioned either," Evelyn yelled back.

"What did he tell you about me?" Kelso glanced at Rollo.

"That you'd be the first tycoon I'd set my eyes on."

"He did!" He grinned. He hadn't thought Rollo would be so kind.

She placed her hand on his chest. "Who do I remind you of?"

"Somebody I'd consider getting to know better."

She took her palm off of his chest. Her blood raged. Having to go through a charade with the individual responsible for Severina's murder was torture.

Kelso summoned the waitress, told her what Evelyn wanted and ordered another round for him and Rollo. When the waitress returned with the drinks, Kelso proposed a toast. "May everyone at this table have their wildest dreams come true."

Their glasses clanged. Somebody's dreams wasn't going to be realized. Each hoped it wouldn't be his.

"You want to ...." Kelso asked.

"Go on a date?"

"Yeah!"

"We'll discuss it later on. My set starts with the next record."

Kelso assisted in moving her seat backward, then helped her stand.

Evelyn was surprised he knew etiquette. She excused herself and went to the stage.

Kelso kept his eyes on her as she began her set. Now he had something else to look forward to besides Kehlmeyer becoming a household word.

Rollo noticed Kelso's stare. Was risking his and Evelyn's relationship worth Kelso's demise?

CHAPTER XXI

DIFFERENCES OF OPINION

Kelso approached Rod Somer in the union vendors' locker room. "Look Rod. Everything you've ever tried outside of vending has failed miserably. I don't think this video rental/virtual reality arcade you're planning to open has a chance of working. You're going to end up sad and pathetic as Lenny Mo unless you rejoin Kehlmeyer."

"I won't end up like Lenny Mo Dinner," said Rod Somer. Kelso sat near Rod Somer.

"Yeah, but you want more out of life than not duplicating Lenny Mo, don't you?" Kelso asked. "Just because you don't duplicate Lenny Mo is no guarantee you'll pay your wife's medical expenses."

"I'm not sure. Lenny Mo's done things that some people only dream about."

Kelso was stunned. "You mean you want to walk around a loser, a has been? Somebody constantly needing the approval of everyone? Trying to be all things to everybody?"

"There are a lot of so-called winners who haven't been to four-teen World Series in person and who'd love to have played stickball with Willie Mays." Rod Somer answered.

"You believe he played stickball in the streets with Willie Mays."

"You don't?" Somer asked, rising from his chair.

"He only tells that story to guys our age or younger. Guys who were in diapers when the Giants left New York. How come he never tells it to men his age? Did anyone actually see him play stickball with Willie Mays?"

"I honestly don't know. Maybe he always wanted to play stickball with Willie Mays, but when the kids chose sides for a game with Willie, he never got chosen. Nobody wanted to play with him. He hung around because Willie Mays was there. Willie came to bat and maybe hit a foul ball somewhere and told him, 'get the ball, Lenny'. He-he went and got it like Willie Mays told him and to this day, in his mind, he played stickball in the streets with Willie Mays."

"That's playing stickball in the streets with Willie Mays?" It was beginning to sound like the chorus of a song. Kelso smacked a locker.

"Who knows. When you got so little going right. When you get all your self-esteem and self-worth from vending. When your wife's glad you're here instead of home with her. When people do their best to avoid you like the plague, why not say you played stickball with Willie Mays? Who-who really cares? Isn't he entitled to a moment of glory? Is it right to deprive him of that?"

"If he's earned a moment of glory, fine, but if he's lying for one, you understand why nobody respects him?"

Kelso looked at Rod Somer and then the lockers. He could do without Rod Somer doubting his logic. "Perhaps you're right, but even if you are, who do you know who'd want to trade places with Lenny Mo Dinner? Who'd say, 'gee. I wish I were in your shoes'."

"I didn't say anybody had to trade places with him. I-I was only pointing out that even someone like Lenny Mo has done something that can be admired, that could make some people feel envious," said Somer.

Kelso gritted his teeth. "I think you've made a big mistake giving up Kehlmeyer. This video store/virtual reality arcade you're opening won't work."

Rod Somer's eyes became as big as the wire frames of his glasses. "Save your breath. Whether it sinks or swims, I won't be torching buildings filled with women and children."

"Do you want to be in a commercial?"

"Are you hard of hearing?"

Kelso glared at Rod Somer, took a deep breath and left the locker room.

Rod Somer changed into his vending uniform. As he was

143

tying his shoe laces, Rollo entered.

Rollo had known Evelyn for a little more than three months - it seemed like a lifetime. She had an effect no other girl had ever had. He had had fine girlfriends, intelligent girlfriends, girlfriends where the many ingredients for a successful relationship worked, girlfriends where only a few ingredients for a relationship were present, girlfriends where none of the ingredients of a relationship were present and females seeking Platonic relationships. Those relationships seemed piddling compared to what he had going with Evelyn. The *difference* between Evelyn and the rest was she cared for him in a way he had not previously experienced. Whether apart or together, there was a stronger sense of trust: for once in his life he wasn't concerned with what was going on while he wasn't around. With Kelso about to become a bigger part of her life, this was in jeopardy. He realized necessity could compel her to be more friendly than either he or she cared for, but he hoped being with Kelso wouldn't bring this about; one thing becoming an adult had taught him - if you live long enough, you learn you can't put anything past anyone. He clapped his hands, held them together and blew on his thumbs. What people go through to cleanse their souls, he thought.

"What's troubling you?" Rod Somer asked.

"How do you know something's troubling me?" Rollo turned to face him.

"I know that look."

"What look?"

"I know you're giving more than a passing thought to something. Perhaps you've lost your best friend?"

"It's not that bad, at least not yet."

"But something bad-bad could-could happen soon?"

"Don't you have a commissary to go to?"

"Don't-don't tell me my business. I'm concerned about someone I've known since he was a teenager."

"Thank you," said Rollo, sarcastic.

"Forget it. Is a girl giving you these doldrums? Hey, you're young, don't shatter mirrors. If it don't work out, you'll get another girl."

"Not like this one."

"What makes this one so special?" Rod Somer stood up.

"I'd give up vending just to be with her."

"Wow, that's serious! You never had this feeling with other girls?"

Rollo shook his head. "It seemed as if they all waited to see what I could do for them before *they cared* - if they did care. Love wasn't unconditional."

"Then-then it wasn't true love. That's what I hear from a lot of guys. I guess that is what love has come to these days. I'm, I'm glad I'm ma-married."

"Let me see a picture of your wife?"

Rod Somer reached into his pants pocket, pulled a picture out of his wallet and handed it to Rollo.

As he looked at Somer's palsy stricken wife's smile, Rollo thought love did work in mysterious ways. He'd discover how mysterious as he and Evelyn either became more harmonious or just another shattered dream.

"Did Copperblum tell you how Kelso's going to be taken care of?"

"Yeah."

"I wish there was another way."

"You're right to be concerned. I wouldn't want my wife near a scumbag like Kelso either. However, from what little I know about wildside women, if you love them, you got to let them do what they feel they must do. They need the freedom."

"As an artist I can appreciate that."

"As long as she balances freedom with responsibility it should wor-work out fine."

Rollo nodded. "There's no freedom without responsibilty."

Uranso entered the locker room carrying a large paper bag. "You see Oasis, mon?"

"No. No Jamaican food tonight?" asked Rollo, breathing heavily through his nostrils as Uranso unloaded napkins, utensils and a quart container of shrimp sauteed in hot chili sauce.

"Me give wife break, mon. She need freedom from kitchen once in a while."

"Funny you should mention that. I'm outta here." Rollo got up and left.

"What dee matter wit him?"

145

"Share the-the shrimp and I'll tell you," said Rod Somer.

Uranso sat down, gave Rod Somer a shrimp, watched him chew. "You better not spit any chili sauce on me while you explain or I knock your teeth down your mouth, mon."

CHAPTER XXII

COUNTING

She let her fingers touch the two dozen flowers: one each for the five mothers, the sixteen infants and her three brothers, hoping the flowers were solace to their spirits. And with each touch the sense of loss became more vivid, the shattered dreams more real and the enmity toward the person who caused it, more potent.

She put the carnation bouquet on Severina's grave, then read a passage from the Koran and wiped away tears. It was the second time she had performed the ritual in the six weeks since the C.U.M. brownstone was destroyed.

She had last seen Severina less than a week before the fire. At the funeral the nun had told her of the strides Severina and the other mothers had made in becoming more self-responsible, disciplined and in showing stronger respect and concern for one another. It was cruel that lives were lost, crueler that those lost were on the verge of new lives.

What she felt now she had never felt. It was different from the hatred for her brothers' killers. She knew political killings had been taking place since people lived in caves. She could rationalize her brothers' murder as a case of rulers doing away with those they felt were serious threats, but she couldn't rationalize the deaths of the C.U.M. arson victims. The children were innocent of the vices their parents had practiced. The mothers had given birth out of wedlock. But had they *harmed* anyone? The mothers and their children were learning to function effectively. Were they lesser human beings while being taught? Evelyn didn't know all the answers. She did know that someone had them murdered and that someone needed a lesson.

But eliminating Kelso wasn't going to be easy. Kelso was cunning. She also did not want to be caught. She had no intention of spending the rest of her life in jail. She placed her hand on Severina's tombstone and prayed out loud: "If there is an Allah, your death will be avenged and I will be the instrument of his will. The swine who put you where you are, will be no more."

She wiped her tears away, got up and left the cemetery. As she passed through the entrance, she wondered who was better off - the souls resting in peace, or those living in such violent times.

She was on her way to meet Kelso at a fashionable men's clothing store. After seeing him twice since Labor Day weekend, she was certain he was a detriment to mankind, even though she couldn't help admiring his ingenuity. He had many legitimate businesses. He was part owner of an Acura dealership and an automotive electronics supply and installation shop. He had an interest in a limousine service, and he had invested in several Off Broadway productions. He was planning to back his first Great White Way production with his Kehlmeyer profits when the baseball season was over. He was brilliant at keeping out of the limelight and remaining inconspicuous to competitors and law enforcement officials. He was a sharp contrast to the other men who tried to pick her up in Betsy's. Kelso didn't shower her with dollar bills. He didn't brag about his material possessions. He didn't try to seduce her by promising to put the world at her feet. What he did do was take a genuine interest in her, carefully listened to what she said, and never acted as if he were her superior. She wondered how someone so callous could seem so genuine.

It was late afternoon when she arrived at Barney's Seventh Avenue entrance. It was the week of Barney's annual warehouse sale and Kelso had asked her to assist him in selecting his fall wardrobe. From there she'd promised to take him someplace that would make the evening unforgettable. Kelso was waiting in front of the elegant department store's glass and brass door, talking to the doorman. When he saw Evelyn, he made a parting gesture to the doorman and moved toward her. Kelso put his arm around her waist and they walked along Seventeenth Street to the warehouse and joined the line of people waiting to get in.

"What are you looking for?" she asked.

"Shirts, slacks, an overcoat."

"What made you come here?"

"A C.P.A. I know told me you can get good threads at reasonable prices here. Must be some truth to it, these people on line aren't waiting to see a celebrity."

"Times are tough. It's been a lot longer in years past."

"Maybe you should start dancing. That'll get people here."

"Not to buy clothes."

"They might even give you something for free for attracting an audience."

"Yeah. A pat on the back and thanks for coming."

They smiled at each other and passed the time looking at the people on line, coming out of the warehouse and cars going past on the street. When they finally entered, inside had the atmosphere of a bazaar. Groups of people clustered around various stalls inspecting garments.

It took Kelso and Evelyn less than an hour to find shirts and slacks. They were walking toward the exit when Kelso noticed a charcoal gray glenplaid suit. He grabbed Evelyn's wrist and brought her attention to the suit, also. Evelyn carefully felt the material. "I like its texture. This is high quality wool." She unbuttoned the jacket and opened it. "It's an Oxxford suit." She checked the price tag. "The price is right," she said.

Kelso looked at the price tag. He dropped it as if it were a request to attend a best friend's funeral. "That's an awful lot for a suit."

"In the main store you'd pay twice as much."

"I didn't come here looking for a suit, remember?"

"Who yanked whose arm to get them to pay attention to it?"

"I really don't need it."

"But you want it, right? This suit'll make quite an impression."

"Most of the business I conduct isn't done in suits."

"With what you've been telling me, that's going to change. You're moving up in the world. You're going to be dealing with people who are going to size you up in the first few seconds."

"And wearing this suit's going to make them fall in love with me instantly?"

"No. But your appearance can help you get your point across."

"All because I'm wearing the *right* suit."

"I said, 'help you' - not do everything for you. If you speak like a retard or say something that sounds senseless, the suit isn't going to make much difference. But a lot of people buy into packaging more than substance. How do you think certain girls in my business earn a living?"

"I see your point. All we got to do is package ourselves properly and everything'll be taken care of." He was tempted to ask her to become a business partner.

"Let's see if they have it in my size," Kelso said.

He went to the suit rack where forty-three longs were hung, took one from the rack, tried on the jacket and went to look in the mirror. The neck and the shoulders would need tailoring, but it fit.

Evelyn gave a nod of approval. Kelso took off the jacket, placed it back on the hanger, took the suit over to the cashier's counter and pulled money out of his wallet.

Evelyn was astounded by the quantity of large bills Kelso was carrying. She had seen and carried thicker wads of money while working, but they were dollar bills. In Kelso's hand were large bills - she didn't see anything less than a ten - and as thick as a popular girl's best dance set. *Some* businesses were more rewarding than others.

Feeling elated she watched Kelso hand the money to the cashier: she had convinced him to do something he was reluctant to. An unexpected opportunity that could recur.

They left the warehouse and walked along Seventeenth Street. Day had become night and they talked about eating dinner, but neither was hungry. They stopped in a coffee shop and drank iced coffee.

"What time is it?" Evelyn asked as they left the coffee shop.

"Ten thirty," said Kelso.

"You want to go with me to a club?"

"I'm not much of a dancer."

"You don't have to be at this one."

"We're not dressed up."

"You don't have to be dressed to the max at this one."

"You don't?" Kelso's mind began racing. Was this to be the night, he wondered. "Where exactly are we going?"

"Let me surprise you?"

"Surprise me," said Kelso, expecting the best.

They got in Kelso's mint condition '64 Pontiac GTO. Evelyn said, "Head downtown."

Traffic wasn't heavy, but there was a smattering of cabs moving through the streets as if they were stray, rolling pool balls. Several ambulances screamed by, headed to the nearby hospitals. Kelso turned on his windshield wipers at each red light to keep homeless children and drunks from washing the GTO's windshield. He felt relieved when Evelyn finally told him to park.

When they got out of the car and he saw where Evelyn was heading, he felt like getting back in the GTO and contending with the perils of driving in lower Manhattan. "We're going in there?" The building looked desolate. Not a site where he envisioned being titillated to ecstasy.

"Come on. You scared?"

"No."

"Then come on."

Slowly, Kelso crossed the street. "You didn't have to bring me here for a surprise," he said.

Evelyn laughed. "Wait till you see the real surprise."

Kelso froze. His excitement at entering a hedonistic swing club was no more; it seemed as distant as a childhood daydream.

Evelyn pinched his lovehandles. "Come on. I'll make sure you walk out of here."

"In one piece?"

"Look at it this way. If you walk out in more than one piece, you're going to be famous."

They went down a flight of stairs. At the bottom, Evelyn pushed open a metal door. The ten feet between the door and the admission booth were dimly lit. From behind a set of bars a pale, androgynous blonde said, "Hi Didi. What's happening?"

Evelyn reached into her purse and pulled out a plastic membership card.

"You didn't have to show me that," said the androgynous blonde.

"Well, he's with me." Evelyn pointed her thumb toward Kelso.

The androgynous blonde looked at Kelso and giggled. "Fresh meat, huh? He doesn't seem too thrilled you brought him here."

151

"I told him it was a surprise."

The androgynous blonde giggled again and pushed a button. A loud buzz came from a second metal door. Evelyn snapped her fingers in front of Kelso's face. "Open the door."

Kelso complied.

Evelyn walked inside and Kelso followed. The door slammed behind them. A gargantuan Black man, wearing black alligator skin cowboy boots with spurs, black Wrangler bellbottoms, a black t-shirt, a black leather vest and a black western chapeau approached and kissed her cheek. "Double D. What's up?"

"Hi Russ. How are you?"

"Who's this?" Russ pointed at Kelso.

Evelyn put her right arm around Kelso's waist. "This is my friend Terry."

Russ ran his thick fingers through his muttonchop sideburns. "You gonna whip his ass, let me do it, or someone else?"

Evelyn hugged Kelso tighter. "I might let him whip mine."

Kelso turned milk white.

"If you need me, just call," said Russ.

Evelyn led Kelso past a square bar where transvestites, transsexuals, homosexuals and their beaus sat or stood around cackling like old women on a park bench. Kelso had trouble looking away from the bar. Several of the transvestites and the transsexuals looked more attractive than the girls in Betsy's.

"You want to go for it at the bar?" Evelyn asked.

"No. I don't go that way," Kelso replied.

"Why are you looking back there then?"

"This is the first time I've ever seen so many of them clustered together."

"Do you look at everything you see for the first time - so hard?"

"Seeing them gave me an idea. Maybe I should open a gay bar."

"And serve Kehlmeyer there, right? If you do, remember gays when they're pissed off - oh, hey no pun intended - can make a big stink about it. They'll start protesting right in front of your place. Contacting politicians, threatening not to vote for those who do not support their views. You'll be on the six and the eleven o'clock news - possibly even the national news."

"If I do open a gay place, perhaps I won't serve Kehlmeyer."

As they entered the next room, a putrid odor unclogged their nasal passages. Kelso looked around, waiting for his eyes to adjust to the gloom, wondering where the stench came from. They moved close to a man wearing black wool, checkerboard emblazoned gangster socks, black wing tip leather shoes, who was tied down to an elevated stirrup chair. He was either meditating or waiting for someone to redden his pale flesh. The odor wasn't coming from him. They moved toward a man standing upright, fully exposed except for a pair of bikini undershorts, bound by chains, ready to receive the next lash from a brunette wearing a black leather mini-skirt, thigh high black patent leather spiked heel boots and metal studded wrist bands. A cat-o'-nine tails would deliver her lashes. Or he'd receive them from a mocha complexioned woman wearing black brushed cotton short shorts, a brass studded leather bustier and seven inch black suede pump heels, brandishing a bull whip. Evelyn and Kelso moved past the trio as the mocha complexioned woman's whip struck and her captive squealed. The two women winked at Evelyn. Evelyn made a circle with her left thumb and index finger. They still hadn't found the source of the odor.

They moved on to a room where there were five stalls offering semi-privacy because chains could be put across their entrances and they had eight by twelve by three feet high platforms. In one stall a man and a woman made a lot of noise. The man had mounted the woman from the rear and was humping. As Evelyn and Kelso looked at the next stall, the woman screamed, the man yelled and their humping slowed. In the next stall a transvestite was jerking himself off while he sucked on the penis of a man dressed as a motorcycle gang member. The stall in the middle featured two lesbians letting a two foot long black dildo explore their insides. Kelso seemed to enjoy this scene most. Once it caught his eyes, he gave it his undivided attention, and when the women moaned he did ankle raises to subdue his anxiety. When she saw him, Evelyn grabbed him by his right arm and pulled him into an empty stall. She put the chain's hook into its latch and said, "Lie down."

"What for?" Kelso asked. There was a pillow on top of a wooden bench with leather and foam padding.

"Shut up. You want me to go get Russ?"

Kelso lay on the pillow and didn't say a word. Evelyn unbuttoned her Swiss Army shirt and took it off. She was wearing a strapless red lace bra. Kelso raised his head to get a closer look.

"What did I tell you?" Evelyn said.

Kelso plopped his head back onto the pillow.

Evelyn snapped her fingers. Effeminate twins walked toward the stall like puppies wanting to be suckled by their mother. They were blond with green eyes, chiseled chins, taut upper torsos and thin legs. One had on black hi-top Reebok gym shoes; the other white hi-top Reebok gym shoes; both wore sweat socks and nothing else. They bowed before Evelyn, arose and together said, "Do you want slaves, mistress?"

"Hurry. Bring me a riding crop and a paddle."

Kelso sat up.

"Why aren't you lying down?" Evelyn asked, turning around.

"I want a better view."

Evelyn grinned. The twins returned with the riding crop and the paddle. Evelyn took the riding crop in her right hand. "Hold him down," she ordered.

The twins grabbed Kelso's forearms and pushed his back onto the pillow. Kelso struggled to get free, but the twins, though effeminate, were as strong as lumberjacks and struggling was useless.

Evelyn unbuckled his belt buckle, unfastened his jeans button and zipper and lowered his jeans and shorts. She wasn't displeased with what she saw beneath the jeans and the shorts: Kelso wasn't the biggest guy, but neither was he the smallest. If she did have to let him stick it in, it would benefit her: after having Rollo penetrating her for three months, her vaginal wall would get a rest.

She cracked her knuckles, put the riding crop in her right hand, and flicked her wrist.

Kelso's facial skin took on a scarlet hue. Sweat beads appeared on his forehead.

Evelyn slowly lowered the riding crop to Kelso's scrotum and tickled it.

Kelso tried suppressing a giggle but couldn't. When Evelyn and the twins heard him, the twins put more pressure on his forearms and Evelyn gently slapped his scrotum with the loop. Kelso stopped giggling. He closed his eyes and gritted his teeth. Evelyn slapped his scrotum again, a little bit harder.

Kelso opened his eyes. Blood was rushing from his arteries to his scrotum, causing it to expand like a blowfish defending itself. Despite the pain, he found it titillating.

"Harder," Kelso grunted.

Evelyn complied.

"Harder" Kelso's grunt became louder and deeper.

Evelyn did as she was asked.

"Harder, harder. You titty bar dancing BITCH!"

Evelyn cocked her arm back and brought the riding crop forward like a jockey about to strike a thoroughbred's rump in the home stretch. The loop met Kelso's scrotum straight on.

Kelso screamed so loud the twins released his forearms. He bolted upright, palms over his face.

Evelyn wondered if she had lost her opportunity. She didn't plan to hit him as hard as she did, but she didn't like anyone calling her a bitch. As she saw Kelso bent over she realized he had another quality she could admire: the assertiveness he displayed in asking for the strokes she delivered. She had once given similar treatment to a Fortune Five Hundred executive who wanted it as much as - if not more than - Kelso; but he acted like a sniveling milksop. She despised beggars. The result being she stroked him with a goose feather. The executive got frustrated and acted more cowardly. While crying, he knelt before her like he was worshipping an idol. Evelyn became invidious. She stomped her five inch heel onto the executive's left backhand. A quarter inch deep impression was left and the executive's wife came, put a studded leash around her husband's neck and led him to a corner where he'd attract less attention.

Kelso had regained his composure. He was sitting upright and his complexion had turned to normal.

Evelyn smiled. "Having fun?"

Kelso nodded.

"Good. Turn around and get your ass in the air."

"What?"

"You want me to do it, or you want these guys," she pointed to the twins, "to assist you?"

Kelso turned around and bent over so that the cheeks of his butt protruded at a sixty degree angle from the floor. Evelyn put down the riding crop and had the twin wearing the black Reebok's hand her the paddle. It resembled a cricket bat; except its fat part was flat and had the word TOWEL engraved on its wood. Evelyn gripped the bat like she was going to take a cut at a softball and swung. She hit Kelso's rump. He sucked his teeth. It hurt, but not like the final blow of the riding crop against his scrotum. Evelyn delivered three more blows. Kelso's butt was turning orange-red. She had planned to originally hit him twenty-five times, but because of the spirit he displayed while she used the riding crop, she reduced it to ten hits. By the time the tenth hit scorched Kelso's rear end, a welt was noticeable on his right cheek.

Evelyn put the paddle down and kissed the palm of her left hand. She placed the palm on Kelso's butt right cheek. She could feel the paddle's friction simmering Kelso's skin. She grinned, released his cheek and said, "Turn around. Put on your pants."

Kelso stood up, reached for his clothes, but the jeans felt as if he were trying to wear jagged glass on his rear end. He did get them on, but they remained unbuttoned with the zipper down.

"Come on. I'll buy you a drink," Evelyn said.

Evelyn put on her Swiss Army shirt and they walked toward the bar. Kelso walked like a soldier trying to maneuver through a mine-field. Evelyn had to almost stand still in order not to leave him behind. When they were within thirty feet of the bar, Kelso said, "I got to take a leak. Where's the Men's room?"

"There is none. Go in there." Evelyn pointed to her left, toward a room along a dark corridor.

"What's going to happen in there?" Kelso asked.

"What do you want to go to the bathroom for?"

"To take a leak."

"Then that's what'll happen."

"Then why isn't it marked as a restroom?"

"Are trees, bushes and secluded spots marked as restrooms?"

"No."

"That doesn't stop men from using them like restrooms does it?"

Kelso nodded.

"Get in there before you pee in your pants."

Kelso walked along the corridor and entered the room. He saw there were urinals for him to relieve himself. The putrid odor's source was no longer a mystery.

A bathtub against the wall opposite the urinals contained a man wearing a bugler's cap reminiscent of those worn during the Civil War. Kelso moved toward the bathtub. The man in the tub had honey blond hair, a full beard and a mustache. He wore a light blue denim jacket, a blue sport shirt and blue jeans and black boat shoes. Kelso covered his nose and breathed through his mouth. It had little effect. The tub was a third filled with urine. When the man inside saw Kelso, he said, "Pee on me. Oh please, pee on me."

The tingling in Kelso's groin grew cumbersome. If he didn't urinate in the tub or the urinal soon he'd do what Evelyn said he could do without being in the bathroom. He reached inside his shorts and pulled out his penis. The man in the tub grew agitated: "Please! Oh please! Pee on me."

"Go ahead, let him have it," said another man entering the bathroom.

Kelso's urine hit the porcelain of a urinal. It took him half a minute to relieve himself. As he was leaving the bathroom, he saw the man who had entered after him doing what he couldn't bring himself to do. The level of fluid in the tub rose like high tide hitting seaside cliffs. The man finished, zipped up his pants and spit in the tub. "You don't deserve it, you bum," he said.

"You feeling any better?" Evelyn asked, when Kelso returned.

"Due to taking the leak? Yeah. Due to what I saw? No."

"Don't worry about it." She placed her left hand where his neck joined his shoulder blade. "Nobody forces Traveler to get in that tub and nobody forces anyone to piss in it or on him."

"The guy in the tub's name is Traveler?"

"His nickname," said Evelyn. "No one's ever asked him his real name, but with that Civil War get up, he's probably more of a history buff than anyone here, so the regulars named him after Robert E. Lee's horse."

"Why doesn't somebody bring him a bugle to play while he's in the tub?"

"Somehow brass, music and piss don't seem like a good mix. What you drinking?" Evelyn asked.

"A double martini,' said Kelso.

Evelyn got the attention of the bartender and told him what Kelso wanted.

"How come you didn't order anything?" Kelso asked.

"I'm not thirsty."

"It couldn't be because there's something funny with this?"

Evelyn took the glass out of Kelso's hand, took two sips of the martini and gave the glass back to Kelso.

"Sorry," said Kelso.

"I understand how you feel. I did the same thing to the girl who introduced me to this place."

"A girl hipped you to this place?"

"Yeah."

"What kind of girl was she?" Kelso took a sip of the martini.

"A girl, girl. She wanted to hang out and get wild, get loose."

Kelso smiled, then frowned then covered his mouth and his nose and put the martini on the bar. He turned around and saw Traveler less than an arm's length away.

Traveler kept moving, but the stench that was disgusting from a distance was lethal at close range. Kelso grabbed Evelyn's right upper arm and they left.

When they got outside, Kelso took a breath of fresh air and zippered his pants, but his groin and butt still hurt.

"I'll take you home," said Kelso.

"You sure you can drive?" Evelyn asked.

"I only drank a third of that double martini."

"I'm not worried about the martini. Let's go."

They walked to the GTO. Kelso opened the passenger side door. Evelyn sat down. Kelso went to the driver's side, opened the door and lowered his backside to sit down. The instant his rear end hit the cushioned seat he sprang up. His head hit the roof.

Evelyn laughed. "See what I mean."

"Right now I'm doing a lot more than seeing it.'

"I'll drive."

"How am I going to get home then?"

"I'll drive you home."

"Then how are you going to get home?"

"Give me money for a cab."

Kelso hesitated, then thought of what could happen if he didn't give Evelyn cabfare. "All right," he said grudgingly.

Evelyn was prepared to leave him by his GTO and let him attempt to solve his problem, but remembering how much pain she had inflicted and how she had to keep him happy to accomplish her goal, she said, "thank you."

She got out of the passenger side, went to the driver side and told Kelso to lie down on the back seat on his stomach. After giving Evelyn the car keys, Kelso lay down.

The city streets were as empty as possible in the early dawn hours and Evelyn had the car in front of Kelso's door in less than twenty minutes. She patted Kelso's back to awaken him. "Home sweet home."

Kelso maneuvered himself upright. "How much you need for cabfare?"

"Give me thirty dollars."

"Thirty dollars! Where you going? To the airport to catch a plane to Argentina?"

"I can't stand a cheap man."

Kelso reached into his jeans pocket and pulled out his wallet. "Here," he said. "Get home safe and I'll see you next week."

"You don't want to see me before then?" Evelyn asked.

"I got to get over the aches and pains." Kelso pointed toward his groin.

"I got a nurse's outfit. I can put it on and nurse you back to health."

"I'll make do with my own home remedies." Kelso got out. They locked the GTO and walked to the corner to hail Evelyn a cab. When one stopped, he helped her get inside. "Call me when you get home," he said and attempted to bend to kiss her, but the pain made him too slow. She slammed the door, and the cab sped away.

Kelso was glad Evelyn had parked the GTO on the side of the street where it could remain all day. He could lie in bed without having to get up in two hours to avoid a parking ticket. He was glad he had let Evelyn surprise him. He had never been with a dominatrix and

159

though the pain would last for a few days he had had fun receiving it. His pain could inspire more unscrupulous business tactics. The kinkier the suffering, the more demoniac the schemes. Now he had material for his memoirs besides his business ventures.

CHAPTER XXIII

GREATER THAN, EQUAL TO, LESSER THAN

"I got to get this over with soon," said Evelyn.

"Don't move too fast," Rollo said. "You don't want him to get suspicious. You sure you still want to go ahead with it?"

"Absolutely. His pomposity and arrogance are getting to me."

"Relax. It gets to most people."

"Relax! How can I relax being around a person who shows no remorse for arson?" She considered hanging up. "This is no person to make a habit of being near."

"Am I still the one you want to make a habit of being near?"

"Get over here as soon as you can and find out." Evelyn hung up.

This was to be her and Rollo's last date until Kelso was out of the way and she had made elaborate plans to insure that it was memorable. She had already put on a custom made white satin corset encrusted with diamond dust. Now she slipped on sheer white nylon stockings and fastened them to the corset's garter straps. The stockings fit properly, but she checked in the mirror to make sure. She was satisfied. She put on slippers, moved to the bedroom closet, and pulled out a strapless royal blue silk crepe dress that revealed a hint of her bosom and upper back. Then she placed a pair of grey pump heels with silver glitter stripes on her feet, added an anklet and a quarter inch wide fourteen inch long necklace, both made of platinum. She didn't like wearing make up when she wasn't working. She wasn't insecure about her beauty. She looked in the mirror once more, went into the living room, sat down on the couch, picked up a National Geographic from her coffee table and began turning the pages. She

161

was viewing a picture of an adult male lion biting into the neck of a young female when the door bell rang.

It was Rollo, awestruck by Evelyn's appearance. He handed her a half dozen orchids. "You look ready for a museum portrait: regal and unique." They always drew a fair amount of stares walking city streets together. Rollo was certain, this evening, people would mistake her for a popular fashion model or a movie star attending the premiere of her movie. He was dressed in a black cotton tennis shirt, cream silk linen blend trousers, black ostrich skin slip on shoes and a black leather sport jacket, but compared to how Evelyn was dressed, he felt tacky.

"I haven't gotten these in a while. You must be thinking of taking me to a tropical island." Evelyn kissed Rollo, put the flowers in a vase and picked up her grey lizard skin pocketbook. "Shall we go?"

"Where to?" Rollo asked.

"Where we can get a meal to match how we look."

"Where's that?"

"Don't ask questions tonight. You should like where I've made reservations."

"The way you look, if they're here, my night's already made."

"You don't get off that easy." She nudged him toward the door and locked it behind them.

As they walked downstairs, Rollo tried to get Evelyn to walk in front in order to better appreciate the view.

"Come on. Don't go pervert on me when I'm all dressed up," Evelyn said.

"I'm not perverted. I want to appreciate a work of art from all angles."

She pushed Rollo gently in front of her. "That'll come later."

"You make it hard to make a choice between sooner or later."

"Don't. Tonight there's no clocks to pay attention to. All right?"

"Sure."

Evelyn told Rollo to drive to City Island, a tiny island considered part of the Bronx with a small town atmosphere that could be mistaken for a New England fishing village. The ride took less than half an hour and once over the bridge connecting the island to the mainland, Evelyn asked if he knew Sambewlu's.

"Yeah. I've passed by it once or twice."

"You ever been there?"

"No, but we weren't that far from coming here when I met you."

"You would've come here on a first date?"

"Sure. I did ask you to go to dinner."

"When it was obvious we had conflicting schedules you opted for breakfast."

"I couldn't wait to see you again."

"Yet, you'll be willing to wait after tonight for how long?"

Rollo put his right hand on Evelyn's left thigh. "As long as it takes."

Evelyn smiled.

The Puegot stopped in front of Sambewlu's, and a husky parking lot attendant pointed out a spot. They walked toward the restaurant holding hands, looking at the sky, and wondering which was brighter - the shining stars or their spiritual unity.

They were thankful Evelyn had made reservations. A dozen people were waiting to be seated. Evelyn and Rollo walked to the maitre'd's podium centered between two forty gallon aquariums, one containing eels, tiger fish, red snappers, blue fish and mackerel; the other, crabs and lobsters with their claws tied. As Evelyn and Rollo walked past the tanks, they wondered if they were looking at their main course. They sat at a table in the center of the dining room, beneath a painting of colonial American fishermen pulling nets from the sea.

Rollo looked into Evelyn's eyes. "It's nice to see how the other half lives."

"You never been in a place like this before?" Evelyn asked.

"Plenty of times, but this is a first as far as someone else picking up the tab."

"No one appreciated what you meant to them?"

"Some did. They couldn't afford to express it like this."

"Why'd you waste your time with them?"

"When you're in love, events like this are nice - they aren't necessary."

Evelyn handed Rollo a menu. "What makes you so sure those girls loved you?"

163

"I'm not one hundred percent sure. If they weren't in love, they could've convinced an awful lot of people beside me."

"Am I convincing?"

Rollo put his hands over hers. "More than convincing. You're the closest to a hundred percent sure."

"How far till I reach there?"

"It's best I don't tell you. You'll get there, become complacent and things won't be the same."

"A petite brunette waitress came to their table. "Love your dress," she said to Evelyn. Evelyn smiled and ordered poached red snapper and Rollo, lobster bisque. They told the waitress to bring a bottle of Veuve Clicquot Brut.

The waitress was back in less than five minutes. She placed the champagne in the middle of the table and left.

Rollo filled Evelyn's glass, then his. "I don't know whether to say, 'Until we meet again,' or, 'will there be a next time'?"

"Why don't you say, 'To the first of many such evenings?"

"With you."

"If not with me, who?"

"With you. And only you," Rollo said. Their champagne glasses touched.

Evelyn took another sip and placed the glass down. "What are you going to do while I'm gone?"

"Gone?"

"I told you I won't be able to see you till I'm finished."

"Then while your gone I'll pray you go somewhere where I can find you."

"Besides that?"

"Pen some lyrics. In solitude if you can concentrate, you can accomplish a whole lot."

"Indeed you can! If you can exert discipline, the world seems to fall in love with you."

"I'll be worrying about you falling in love with Kelso. You, me falling en amor with a world full of people."

"Aren't you already in love with a world full of people?"

"Not as much as I am with you." He placed his hand on top of hers.

164

The waitress brought their food.

They sampled each other's entree before eating their own. The chunk of lobster felt like it melted in Evelyn's mouth. Rollo slowly chewed the red snapper in order to savor its texture and the herbs and spices used to season it. They took their time over dinner, and when they were done at last, a mischievous grin came over Evelyn's face.

"You ate that like a child eating cake and ice cream," she said.

"Dessert here would be a waste then?" Rollo wiggled his eyebrows.

"Not to me." Evelyn signaled for the dessert menu.

"Your insides aren't busting from eating that fish?" Rollo asked, when she was out of earshot.

"This is my first real meal today."

"So you're having an eating orgy to make up for it?"

"What do you know about orgies?"

Rollo grinned. "I'd like to learn more. I thought you weren't into the group scene."

"That doesn't stop me from being a fabulous teacher." Evelyn nudged his foot. "I'll order dessert to take out."

When the waitress returned, Evelyn ordered carrot cake and German chocolate cake. Rollo smiled when he heard her ordering two selections. "When I start eating, chances are you'll get hungry, too."

"I doubt it'll be for food."

"Then I'll require even more energy."

"You're right." A sly grin covered Rollo's face.

The waitress returned with the dessert in a doggy bag and the check on a small plate. The total was customary for a typical City Island restaurant. Bringing him here and treating him to dinner, Rollo knew Evelyn cared. Evelyn placed money on top of the check. She was leaving a fifty percent tip. Rollo said, "that's a hefty gratuity."

"She deserves it. I know what it's like to be a working girl and deal with penny pinchers. Let's go."

When they got back in the Puegot, Rollo asked, "Where to, my dear?"

"The Asgaard Chateau."

"We're going there?"

"No, I mentioned it to see what kind of reaction I'd get."

165

"Your place or mine would have been good enough."

"We know those like bats know their caves."

"Then away we go." Evelyn slapped Rollo's thigh.

The Puegot accelerated to forty miles per hour.

In Rollo's mind, there was no longer any doubt. Dinner at Sambewlu's was a nice treat; a night at the Asgaard Chateau was like being summoned to heaven's foothills. It was a year round resort nestled in New Jersey, fifty miles due west of New York City. If they didn't find enjoyment between the sheets, there were plenty of other recreational activities to partake of. There was an eighteen hole golf course where an annual Pro-Am Celebrity Tournament was held, twelve tennis courts, a horse riding trail that carved its way through lush forest greenery ski slopes never empty in season, two swimming pools, and a trout-stocked lake for fishermen. Rollo wanted to see all the Asgaard Chataeu had to offer but not on this visit.

The Puegot had crossed the George Washington Bridge and was heading down Interstate Eighty as midnight approached. Rollo dodged eighteen wheelers going faster than he was, but the highway soon became more his and Evelyn's. "I know you probably can't stand me being so inquisitive, but how many times have you done the Chateau?"

"Does it make a difference?"

"Not really."

"I don't ask you how many times you went to the swing clubs."

"I can't count how many times I went, but tonight you're the only one I'm swinging with." He put his sinewy right forearm around her neck, pulled her close and kissed her cheek.

"What about after tonight?"

"After tonight it should be a moot point."

Evelyn whispered into his ear, "If it isn't, it ain't going to be no fault of mine."

Soon the Asgaard Chateau's medieval castle was in sight. Its sand colored bricks clearly visible under wall lights.

The receptionist, a well-tanned brunette, smiled, revealing a mouthful of perfectly arranged pearl white teeth. "May I help you?"

"Reservations for B. Diaz."

The receptionist pressed computer keys and looked at the screen. "Do you want the Midnight Sun suite or a something more economical?"

"The Midnight Sun suite'll do just fine, thank you."

From a cupboard full of dark rectangles the receptionist pulled a set of keys, turned toward Rollo and Evelyn and gave them to Evelyn.

"Checkout time is twelve noon," said the receptionist. "Do you want a wake-up call?"

"No," Rollo and Evelyn answered in unison.

The receptionist smiled. "Breakfast is served until 10 A.M. in the Cornucopia room."

When they let go of each other as the elevator opened on their floor, Rollo asked, "That receptionist's attentiveness was a bit too much for you?"

"Yeah."

"She was just doing her job."

"A lot of people who don't want to use their minds 'just do their job'."

"Once we get behind the door," he pointed to the Midnight Sun suite's door, "how much are you and I going to be using our minds?"

She put her arm around his waist as he put the key in the door.

Rollo ran his fingers through Evelyn's curly hair. "We're entering a room where not being too smart will be very smart."

They entered the Midnight Sun suite. Rollo took the "Do Not Disturb" sign, placed it on the outside knob and closed the door.

The suite was appropriately named. There was a dark spacious fireplace with bronze overleaf leading toward the ceiling, a sunken living room and a velour couch and loveseat whose color matched that of Rollo's trousers, bay windows that filled two of the four walls and looked out upon the lake, rust colored llama hair carpet, a thirty-five inch Mitsubishi console television and levelour blinds against the windows for when privacy was desired. There was a small kitchen, but compared to Evelyn's, it was a banquet hall, with ultra modern appliances.

In the bedroom there was a three feet deep, seven feet long jacuzzi beside a ten feet square platform bed. One wall had a sizable closet.

167

A bathroom was ensconsed behind a door on another wall and on the remaining wall, there was another bay window. Rollo was so impressed by the suite's design and decor he continued looking at it like a potential buyer inspecting a model home.

Evelyn had slipped into the bathroom while Rollo continued looking at the suite. When she came out and he caught a glimpse of her glistening in the diamond dust corset, the necklace and the anklet, the glitter and her doe eyes. He was in a trance. The suite was suddenly far removed from his mind.

They weren't married, yet they did everything newlyweds would, and with more intensity since they didn't know when they'd see each other again. When they could take their eyes off each other, they looked out the bay window and saw a refulgent half moon high above the lake. The water was calm, so still, the view from the bay window resembled a picture postcard. Their bodies were heaving as if they had the rhythm of gentle tides, tapping each other like wave crests on the same path. Time was marching on, yet during their between the sheets adulation, it advanced in an amorous crawl. Every moment savored, every touch relished, every thrust delectable, every drop of moisture an ambrosia, culminating in an Elysian nirvana shared by true lovers.

As the moon disappeared and the first traces of daylight came into view, they lay on the bed facing each other, their eyes closed till the increasing sunshine caused them to blink. Rollo looked at Evelyn. She was still pretty after tossing and turning throughout the night. "You want me to call room service for breakfast?"

She pointed toward the corner between the closet and the bedroom. There was a plastic covered straw basket filled with apples, oranges, pears, peaches, plums and red grapes.

"Between that and the cakes, we're set, unless maybe you want to leave the room today?"

"What are you, one of them love 'em and leave 'em guys?" She sat up and pinched his arms.

The sun's rays were hitting the corset's diamond dust, causing Rollo to blink. She had taken it off during the night but left it on a corner of the bed.

"You're not looking me in the eyes."

"Your corset's blinding me."

"I guess I should put it in the closet or a drawer."

"You should. I'm looking at the best jewelry, now." He rubbed his palm against her flat tummy.

Evelyn smiled, got up and took the corset off the bed. As Rollo looked at her smooth skin and lithe torso, he seemed eager to resume the evening's entertainment.

He reached across the space separating them and he swept her toward the vigorous chest she panted for.

"I thought you wanted us to go outside?"

"It doesn't have to be right away."

Evelyn moved her hands over his chest, slid them to the top of his shoulders, spread her legs and mounted him. A warm tingling spread through their bodies and soon they were feeling greater sensation: her legs hung in a V over his shoulders, allowing his hands to touch her outsides and something far more powerful to fill her insides. They kept going like teenagers who didn't know when to nor want to stop. Finally, when the bed linen was moist and sheets resembled dunes, they took an intermission.

Evelyn took a bath in the jacuzzi, and Rollo used the shower in the bathroom, knowing that if he joined her in the jacuzzi, water would be bubbling and splashing without the benefit of modern technology. A towel covered Evelyn from her upper body to her thighs when Rollo walked out of the bathroom. He moved toward the fruit basket, grabbed a pear and bit into it. As he munched on the juicy fruit he said, "I'll get dressed, go downstairs and buy us something more casual. You want running shorts, Bermuda shorts, sweat pants or jeans?"

"Bermudas'll be fine."

"Sure you don't want spandex?"

"I didn't come here to attract attention, and the only serious physical activity I'm doing here doesn't require spandex."

Rollo looked at the bed, her dress hanging in the closet and the corset. "I get your drift. What size do you wear?"

"Twenty-three inch waist. Women's medium shirt. Don't bother with a bra."

Rollo put down the pear and walked toward the living room. "I won't be long."

Evelyn went to the fruit basket and grabbed an apple. Holding it in both hands, as if it were a small melon, she took a large bite and slowly chewed. As she finished the apple, Rollo re-entered with two large white paper bags. "You went on a shopping spree."

"I'd rather spend my money on something you can walk away with." He placed the bags on the bed, opened one and reached into it. "Besides, after a while, we'd look tacky in the same clothes - even if they were cleaned and pressed."

Rollo pulled out a pair of sky blue Bermuda shorts, a pink tennis shirt and black running shorts and handed them to Evelyn.

She took the tags off the various garments and tried them on. They weren't perfect fits, but they would suffice while they were at the Chateau.

"You almost look like a tomboy," said Rollo, putting on a pair of knee length maroon sweat shorts, an ash grey tank top shirt and thongs.

They held hands as they walked out of the suite. When they got downstairs people were checking in, lounging on chairs and couches and sipping drinks. They went outside and walked toward the lake, where they found rowboats bobbing in water. Rollo moved the boat away from the others and held Evelyn's arm as she got in. She sat down and Rollo said, "Bye," and pretended to push the boat away. He saw a blank look on Evelyn's face.

"I was only kidding." He pulled the boat back and jumped in.

"Fall overboard and need someone to rescue you, that's when I'll kid."

Rollo grabbed the oars from under the planks. "You'd let me drown?"

"I didn't say that."

"What a relief!" He placed the oars through the metal circles atop the port and starboard sides and began to row. Using a combination of powerful and gentle strokes, the boat was in the middle of the lake in fifteen minutes. He took the oars out of the circles and placed them inside where they'd be out of his and Evelyn's way. He slid off the plank onto the boat's bottom.

Evelyn's eyes became as bright as a light on top of a slot

machine when it hits a jackpot. She gazed deep into Rollo's eyes, slid down, turned her back toward Rollo, moved close to him and used his lean upper body as a cushion.

Rollo put his right hand under her chin and turned her head upward. "What are you going to do now that we're here?"

"Let nature take its course."

"We can only go so far in this boat."

"I wasn't referring to what I think you're thinking." Evelyn took her flats off and put her toes in the water. "You think we can make this last forever?" she asked, putting her arms around him.

"No," said Rollo. "We can do it over and over again."

"That's more realistic. You wrote anymore lyrics about me lately?"

"None you'd want to hear?"

"Why do I - deep down - doubt that I'll be missed while I'm gone?"

"Fear. You're letting insecurity cast your true feelings aside." He stroked her hair.

"Does that mean I'll hear songs about me on the radio when I get back?"

"I'm not promising you that. One day your song'll be on the airwaves. In the meantime, I'll greet you with open arms when you get back."

"You worried something might happen to me while I'm gone?"

"Concerned. Worrying isn't going to help either of us."

"If the worst happens, you going to go looking for someone new right away?"

"Girls might come looking for me before the worst happens."

That wasn't what Evelyn wanted to hear, but she knew it was a possibility. With Rollo's Mediterranean complexion, athletic build, and talents, it wasn't hard to figure out why he was popular at the swing clubs - or why he'd be popular almost anywhere. She wasn't foolish enough to believe there weren't any places left where complexion wouldn't make a difference. "Does that mean your going to be sleeping around while I'm gone?"

Rollo tilted her face skyward and kissed her forehead. "Too much risk involved. Risk losing the love of my life, risk catching disease, risk fathering a baby with someone I don't want to be the mother, paternity suits, risk you coming back looking to kick my ass."

"Most of those are easily avoidable."

"There's a simple way to avoid them all: be patient until you return." He kissed her lips.

"I won't let you test your endurance. And if the worst does happen - after you've gotten over me - find a girl you want; not whatever comes your way," said Evelyn. She kissed Rollo's lips.

The suite was clean and fresh linen was on the bed when they got back to the suite. The suite remained clean; the linen didn't remain fresh. They didn't go out for dinner. They had room service send hamburgers and daiquiris. Once they had replenished their energy, they resumed.

The following morning they were exhausted. They did not awaken until mid morning. Only their eyes moved at first. Winsome glances were exchanged and Rollo reached for the television's remote control. An NFL game on a cable channel made Rollo stop pressing buttons.

Evelyn had buried her head into her pillow. Upon hearing the announcers describe a play, she said, "You're not going to watch those behemoths slam into one another, are you?"

"I shouldn't with this being the last I see of you until you kill someone."

"We make love and you have pangs of conscience?" She had moved her back against the bedrest.

"Have you considered something could go wrong and you end up the victim?" Rollo turned the television off.

"So the alternative is letting the rapacious murderer off the hook? No way. As far as I'm concerned, his days are numbered."

Rollo studied Evelyn. "You can't let blind hatred warp your mind. You're not that vicious."

"Am I supposed to let greed and avarice warp other people's minds without them having to answer to anyone?"

"Eventually we all - even Kelso - have to answer to someone."

"Did eventually come soon enough for my brothers or Severina and her baby?"

"Is killing Kelso going to bring them back?"

"Is leaving him be going to mend his ways?"

"How do you plan to live with yourself if you pull it off?"

"You mean *when* I pull it off. I imagine a lot better than I do now."

"Even if you take out someone as repulsive as Kelso, you think you're going to be able to go on living as if everything's peachy keen?"

"I'm not that naive, but I'm confident I'll be able to cope with whatever the aftermath is."

"Let's see if you feel the same way when you're done."

Rollo looked at the corset. The rays glistening from the diamond dust seemed ephemeral, like shooting stars that burned brilliantly but soon died out. He wondered if they were a harbinger of his and Evelyn's relationship.

CHAPTER XXIV

OF IMAGE & INCOME

The initial public offering (IPO) of Kehlmeyer Inc. had commenced. The bid price went to $3.50 within thirty days of going public. Kelso watched Financial News Network as if he was an avid soap opera fan and charted his stock's progress.

The ad campaign began shortly after the IPO and established Kehlmeyer as a real competitor with its more prominent rivals. Kehlmeyer posters were displayed on the walls of inner city buildings, subway stations, highway billboards and bus shelters. Besides the bikini clad blonde there was a poster with the silhouette of a stallion standing on its hind legs and the slogan: "Kehlmeyer, the brew with the kick to put you on top." Where Kehlmeyer's ingredients were listed, horse urine was replaced by the euphemistic "other natural ingredients."

He figured if he could achieve critical mass, breaking through whatever barriers remained would be a cinch. He had read Ken *Keyes,* "The Hundreth Monkey," and at first thought it was scientific fodder. Then he reread it and examined real life examples of critical mass (the theory that once a critical mass number is reached, the same behavior or thinking begins to show up in all other members of the same species). After a critical mass of teenagers wore a particular brand of sneakers, other teenagers had to wear it - no matter what the cost. After a critical mass of senior citizens used a specific drug, other senior citizens had to use it - no matter the side effects. If a critical mass of beer drinkers consumed Kehlmeyer, other beer drinkers would - no matter what its ingredients.

Critical mass. Reach it, surpass it and live on easy street.

174

Hesitate, procrastinate and let it slip through his grasp, and he would be just another American struggling to remain in the top five percent of wealthy individuals. Far less than what he wanted.

No indecisiveness, no wishywashiness. He wrote it as a *mission statement* and hung it on his office wall.

He still had one ballpark partner - Andy Metzger. Kelso knew Metzger wasn't loyal to him but to Kehlmeyer's profits. Metzger's son was a high school senior, had good grades, good college board scores and extra curricular activities to impress college admissions committees. Metzger, another teacher moonlighting as a vendor, provided his family with food, clothing and shelter and not much else. Metzger didn't want to tell his son he'd be limited to attending a college that gave him a scholarship.

Kelso combined his need for an alibi and Metzger's need to provide for his son to induce Metzger to remain loyal. The proper bait could catch the appropriate fish.

With the IPO of Kehlmeyer, Kelso had to make sure the public didn't become aware of his beer's authentic equine qualities, but he figured if the horse urine was discovered, he could claim somebody had snuck the ingredient in without his being aware. Kelso had Metzger collect money from Beezer and other club owners. Beezer's and the other clubs, inner city holes in walls, weren't the primary target market, but they could help him achieve critical mass, so he was going to look after them like a big brother protecting a younger sister.

Beezer's club was four blocks from Yankee Stadium. It might as well have been four time zones away. Many buildings were gutted. People milled around on the adjacent sidewalks gossiping, drinking alcoholic beverages, selling drugs and playing dominoes. It wasn't a moat he was crossing, Metzger thought, as he prepared the club's door; but if he was wounded before entering, what was the difference?

Metzger knocked on the brown metal door. Eyes looked through the door's security viewer. There was a ringing sound. The door opened.

Andy Metzger entered. Beezer, with the solemn look of an Indian chief examining a disappointing warrior, nodded. "What's up?"

"Kelso sent me. I think you know what for?"

Beezer closed the door. "He couldn't come himself?"

"You're a business man, too. You should know a business owns its owner, not the other way around."

Beezer shook his head. "Competent businessmen strive to eliminate that. It's bad enough when people think they can own you. When something you created is your master, that's fucked up."

Metzger gave a knowing smile. Hearing this from someone who was as likely to be on the cover of FORTUNE as the Pope would be on the cover of PLAYBOY made it lose something in translation. Metzger got serious. "Are you competent enough to pay for your inventory now?"

"Sure. Stick around tonight and I can pay you next month's before you leave."

"I'll wait till next month. I have faith in your competence to keep this afloat till then. Nighttime's no time I want to be in this vicinity."

"You dissin' my enterprise? You faggot ass schoolteacher," said Beezer.

"Did I say that?"

"You didn't have to." Beezer walked behind the bar, opened a metal box, picked up a pile of money and counted it. "I need more kegs for next month. Customers have been sousing Kehlmeyer since those ads started appearing."

"Shouldn't be any problem. How many more do you need?"

"Sixty."

"Sixty! You going to be able to move that plus your regular inventory in a month?"

"Yeah, with the Play-offs and the World Series coming up next month; as well as Football and more people coming here as the weather gets cold. I might even need more than that."

Metzger looked around the club. The two twenty-inch Toshiba television sets would attract people who wouldn't watch these events at home. It looked as big as the finished basement of a middle class one family home. To envision enough people visiting it in a month to drink more than two kegs per day of Kehlmeyer tested his imagination. Then he remembered he had been the most skeptical original partner, believing Kelso just wanted to prove he could get people to do anything as long as he promised them ample money in return. He also remembered ten years into his teaching career people made Pet rocks the chic commercial fad for a few years. Anything was possible. "Yeah, you just might."

"Do I get in touch with you or Kelso if I need more than sixty?"

"Me first."

"Good." Beezer handed Metzger the cash. "You want a Heineken or a drink before you leave?"

"Mix me a highball," said Metzger.

Beezer put the highball on a table in front of Metzger. He carried a twelve ounce bottle of Heineken to drink himself.

"Salud," Metzger said, picking up his drink.

The highball's tart tangy taste felt good going down Metzger's throat. He looked at Beezer, sitting across the table, guzzling down the Heinekin. He had been teaching laudable kids who grew up to be like Beezer for years. He had followed the New York City Board of Education's guidelines in administering the curriculum and discipline, and added his personal touch in praising and encouraging students worthy of it. Over the years, a few had looked for him when they were at the ballpark to say, "hi," and "thank you," but those were the exception to the rule, and he pondered whether the school system had failed, or if people like Beezer had failed themselves. "Beezer, what you doing with the money you raking in?" he asked, figuring he could find out how such a mind worked.

"Taking care of business."

"What exactly do you mean by that?"

"Keeping my clubs up to date, providing for my children, looking out for my homeboys, finding more ladyfriends and helping relatives."

Metzger took another sip of highball. Hearing Beezer sound altruistic was like a terrorist vowing to become a monk: It was going to take a lot more than Beezer professing a belief in God or chanting hymns to make Metzger believe it. Women had come to the Stadium seeking Beezer for child support. Judging by its interior, Metzger felt Beezer was concerned about his club: with the talent he was wasting, if he didn't make money what was Beezer doing - besides personifying an image the media loved of black men. He did create jobs, but was allowing friends to assist him in pushing dope really being a friend? If his folks knew how Beezer got money would they be proud. "The 'humanitarian' mission you describe, is this how you intend to pursue it? What you're doing is illegal. Changing could make the difference between you surviving five years or living five decades."

Beezer banged his fist on the table. The bottle and glass jumped and came straight down. "No Teach, you got it wrong. If I give up what I'm doing, maybe I'll survive fifty years and live perhaps five of 'em."

"Don't you want to live long enough to see the bastards you created grow up and try to make something of themselves?"

"Their mothers can do all that shit."

"Why'd you get them pregnant?"

"If I didn't, somebody else would have."

"They might have married them."

"Then you would have seen *surviving*. The asshole would what - work nine-to-five? Even so, his family would still be wanting, even if the wife worked and especially if they were like me." Beezer pointed to his skin. "What would've happened when they were laid off or fired? What would happen when they found out that home with the white picket fence wasn't utopia and getting one in an 'upright' community was like hitting the number?"

"Families - help each other in times of crises."

"Does it look like I'm suffering through a crises, Teach?"

"No, but how far away ..."

"How far are you from a crisis since your *'down'* with Kelso?"

Metzger finished his highball. "Nothing regarding Kehlmeyer's ingredients has been established as illegal."

"I ain't worrying about shit. I can take care of friends and families if I'm in jail."

"Don't you want people to be proud of you?"

"Funny. When people were proud of me, I had no money and most ignored me."

"Why don't you use your money to get into something legit? How long is it going to be before you're busted? You know your ancestors died to establish your right to enter into legal business."

"No thank you. And since when are you so knowledgeable about my ancestors?"

178

"You learned one thing in school and the culture taught you another. I remind you of your ancestors because they had a tougher experience. You haven't had to overcome as much blatant racism."

"I'm a graduate of the college of the streets. The results of any form of racism are exactly the same."

"This club is your doctorate thesis? If you had learned something respectable, you and I probably wouldn't be here." Metzger got up.

"Don't forget the kegs."

"I won't."

"Yo Teach. Did you ever think when you were attending high school, then college, and doing all that goody two shoes shit you'd be depending on me and Kelso to help you earn a fortune?"

Metzger shook his head like a man who had heard someone, though talking clearly, clinging to life on a hospital respirator.

Twas the night Metzger was delivering the club owners' proceeds and Kelso was beaming like a child seeing his first Walt Disney film. Critical mass was no longer just a theory, it was something he was applying to his own circumstances.

Kelso liked the commercials using the bikini clad blonde, other models and aspiring actresses. It reminded him of the night Rollo took him to Betsy's. There were a few male models thrown in females would consider "hunks," insuring women's groups wouldn't call the commercials chauvinistic. There was the possibility the Moral Majority would call the commercials sexist, but they were no more sexist than other ads Kelso had seen and since people loved to do what other people said they couldn't, ad bashing would work in Kelso's favor: more people would want to taste Kehlmeyer. The ads would air on a Monday Night Football game. Critical mass could be reached by fall *sweeps* week.

The bell at his home rang, and Kelso went to answer the door.

Metzger handed Kelso a brown attache case. They entered the den. Kelso opened the attache case. Inside, six rows of neatly arranged hundred, fifty and twenty dollar bills were separated by vertical rows of fifties and twenties. Kelso smiled. "Any surprises?"

"Beezer and a few other club owners said they need more kegs

179

next month. They want between fifty to ninety kegs apiece - on top of their regular inventory."

"What!?" Kelso stopped counting the money.

"You heard me."

"A pleasant surprise. Damn!" Kelso completed the count and tossed Metzger a roll of bills.

Metzger grinned and put his fee in a small gym bag, like a teenager admiring a trophy. "I'm going to be doing this monthly?" It was dangerous going to Beezer's club, but if pocketing five times his regular bi-weekly teacher's salary was the reward, it was worth the risk.

"For the time being. You don't have a problem making the rounds?"

"Not at all."

"Good. Go home and tell your wife and your son I said, 'hi'."

They walked to the door, shook hands and Metzger left. Kelso closed the door and shook his head. The effect money had on certain individuals. Metzger acted like a deprived housewife grateful to her spouse for buying her expensive jewelry or an exotic fur coat. Kelso had learned that people who showed emotion regarding money were often parted from what little they had. And that, he didn't plan to do.

CHAPTER XXV

WITHIN SIGHT

As critical mass approached, Kelso was splitting his free time between Evelyn and the ballpark - not necessarily in that order. One September night game when the crowd was sparse due to the hometeam being out of pennant contention, he checked out, washed up in the men's room and drove to Betsy's to get Evelyn.

When he arrived at Betsy's, the only people there were the barmaids and the manager counting the night's cash tally. He was tempted to speak to the manager about having Kehlmeyer sold in Betsy's, but just then Evelyn came out of the dressing room, carrying a weekend suitcase. Kelso took the suitcase out to the GTO, made sure Evelyn locked the passenger door, and began the ride to Yorktown Heights.

"You made a mint tonight?" Kelso asked.

"Not the mint your thinking of. You're the only one who can make that kind of mint."

"I don't know if I'm the only one, I'm the only one you know."

"That's what you think."

Kelso took his eyes off of the road and glanced at Evelyn. "How many other mint makers do you know?" She was beautiful enough to have any man she wanted, thought Kelso, but only men like himself could provide her with an abundance of material comforts. Still, to live lavishly often meant a woman being with someone she didn't want to be with. He didn't fool himself.

"What's it to you?"

181

Kelso resumed looking at the road. "I might want to meet them."

"So what? So you can part them from their money?"

"It'd be purely social."

"Bullshit!"

"It'd be mutually beneficial."

"That's debatable. With people like you, relationships aren't usually win-win propositions."

"If all I'm interested in is money, why am I with you?"

"I never said all you're interested in is money. Do you have a guilty conscience? And you're with me because you haven't had a decent piece of ass since your divorce, but while we're on the subject, what are you interested in besides money?"

Kelso's right foot got lighter on the gas pedal. "If you believe what you just said why are you with me?"

"You're not the most exciting guy I've met; you are the most interesting."

He wasn't certain it was a compliment, but it was the most authentic tribute a female had ever given him. "You're the girl who's most aroused my passion - ever."

"Does that mean you love me?"

Kelso gulped. His adam's apple grew more noticeable, as if a mole was attempting to burrow its way out of his neck, then it receded. "It wouldn't be honest to say that I do, but I do love what you do to and for me."

"Look who's being honest now!" Evelyn playfully slapped Kelso's thigh. It wasn't what she wanted to hear, but it was a seed of opportunity she would fully utilize. "You still haven't told me what you're interested in besides money."

She didn't become belligerent when told she wasn't loved. Was that reassuring or discouraging? Kelso wondered if he really cared? "I like to travel, and I like challenges."

There was a long pause. A moment where the only movement and sound was from the GTO.

Evelyn finally broke the silence. "Anything else?"

"Business related. Things not worth mentioning."

"Like getting off on S and M."

"S and M does present challenges."

Evelyn shook her head. As sparse as she found his non-business interests, at least he wasn't a guy hurrying home from work to eat dinner, watch television and *ignore* his lady - if a guy like this had a lady. She didn't like being with that type of man. She didn't know any woman who did. Men like that actually made Kelso appear attractive.

Kelso pulled the GTO onto the hundred feet long driveway of the Elizabethan Manor house and stopped it in front of the garage door. He could leave it there without losing sleep about whether the vehicle itself or parts would be stolen. Car thieves rarely ventured into his neighborhood. The house was set on a small bluff. Kelso's property was about an acre and a half square and undeveloped. He and Evelyn went inside. Kelso left Evelyn in the master bedroom while he removed the sweat and beer a ballpark wash basin couldn't.

Evelyn debated whether to shower when Kelso was finished. She hadn't worked up a serious sweat at Betsy's, she wasn't going to let Terence get *that* close. She took off the denim skirt, the t-shirt, the sneakers and her white cotton panties, put them in her suitcase, and pulled out what she felt was more appropriate - red satin panties, sheer bra, garter belt, stockings and high heels. She sat on the canopied King Henry VIII bed. It had a mirrored/illuminated headboard and she flicked its lights off and on. Then she went to the bedroom closet and placed her suitcase on the closet floor. As she straightened, she saw something she hadn't seen in a long time. She picked it up. *Ideas came to mind.* She gripped the long hard wooden shaft of the item and placed it back in the closet. It reminded her of something else long and hard she'd recently held. If her plan worked, that could reoccur. She smiled and walked toward the canopied bed as Kelso came out of the bathroom. A white towel wrapped around his waist. He walked as if he were lost; not knowing whether to lie on the bed, sit on one of the bedroom's chairs or embrace Evelyn.

"For a businessman accustomed to making decisions, it verges on stupidity you don't know what to do." She did.

She struck what seemed like a cross between an aerobic and martial arts stance; her legs one behind the other, contracting her abdominal muscles and her arms curled like a late nineteenth century boxer.

183

She pointed her index fingers, then curled them toward her. Like a child being beckoned by his mother, not sure if he was going to be admonished or praised, Kelso moved toward Evelyn. When he was within arms' length, Evelyn straightened her arms and placed her palms on Kelso's shoulders. She nudged him backward, in the bed's direction. He offered no resistance. When she got him within distance of the bed, she pushed. His body settled into the mattress as if it were striking a trampoline, indenting the surface, bouncing up and down. He looked at Evelyn.

His eyes still registered uncertainty - or was it fear; the rest of his face by its appearance - turning scarlet and its muscles growing taut - seemed to know what was in store for the rest of his body. Evelyn continued her slow parade, swiveling her hips as if she could start a hurricane. Of course, *she couldn't; though Kelso had experienced one of her storms.* She reached the bed, stretched her right arm and tickled Kelso's chin. "Prepare yourself," she said, moving her face close to his and tossing him a clothesline.

Kelso sat up and grabbed the clothesline Evelyn had tied to the posts while he was showering. He tied its loose end around his left ankle, then grabbed the rope attached to the other end and tied his right ankle. Finished, he looked at Evelyn. She had the look of a house cat having a pesky mouse where she wanted it.

"Lie down," Evelyn commanded.

Evelyn moved from the bed's end to the headboard. She grabbed the rope tied to the left front post and tied his left wrist. She climbed up on the mattress, stood and placed the sole of her right heel shoe on Kelso's free palm, then she bent down, aiming her crotch so close in proximity to Kelso's face that he could sniff it but couldn't touch. She tied the rope around his right wrist. Before standing she was tempted to lay a fart, but resisted the urge, feeling it superfluous and in bad taste. Then she climbed down from the bed, went to the closet, picked up what she had found before, held the object behind her back and returned to the bed.

"Worthless swine." She used a condescending tone of voice. "You ready to be rocked senseless?"

"Yes, mistress."

Evelyn brought the object from behind her back.

184

Kelso struggled to pull his limbs free. It was a wasted effort.

"Hard or soft?" Evelyn asked. She twirled the object's ends against Kelso's skin, which was starting to grow goose bumps.

"Oh baby, does it make a difference?"

"Don't call me baby. You excuse of a slave." She rubbed the long hard shaft between the cheeks of Kelso's butt.

"Soft mistress." Kelso pleaded.

"Why should I be so merciful?"

"Because I've been faithful to you, mistress."

As if he had much of a choice, thought Evelyn. She removed the shaft from his butt and turned it around. What she placed on his scrotum was vastly different from the riding crop tip used in the S and M club.

She had granted his request. "Oh ecstacy!" It felt as if thousands of hungry centipedes were tip toeing across his testicles.

She twirled the shaft as if it were a baton and the end with feathers was replaced by the wooden shaft. She brought it down hard.

Kelso screamed. His pubic skin turned a purplish red, resembling the shade of a baby mammal that incubates in its mother's pouch. "Why'd you do that?" he hissed.

"Why have you been neglecting me?" Evelyn responded.

"In order to better provide for you, mistress."

Evelyn stabbed the long hard wood into Kelso's butt. His face contorted, his mouth opened wide, but no noise came out. "You expect me to believe that?"

"We're very compatible."

She was tickling him with the feathers again. "What makes you think your the only man I'm compatible with?"

"Oh Didra." From his tone of voice, she couldn't tell if he was responding to what she just said or the feathers stroking his scrotum. "If one were more compatible, you'd be with him now, instead of me, right? After all, it isn't as if you need me, you must want me."

Whatever doubts had been lingering in her mind, were removed. It was no longer a question of whether or not Kelso had an inflated ego, just a matter of how much. Arrogance, pride; whatever term she chose seemed like a mild description of his personality. She wondered if he suffered from megalomania. She picked up the feather duster and

185

was tempted to stick its shaft deep into his rectum. Instead, suddenly disgusted, she took it back to the closet. Reacting violently would have been admitting he was correct.

She danced on the Indian rug occupying most of the bedroom floor. She was tired and, if anything, should have been lying down sleeping, but determination and vengeance kept her body moving as if she were in front of a horde of fawning fans.

The pain and titillation in his groin had subsided enough for Kelso to pay more attention to Evelyn than what she had done to his testicles. He didn't know if her dance was stimulating or debasing; he did know being with his ex-wife had never been like this - and that made him want Evelyn all the more. While he didn't verbalize his desire, it was starting to show.

His limbs, like his testicles, had become rigid. If he could have broken the bed's oak posts, he would have. Instead, his body floundered like a squealing pig being prepared to roast over an open fire pit.

A grin of growing satisfaction creased Evelyn's face. Blustering ego or not, he wasn't much different from most men. She moved closer to the bed, brushed her thighs against the soles of Kelso's feet as she danced. "Now tell me. Who wants who?" She asked.

Kelso struggled to control himself, but what was between his legs kept growing, becoming more rigid, "We're our own mutual admiration society," he responded.

"Why don't you relax?"

"What do you think I'm trying to do? If you untie me, I'd probably find that easier to accomplish."

"Do you find this poetic justice?" She moved close to him, again. "You being so hard driven and now your ....."

"You'd like to hear me say that, but no. This is nothing more than two people having fun after a hard day's - or night's - work."

"Is this as much fun as you want to have?"

"Whatever additional pleasure you provide, I'd be eternally grateful for. I'd be the happiest man on the face of ...."

"Shut up! You fuckin' liar." She stopped dancing and slapped his face. "What makes you think I or anyone else believe you'd get more satisfaction from human companionship than making money?"

"What can I do to prove it to you?"

"You said you haven't traveled recently?"

Kelso nodded.

"Let's go on a trip?"

"I'd like to, but I've got business concerns I got to stay on top of."

"See, what did I tell you?"

Kelso's body - his entire body - went limp. His last vacation had been while he was married and though he was accustomed to financial success, not having a social life had taken its toll. He could devise money making schemes as easy as most people changed underwear, but if what he was doing with Evelyn was how *he had* to enjoy himself - was it worth it? "Where do you want to go?" he asked.

"Let's go to Africa."

"What do you want to go there for?"

"In the rural parts, it'll be easy for you to unwind. Your business concerns won't constantly be on your mind."

If he did go on a vacation who was going to make sure critical mass was achieved? He could depend on the advertising agency to see that it was reached. "What makes you so sure I'm not happy with the way things are?"

"Your going to lie there and honestly tell me having a girl beat you up and 'business', are how'd you want to spend the rest of your life? Suppose I get the feather duster and stick the hard part up your ass again - at a sharper angle. Would you say the same thing?"

"No I wouldn't. But you don't know what I'm going through."

"Why don't you set the record straight, Terence?"

"I want to go, but ...."

"But what? You got a money making scheme going that's going to get you over the hump forever, right? Aren't you already on 'easy' street? What do you need more money for?"

"I don't need it. I want it. I want it because it's there and if I don't get it while it's there, somebody else will. Somebody I don't think is as deserving as I am.

"And you might think I'm on Easy Street, but even on Easy Street there are no free lunches. I've been through enough to know that 'easy' street can turn into hard times just like that." He snapped his fingers.

187

"So Didra dear, going to the dark continent with you isn't all that easy."

"You didn't hear me say it was easy."

His mouth opened. A bemused look swept across his face. "Then what is it?" he asked.

"You and your business associates have mutual interests. If you go on the trip and they screw up your plan or screw around with the money you got coming to you, you can make life miserable for them, right?"

Kelso nodded.

"And you'll get by if they don't give you the last dime?"

"Yeah, yeah. I'll get by."

"Well ..."

"You want to go by the middle of next month?"

"Do you have a passport? Your going to have to get Visas, shots. I'll plan an itinerary once you purchase tickets and make reservations."

"Why don't we go by charter?"

"Don't you want a little more privacy - a little more intimacy - than a charter offers?" She tickled the soles of his feet.

"Yeah. Which country do you want to go to first? I'm not ticklish."

"Kenya."

"I'll get to work on it on Monday. He looked at the radio alarm clock on the lamp table. He was astounded by the time. "Untie me. I got to take you home and go to work."

"Work where? It's Sunday."

"I want to go to the ballpark."

"What?!"

"You heard me."

She was tempted to throw a temper tantrum, but she had got what she wanted and didn't want to jeopardize losing it, so she untied him. She wondered why he was divorced. She could conceive countless theories, but one thing stuck in her mind: his insistence on working Sunday when he could have been with her. Having been in love, she knew to love one had to pay attention. Kelso could be quite attentive, but the timing and aim of his attentiveness could stand drastic improvement. Not that she wanted to, but she was going to have an opportunity to work on it. As much as Kelso enjoyed the masochism Evelyn had grown tired of inflicting it. The fact that Kelso did enjoy it, confounded her. Anyway, if he truly enjoyed pain she'd see to what extremes he was willing to go to in Africa. There there were places she could make use of her firearm's expertise - and get away with it.

She finished untying him; they got dressed and left the house.

CHAPTER XXVI

NO OLD COBBLESTONES

They sat below fluorescent lights in the empty locker room, staring at the rows of metal lockers, reflecting upon what had come to pass and what might have been. How they had almost lost their souls participating in Kelso's venture. How Rollo still had the opportunity to become wealthy, while Uranso would continue meeting his financial obligations through labor and mental drudgery.

"It wasn't a total loss," said Rollo. "I donated half my money to C.U.M. The rest I'll use to re-establish my songwriting career. Maybe I'll write a song for them in the collection I'm putting together. Teenagers listen to musicians more than they do most other people. Maybe I'll inspire someone to go on the right track."

"Is dat going to bring back dose women and childrin?" Uranso asked.

"No, but that fire didn't put an end to C.U.M.'s activities. They have other facilities, more unwed mothers and children that needed help."

"Why don't C.U.M. or anyone put more emphaasis on girls not becomin mothers before dey can provide child wid decent upbringing?" Uranso rocked his chair.

"All the emphasis in the world can be put on. It will make a difference, but there'll still be unwed mothers. Boys and girls aren't necessarily going to be any more careful because of emphasis."

Uranso nodded.

Rollo looked at Uranso, sitting opposite him in a wooden folding chair. Uranso could be quite charming. He could persuade a

190

vendor who swore he wasn't going to give him subway into giving him anywhere between two to ten dollars. Though there were those who despised this quality, there were far more who admired it. Rollo wondered why Uranso didn't apply charm and ingenuity to something beside Kehlmeyer. Often Rollo had seen the middle aged dark skin Jamaican, wearing golashes, rapping to girls young enough to be his daughter - some young enough to be his granddaughter. Rollo knew Uranso could have taken some of these girls home, but didn't out of fidelity to his wife. If Uranso could use his charm for purposes beside extracting subway and pulling girls, there were infinite possibilities.

"Uranso, you got to get off 'the beaten path', man."

Uranso tilted his torso forward. "I am off dee beaten path. I got part of dee money for beach front property in Jamaica."

"What are you going to do for the rest of it?"

"Maybe I pull off scam, mon. Cept mine won't be as wicked as Kelso's."

"At least it's a start. But you're crafty enough. You don't have to resort to that." Rollo shook his head. "Hey, I know what you can do! You and your wife can write an organic Jamaican cookbook.

"Once you and your wife write it, you contact a media services company, see how much it costs to produce an infomercial. You can be the guru who's hoisted organic Jamaican cooking and its benefits upon the world. You have the same heart-stirring persona as these television entrepreneurs. And Errol can be the host - an electronic shill."

A somber appearance took over Uranso's face. "Sounds like it got potential, and it is getting off dee beaten path."

Rollo tapped Uranso's shoulder. "use your imagination."

"How can I use my imagination when I have family to provide for?"

Rollo folded his knuckles between each other, gripped them tight and shook his hands. "Imagine how you'll be better able to provide for your family as an entrepreneur. As an example, you ever made love to your wife someplace besides your place after you took the vows?"

"What dat have to do with my imagination?"

"What prevented you from making love in an 'out of the way' place?"

"Dee tought never occurr to me."

191

"What if it had?"

"It a lot easier to tink about different sex than changing one's way of life, mon."

"You seriously believe that? If your wife loves you, you don't think she'd go along?"

"How many women you know willing to risk seecurity for dee unknown?"

"You want me to introduce you to some?"

Uranso started to say yes, but remembered some of the girls Rollo was known to associate with. "Dat's all right, mon."

"Now what's holding you back?"

"I don't know. Maybe dee example you use isn't persuasive enough. You ever made love in an 'out dee way' place?"

"Sure."

"Oh yeah, dee swing clubs. You nasty mudderfucker."

"Those weren't out of the way places. They got free publicity in PLAYBOY, the tabloids, porno movies; some were very commercial, sold souvenirs with their names plastered all over them. They attracted customers with daring minds and ravenous sexual appetites like scrap metal to magnets. To the casual observer, they might have been 'out of the way' places, but for swingers, they became 'beaten paths'."

"Now what? You going to tell me you made love in the Statue of Liberty?"

A lecherous grin came across Rollo's face. "I'm working on that. However, I have made love at the foot of the Manhattan Bridge."

"Where?"

"The bridge between the Williamsburgh and the Brooklyn Bridges."

"How dat happen?"

"We were coming from this club in Midtown that catered to upscale couples. We had been with three or four couples that night. I was driving her back to her apartment in Brooklyn Heights. As we got near the final turn before Chinatown under the F.D.R. drive, she reached below my waist. I kept my left hand on the steering wheel and reached for a part of her body above her waist. We connected. So well, in fact, that I pulled over to the side of the cobblestone road by the East River, facing the Manhattan Bridge.

"There was a full moon above. It made a beautiful reflection on the the East River. At that time of night there was hardly any traffic so we let it all hang out; must have done about a good - make that unforgetable - forty-five minutes of the nasty. An indescribable fever was swirling inside me, yet cold sweat beads were dripping from my forehead. She screamed. We came at the same time.

"When we were through, the car's windows were fogged. We cuddled for a little while, then I reached for my shorts and had them up to my knees when we heard sirens.

"Suddenly, two cop cars and an ambulance screeched to a stop along side us. The cops approached and rapped on the window.

"A male cop went to my girlfriend's side and asked what was going on. She explained - in general terms - what had happened. The officer understood. On my side was a female cop. She acted hysterical. Calling me everything but a child of God. Threatening me in ways one human being shouldn't threaten another.

"I sat there frozen - goose pimples popping up all over me. Not even bothering to pull my drawers over my balls and my ass. It was quite a swing of the pendulum: one moment I felt as powerful as a charging elephant; the next, as helpless as an earthworm.

"The paramedics were laughing in the ambulance. The male cop came over to calm down his partner and tell her me and my girlfriend were in love. The other cops never got out of their car."

"Was getting off 'dee beaten path' worth all dat?"

"Yeah. Look at all the fun and excitement I had."

"Why didn't you marry dat girl, mon? Sounds like you would have great sex life."

"We would've. One problem though. When the clergyman would have said, 'forsaking all others', I couldn't picture her doing that."

"Yeah. You didn't want to be in one of dese 'Ken and Barbie' marriages where you show friends and relatives, 'see I have a spouse'. And dey be no internal harmony - you feel like shit, mon."

"That might be too complimentary a description."

"It dee best I can think of."

"Once your off 'the beaten path', your imagination'll expand.

Think of all that great Jamaican cuisine you'll be offering to America!"

"I wonder if it's worth it."

"If you keep doing what your doing now, simply working and providing, not doing anything else, are you going to have any stories to tell your grandchildren? Stories that put their train of thought on the right track, stories that'll keep them from becoming a prisoner of the streets and t.v. - or a pawn for someone like Kelso? So they don't end up doing what someone's programmed them to do? So they can express real freedom?"

Rollo noticed Uranso's perplexed facial expression slowly change to comprehension. "Tell you what," Rollo said. "When I do make love at the Statue of Liberty you're going to be there. You want to videotape it?"

"What? You lose your bloody senses, mon!" Uranso said incredulously. "Well, is it going to be with one of dee hit it and quit it girls or someone special?"

"You can be the judge of that while you're taping." Rollo answered. He didn't want to have too many lengthy discussions about the only girl his heart was beating for.

"With the acoustics in there, the way sound carries it can be surround sound erotic video."

"And you want me to tape dat?" Uranso asked.

"NO! I wanted to make sure you're paying attention."

"Believe me. I pay attention. Still, I no want to intrude on your special moment."

"You won't be intruding. How does that saying go? Existentially, you're always alone. There might be boatloads of people around, but only the girl I'm with and I can experience it the way we can as individuals."

"Since you put it that way ...." The traces of a smile creased his countenance. "A girl who makes love to you dere must seriously be interested in commitment."

"She's committed to exhibitionism. What else, there's no guarantee of."

"Still, not just any girl would do dat."

Errol walked in.

"You going to be on t.v., mon!" said Uranso.

194

"Who found out what I did?" asked Errol.

"Not for Kehlmeyer, but for my infomercial."

"What infomercial?"

"Dee one we're making to promote my great organic Jamaican cookbook."

"The what?"

"Don't you see? I'm getting off dee beaten path."

"You been beating something, but I don't know if you're getting off on it."

"Chill," said Rollo. "I got him in the entrepreneur mode. Uranso and his wife are going to write a cookbook, and he wants you to host the promotional infomercial: the shill to his rags-to-riches, gee, aw shucks, pull yourself up by your own bootstraps story."

"He should have said that from the get go. Those things make tons of money. Fuck beach front property! Your going to *own* Jamaica. All you gotta do is promise me the sole restaurant franchise."

"You got it, mon!"

CHAPTER XXVII

ARMAMENT

Evelyn had packed three suitcases. She didn't anticipate staying longer than two weeks. If her plan worked, it would be even shorter. She sat on her bed and looked out the window at the teeming masses scurrying along West Fifty-second Street.

Once she and Kelso were in Kenya, she had to make sure she stuck to her plan. It was simple: he'd be out of his environment and dependent on her. She could work more of her womanly vices on him, that would put him in a more receptive mood and increase his curiosity. She would let nature take its course - well, not quite. Then she'd return to her adopted country.

As far as she was concerned, the world would be far better without Kelso. Yes, he showed - at times second to none - capitalist skills. But in moving toward his goals he'd lied, cheated, had women and children killed. Though still an agnostic she remembered from the Christian Holy Book: "What good does it a man to gain the world and lose his soul." She wondered how much different he was from other entrepreneurs.

A lot, she told herself. When Kelso was no more, other entrepreneurs would come forth, but hopefully, they'd use more scrupulous business methods. She knew she was letting hatred and what she perceived as noble intentions obscure the evil she was about to do. Fleetingly, she saw she was reducing herself to his level, but when she thought of Severina and her baby being burned to death, she saw that Kelso was worse than the men who killed her beloved brothers. She

196

vowed to make dying the easy part of what she'd do to Kelso.

Thirty blocks north of Fifty-second Street, Kelso was also looking at something. He had conceived it. He had nurtured it. He believed in it. He never got tired of watching. It didn't look much different from what he saw the night he met Evelyn. Only now, there wasn't quite as much skin revealed, and it was being shown on television screens all across the country. The bikini clad blonde now had on a sequined teal mini-dress, matching pump heels and nothing else. Beside here there were a brunette, a well tanned redhead and a Black with hair so straight and long it could easily have been a hair-weave. Dressed alike, they shook so alluring and provocatively it seemed they'd burst out of their outfits and through the screen. There was a deep bass voice asking the question: "If thinking about Kehlmeyer can get this reaction, imagine what drinking it can do?"

It wasn't hard for Kelso to imagine people who viewed the commercials asking for Kehlmeyer the next time they bought beer. Most would find Kehlmeyer more potent than what they were accustomed to - and they'd be willing to drink it again. They would stock up, buying by the case. Kehlmeyer's share of the market would improve. With the continued use of sexy ads, more people would sample it. More people would make it their beer of choice.

Kelso punched the remote control, placed it on his desk, picked up the Wall Street Journal, and turned to the pages where the National Association of Securities Dealers Automatic Quotron (NASDAQ) stock prices were listed. He put his finger on Kehlmeyer's line to make sure he'd found the correct quote. He had. The elation of a parent seeing his son or daughter graduate from college swept through him. Kehlmeyer's price per share had skyrocketed. If its rate of appreciation continued, he'd have to worry more about a Securities and Exchange (SEC) investigation than critical mass. He shrugged. He had nothing to worry about.

Still, he was losing sleep worrying about whether he and Evelyn should leave for Kenya before critical mass was achieved. On the other hand, what he had set in motion had reached the stage where it could be managed by the investment banking firm and subordinates within Kehlmeyer's corporate structure - none of whom came from the ballpark. He could go to Kenya. On the other hand, it was devastating to realize he wasn't indispensable. He could postpone the trip, but that would involve lying to Evelyn, changing tickets and hotel reservations, which could cost him money - something he still hated to waste. Would she still want to go if he made it an open date and delayed the trip until critical mass was achieved? There'd be no postponements, he decided. He picked up the phone.

Would Rollo still be in love when she got back? She had fallen in love with a philanderer. Though he professed to be faithful - as she understood men - it was contrary to their nature to remain celibate for long. When she considered Rollo's past, it was like expecting an archbishop not to pray. Still, he did seem attentive, and she hadn't found any telltale signs of infidelity: lipstick on shirt collars, female phone numbers in pockets, women's fragrances besides her own when she got near him, and no lack of virility during their lovemaking. The Asgaard Chateau weekend had convinced her he was sincere.

What would be their routine when she got back? If they made a long-term commitment, what they had in common could cause problems as easily as it could cause their bond to grow stronger. Both enjoyed the limelight. She knew she needed it more than Rollo. And both craved independence - neither liked being subservient to anyone. And how would they provide for each other? Rollo had written hit songs. She believed he could do it again. But how soon and how consistently? Had he maintained contacts with people who could get his material in front of important people?

She sighed and sat down on the bed. So many what if's. Still, she was optimistic. She pushed in the locks on the last suitcase. When she returned she'd go back to school and get her degree. Geologists were still needed by oil companies, building contractors and government agencies. She had saved enough to pay tuition and live for five years, as long as she didn't engage in rampant materialism. She had discovered she could do without most material things - no matter how much the culture said otherwise.

The phone rang.

She stretched across toward her night table and picked up the receiver.

"Didra honey."

"What is it?" she asked, exasperated.

"The trip's set. We leave next Thursday."

"Oh Terry, that's fabulous. Which airline?"

"I tried Pan Am first. But they uh, they, wow, I see why they're on the verge of going out of business. We're going on Kenya Airways."

"We land in Nairobi, Mombasa, Malindi or Kisumu?"

"Nairobi." He hadn't heard of the other destinations.

"That's cool."

"I got us a room in the Norfolk, too."

"Well, well, well! The Hemingway Hotel!" While in Kenya, Ernest Hemingway had often lodged there. That made it one of the most sought after spots for tourists. It also made staying there expensive. Evelyn had had to lie to get Kelso to consider staying there. She had told him if he didn't get them a room at the Norfolk he'd be very sorry. "You got your pills and vaccinations yet?"

"No. But I have a doctor's appointment next week."

"Good. No point in getting sick over there." Especially when he might not come back. She giggled. "Oh Terence your going to love it. We'll go to the coast, the lakes, see the Maasai, go to the game preserves. You have a rifle?"

"What for?"

"In case you want to shoot some wildlife."

"I'm no hunter."

"You may not be, but you *are* competitive."

"So what?"

"You see those animals and your not going to be satisfied just looking. Besides, you never know if you'll be in a situation where you have to shoot one."

"Wouldn't someone be with us who can do that?"

"Most likely, but wouldn't you feel safer in command of your own gun? Look, do you want to be in a situation where you have to defend yourself against wild animals with your bare hands?"

"No."

"Get a thirty caliber. Either a Remington or a Smith and Wesson."

"How do you know so much about rifles?"

"Long story. You don't want me running up your phone bill, do you?"

"No."

"Gee. Why am I not surprised? I'll explain it to you some other time."

"I wonder when that'll be?"

"Call me after you get your shots."

"I will."

Evelyn hung up.

She had learned how to manipulate men before reaching puberty. Kelso, for all his business acumen, once she pointed him in proper directions, was just another toy in her hands.

CHAPTER XXVIII

BIRTH OF A UNIT

There was not a cloud in the sky. It was the Yankees last home game, but as they were also rans, the stadium was almost empty. From a distance the few fans present resembled flesh buoys amongst the sea of blue seats. Pro football was off to a fast start, and fans starving to identify with winners were home in front of television sets, ready to cheer local gridiron heroes. Staying home was logical. The fans could rest on their couches, adjust thermostats; if they had companionship of the opposite sex, they could create their own heat and give new meaning to an end run.

Meanwhile, many of the ballpark fans were shivering under blankets. Rollo wondered why these fans bothered.

At least Rollo could go inside the commissary. There was only one open on the lower deck. Most of the union diehards were there - those who needed money or had nothing else to do - the football games not withstanding. Alouiscous, Lenny Mo Dinner, and Kelso had the beer spots. Oasis, Rod Somer, and Copperblum had hot dogs. Rollo, not wanting to lug around heavy containers today, had opted for peanuts. Rookies who didn't know any better were stuck with ice cream and soda; and Mordecai Kaplan had pretzels.

The plan to administer justice. A justice they felt the courts couldn't adequately administer. Along with keeping themselves off witness stands and outside of prison cells made the conclusion of another baseball season anticlimactic. The tragedy had taught them that making all they could and winning at all costs were credos more expensive than the gains they had garnered.

201

Rollo had gotten everyone to contribute to a C.U.M. memorial fund. He had taken the collection to one of the nuns. "It's from those who want to turn the sorrow and grief into hope and opportunity," he told her.

Rollo looked around the commissary. He shook his head. It was easier to be optimistic with the nun than amongst his co-workers. Lenny Mo was by the checker's desk babbling about how he had been dealt another cruel blow by withdrawing from Kehlmeyer and being relegated to vending and hacking.

Alouiscious stood in the middle of the commissary ranting and raving about the "woomen's" phone numbers he had gathered the previous day, how many he had met at a nearby bar after the game and how he'd have a retinue of "woomens" at his end of the season party. Kelso sat in a corner, looking around the ceiling, not saying anything. Rollo wondered how long he had left on this planet. Nobody included Kelso in conversations anymore - except Metzger, Beezer and Kaplan. If he asked a direct question to anyone beside them, he'd hear a terse answer. Despite having faith in Evelyn, her plan could fail. Oasis was by the refrigerator placing bets on the NFL games with Iggy Biggy. Rod Somer stood nearby telling everyone who'd listen - he was almost talking to himself - why the teams he had chosen would win. Rollo was glad they had shunned the cut throat ruthlessness of Kelso's business methods, but he was disappointed they weren't putting together plans to achieve goals, and refusing to give up on themselves. Even if they no longer wanted to be financially independent, goal setting could help them in life's other aspects. He had done it to establish himself as a songwriter. He was applying it again to re-establish his songwriting career. Only this time he would be more disciplined and not get complacent when he reached his goals. And this time, he'd have a more suitable woman by his side.

Mordecai Kaplan walked into the commissary and yelled, "Guess who was in the courthouse, Friday? Getting ready to go to trial."

"Beezer," said Oasis.

"Why'd you say him?"

"Who else would you tell us about? Who else was most likely to pop up where you work as a court officer?"

202

"Larry Davis, Julio Gonzalez - the Happy Lands Social Club murderer, the slumlord I had to protect from his tenants before their suit against him started."

"Yeah, but they don't work with us. You get to see people who make 'Bronx Madness Sadness', common."

Kaplan grinned. His eyelids came together like piggy bank slots hiding his bloodshot eyes. "Beezer's one of 'em and his trial starts next week."

Kelso took his eyes off the ceiling. "What's he going to trial for?"

"Drug trafficking."

"Which drugs?"

"They busted Beezer up on the Concourse near 167th Street doing Ice."

Kelso stood up. "What's in Ice?"

"Frozen H2O," said Kaplan.

Kelso gave him a look.

"I think valium, methodone and cocaine, but I'm not sure," said Kaplan.

"Is drug trafficking the only charge Beezer faces?"

"As far as I know. Why so interested?"

"He's an ex-schoolmate."

"How come your other ex-schoolmates don't interest you as much?"

"We haven't stayed in touch, we're not close friends."

"You and Beezer are close friends?" Kaplan lowered his glasses to better stare at Kelso.

"No, but we share mutual interests."

"Does that mean what I think it means?"

"No." Kelso described his business arrangement with Beezer.

"If he's sent to Mid Hudson Correctional facility, you can take over the clubs."

"Thanks but no thanks. I have no interest in Beezer's clubs."

"Then let his trial proceed and stop acting like you want to be his lawyer."

"Will you keep me posted as to how it's going?"

"Yeah."

"Give me your seven digits. I'll call you before Halloween."

Kaplan walked to the checker's desk, picked up a currency wrapper, a pencil and wrote his name and telephone number and handed it to Kelso.

"How much time is he likely to get, Kaplan?" Oasis asked.

"Does it make a difference?"

"What a waste," said Oasis. "What'll happen to his children and their mothers?"

"You probably care more about 'em than he does. They virtually don't depend on him now. They won't do noticeably worse while he's gone. Come to think of it, they might receive their support on a more regular basis, knowing where he can be found."

Oasis looked at Rollo. "Want a ready-made family?"

"No thank you, Oasis. I prefer starting from scratch."

"I don't blame you. How long you going to wait for a 'start from scratch' family?"

"Not as long as you might think. It'll be either that, or I'll invite you to the island to see the confines and the concubines." He wasn't going to talk about Evelyn with Kelso in the room. "Look, I'm not greedy. I'll be sought of a modern day Van Gogh or Gengis Khan with my ears intact and without the rape and pillage."

"In exile."

"If it comes to that, an exile I've chosen. Nobody's forcing it upon me. What did Lao-Tsu say: 'The greatest conqueror wins without a struggle'."

Kelso, more than anyone else, looked at Rollo when he finished the quote. The remark made Kelso think about his father. How could Rollo appear so mellow, while Edgar Kelso had allowed adversity to kill him. After thirty seconds of silent staring he left the commissary.

"Who was Lao-Tsu?" Oasis asked.

"A king in the Tah Teh dynasty."

"You studying Far Eastern culture now?"

"Look what the Japanese have accomplished by studying our culture and combining it with theirs."

"You're striving to be the universal man?"

"Whatever man I am, there's always room for improvement."

"You looking for the complete package then?"

Copperblum moved toward the checker's desk and looked at the cards.

"You still seeing that girl you brought to the day game?" Copperblum asked.

"Sought of."

"What does that mean?"

It means I'll be seeing her a lot more frequently in the future."

"You going to ..."

"I might," said Rollo. "I'm seriously considering it."

"What about all the hearts you'll be breaking?"

"They'll get over it. Besides, someone'll follow in my footsteps."

"Like Alouiscious?"

"I said, 'follow', not turn my path to fertilizer."

"You're too kind."

"How does that saying go: 'It's nice to be important, but it's more important to be nice."

Oasis tapped the back of Rollo's hand. Alouiscious approached the checker's desk, an ebullient curiosity etched on his face. "What's this I hear about you following in my footseps?"

"Alouiscious, I don't think the world's ready for anyone to follow in your footsteps. Except maybe," Rollo looked around the room. His head stopped turning when he saw Lenny Mo Dinner.

"He's not even a man. And you think he's worthy to follow in my footsteps?"

"If he's not a man, what is he?"

"Yesterday he didn't even rate beer, and he's been here longer than me. You think you're a man like me, Lenny?"

Lenny Mo walked toward the checker's desk and stood in front of Alouiscious. "Not only am I a man like you, I'm more of a man than you."

"Why don't you prove that by kicking Iggy Biggy's ass?"

"That's not necessary." Lenny Mo blushed, knowing if he raised a hand toward Iggy Biggy, he stood a good chance of losing it. "I don't have to prove to you nor anyone how much of a man I am."

"Then how come you were so sad yesterday lugging around a hot dog bin? The great Alouiscious is never concerned what product he sells and never asks the fans to buy it."

"Selling beer would make me a man like you?"

205

"Not hardly, Lenny. But, at least, you'd be called a beer man."

The remnant of a smile creased Lenny Mo's face. The final home game he did rate beer and Alouiscious was right. He did feel like more of a man.

Alouiscious, noticing the smile, said, "Come to think of it, Lenny, you'll never be a man like me, but you can follow in my footsteps. Your always going to be following someone. It might as well be me. You could do worse."

"Or better."

"I don't think *better* people would let you follow them, Lenny."

"I'm going out."

"Go ahead."

Lenny Mo picked up a beer tray and left the commissary. The other beer men did the same.

Rollo, Oasis and Copperblum observed Alouiscious remaining stationary. "Aren't you concerned that the other beer vendors are jumping you?" Copperblum asked.

"Not during the last home game of the year. Besides, I have people waiting who'll only buy from Alouiscious."

"What makes them so loyal to you?" Rollo asked, screwing up his nose to keep the effect of Alouiscious's funk to a minimum.

"The 'woomen's' know there are things only Alouiscious can do for them."

"They'll be at your party after the game?" Oasis asked.

"Of course." Alouiscious picked up his beer tray and left.

Everyone left in the commissary resumed normal breathing and laughed.

"That's one of the fabulous things about working here. When sales are slow, you can get a laugh listening to Lenny Mo or Alouiscious," said Copperblum.

"Who's funnier?" Oasis asked.

"I don't know," said Rollo. "Lenny Mo is more tragic. You'd think someone who played stickball in the streets with Willie Mays could've accomplished something meaningful."

Oasis, Copperblum and the other hot dog vendors moved to the back of the commissary, took their bins and went outside.

Rollo went to the corner and opened two boxes of peanuts to

serve fans. After telling the checker he had two boxes, he left.

When he got to the seats, it was ten minutes till the start of the game. He wished it was ten minutes till it was time to check out, but wishing it wouldn't make it so, and he preferred dealing with life the way it was than dreaming about the way he wanted it to be. It was a perspective that made the absence of Evelyn bearable.

He wasn't pursuing other women while she was gone - that didn't stop other women from pursuing him. Part of making life the way he wanted it to be was realizing he had to keep certain hormones and a particular organ under control. Devoting most of his waking hours to songwriting, the thought of Evelyn returning and what could happen if lyrics and love were in synch allowed his libido to remain in a state it was unaccustomed to.

The songs he had written while they were apart had to be put to music. He'd contact his agent to show him the first drafts. He didn't know how much of an advance could be obtained. Anything less than five figures would have him looking for a new agent or wondering if neglect had caused one of his best talents to abandon him. He relaxed. If his talent had eroded, he could keep practicing until he got it back. The advance would probably fall short of the money he had earned with Kehlmeyer, but that didn't bother him; songwriting let him sleep with a clear conscience, and he didn't need a fortune to be happy.

A fan bought the two box loads of peanuts and began throwing peanut bags to fans around him. Rollo counted the money the fan had given him and handed him five dollars change. The fan told him to keep it. Rollo thanked him. The mid six figures he banked with Kehlmeyer would've come in handy during the winter. Still, the nuns needed the money to help the mothers and children. He walked back to the commissary telling himself he was closer to having more time to create lyrics. He saw Kelso near a public phone as he got close to the commissary. He looked at him and continued walking. He wasn't going to let anything ruin his concentration.

"Hello." Her voice sounded as if it were in the stupor between sleep and wakefulness.

"Didra, you awake.?"

207

"Could you call back?"

"I got good news for you."

"Can't it wait?"

"If you spent a Sunday with me, you wouldn't be sleeping." The assertiveness she admired was turning into aggressiveness.

"Yesterday I bought a .22, a shotgun and a .30-.30 - an elephant gun."

"Did you buy bullets, shells and carrying cases?" Grogginess was no longer in her voice.

"I got all that. I still don't know how to load bullets."

"Don't worry, I'll do that for you." She was elated but kept her voice under control.

"You know how to load a rifle?"

"Yeah."

"When did you learn how to do that?"

"I'll tell you on the plane ride over."

"Another long story?"

"It's up to you. You're the one paying the bill."

"I'll wait till the flight."

"I want to see what you got before we go."

"Tuesday afternoon good?"

"Yeah."

"I'll pick you up at your place."

"Two P.M."

"See you then."

"Bye." Evelyn hung up. She smiled, got up and went to her dresser. She liked the way her plan was progressing.

CHAPTER XXIX

KELSO'S SAFARI

In thirty minutes the 747 would land. Evelyn looked out of the window, Kelso's snoring soaring over the engine's muted roar. Six miles above land, she glimpsed the stretches of green and brown vegetation beneath the plane, and reflected that the vegetation and her companion both seemed peaceful but deceptively so. The vegetation was home to numerous species, some of which were predators. They behaved according to their instincts. Kelso was a predator all right. On the other hand, his behavior wasn't natural. Most people - including most businessmen - weren't willing to go to the extremes he did to get what they wanted. Still, he was a man who thought things out and executed his plans with more determination than Evelyn was accustomed to seeing. He wasn't a fool. She had taken that into account when planning the trip.

Having come this far, she felt there were only two obstacles to her mission's successful completion: depending too much on mankind's benevolence and underestimating her opponent. She knew mankind's benevolence existed - witnessing it restored her faith in the human spirit, but depending upon it was asinine. Kelso was as benevolent as a shark on a feeding frenzy. And though she knew how to manipulate him - she didn't underestimate him. She turned and watched his facial expressions change subtly as he slept, like a body of water experiencing ripples.

She looked outside again. She would have preferred landing in Malindi, a coastal town heavily influenced by Arabs; then catch a flight to Lamu, the archipelago two hundred miles northeast of Malindi. She had been there once with her brothers. If she could have been certain the roads were dry, they could have taken a four wheel drive there. But though it would have been easier for her to blend in in the Arabic environment, it wasn't essential, and she didn't want to argue over the landing site. Besides, what she planned to do was better suited to Nairobi and its easier access to the game preserves. The ping of the "Fasten your seat belts" and "No Smoking," indicator echoed throughout the plane. Kelso woke up, fastened his seat belt, and leaned over Evelyn's lap to look out the window.

Since purchasing the firearms, Kelso had discovered a whole new world. Twice she had taken him to a firing range. And while no one would mistake him for a sharpshooter, neither would anyone believe he was a novice. She had loaded his weapons out of his sight and brought them to him - one at a time - demonstrated how to hold, aim, shoot and handle the weapon's recoil. Kelso shot at targets ranging from twenty to thirty yards away with either the .22 caliber, a Winchester, or the .30-.30, a Smith and Wessen - called an elephant gun. He scored no bullseyes, but often hit each target in positions to do serious damage. In two lessons he had gained enough confidence to hunt, or rather poach, since Kenya's government outlawed hunting nationwide in 1977, animals that were prey for other animals.

The 747's wheels lowered. The wing flaps opened. The runway seemed close enough to touch. Soon it would be. "You had a nice nap?" Evelyn asked.

"Slept like a baby and dreamt about you."

Evelyn's lips became an upward pointing crescent. "Didn't you sleep at all?"

"A few minutes here and there."

They felt a bump and heard a loud grotesque screech as the plane touched down.

When Evelyn stepped onto the tarmac, she felt both elation and consternation. After a seventeen hour flight through eight time zones, it felt good to stretch her legs on the ground of her native continent. Though Kenya wasn't her native country, she knew it would be easier to get along with her fellow Africans than it would be for Kelso. Despite the long colonialist period that ended in Kenya in 1963, they would not know what to make of this white American. It seemed unlikely any part of the world was prepared for Kelso's business tactics. Besides, as she spent more time in the sun and got browner, she'd look more like a native, or at least an Ethiopian or a Somalian since her hair was straight. Abashed to be seen here with Kelso, she only hoped she could accomplish what she set out to do and get out of Kenya as soon as possible. She could always come back with Rollo - provided he still loved her.

Except for the passengers from her flight, the terminal wasn't crowded, but the line at the customs counter moved as if it were the ticket line for a popular event. After getting their passports stamped and showing immunization cards, Evelyn and Kelso walked to the currency window, where he exchanged $3,000 into Kenya shillings. Then they walked to the side of the terminal facing Nairobi and got into the taxi queue.

Before either of them could raise their arms, a cab stopped in front of them. An ebony-skinned man with the wiry build of a distance runner lowered his head to the passenger window. He had salt and pepper grey hair. "Where you going?" he asked, his English fluent, his accent British.

"Hotel Norfolk."

"Come on."

"How much?" Kelso asked.

"Four hundred shillings." The cab driver got out, opened the trunk, and he and Kelso put in the luggage. The driver introduced himself as Basil and shook hands with Kelso and Evelyn.

The Fiat pulled away from the curb. Basil looked through his rear view mirror. "What are you here for?"

"A vacation." Kelso and Evelyn answered simultaneously.

"What do you plan to do on your vacation?"

"Sh ..." Evelyn gave Kelso's knee a warning tap. "... Observe wildlife," said Kelso.

Basil grinned. He had a funny feeling the "sh," Kelso started to mention wouldn't have been the solid waste material that came from his behind. "Where are you going to observe wildlife?"

"We haven't decided yet," said Evelyn.

"You're going to need a guide, right?"

"You one?" Kelso asked.

211

"I can get you one."

"Give us your phone number. When we've reached a decision, we'll give you a call," Evelyn said.

"Ahsante. I'll give it to you when we get to the hotel."

"Karibu," Evelyn answered.

"Where'd you learn Swahili?" Kelso answered.

"You two married?" Basil asked, before Evelyn could answer.

"No." Again Kelso and Evelyn answered simultaneously. Kelso's "no," was casual. Evelyn's no was obdurate, as if he'd asked her if she would enjoy contracting malaria. Basil was tempted to ask if they'd be staying in the same room. They weren't acting like lovers. Maybe he should warn them they were in a country where people were zealous in expressing religion - whichever faith they were devoted to - and British Victorian morals were still prevalent. Their accents sounded American. In America, sleeping with someone you weren't married to was frowned upon less than in his country. He decided against it; it was none of his business. "You Americans?" he asked. Americans tended to be the strangest - though not the most obnoxious - tourists.

"Yes."

"I recognized the accent."

"If you want, I'll tell you the major sites as we drive toward the Norfolk."

"That's all right," said Kelso, who wanted to observe the sites in silence without the standard tourist rap.

Until they arrived at the Norfolk, Basil didn't say another word.

Kelso and Evelyn looked outside to see downtown Nairobi.

In many respects, it resembled a major American city. There were skyscrapers, some finished, others still being erected. Streets were wide - even the side streets accommodated two-way traffic. There the resemblance ended. Cars from every major manufacturer were driven on the left side of the road in a far more orderly fashion than in Manhattan. Instead of pigeons, a few adventurous vultures from Nairobi National Park were flying above the buildings. "I didn't expect to see this many colored people," Kelso said as he tapped Evelyn's thigh. Most were Africans, native Kenyans, some were Arabs, others Indians and a few Japanese businessmen. This was his first visit to a third world country. "Where do the whites live?"

"You can't be serious. This isn't New York, where you take a train a few stops past 125th Street and it's as if you've moved to Europe," said Evelyn. "The white man doesn't predominate everywhere, you know."

"Okay, forget it. Sorry I asked."

At last the taxi pulled in front of the Norfolk. A bellhop immediately appeared and took Kelso's and Evelyn's suitcases. Basil reached into his pockets and handed Evelyn his business card.

"Call me anytime," he said.

"You'll hear from me."

Kelso gave him four hundred shillings. Basil got back in the cab. He wondered why the woman said, "You'll be hearing from me," instead of us. Perhaps it had to do with Kelso not giving a tip. Basil was perturbed, but tourists were the best customers and even if Kelso continued not giving tips, he'd do quite well with the fares he collected, since he doubled the fare he charged tourists.

The Norfolk looked like a Hollywood studio prop setting - except there was substance behind the image. It stood twenty stories high with charcoal grey bricks as the backdrop to windows with alabaster linen curtains. The renovation, though giving it a touch of the latter twentieth century, made it look like an upright Chessboard.

"It's doubtful Hemingway would have been pleased with the Norfolk's modernization," said Evelyn.

The bellhop took the luggage past steps connected to a dark oak porch with bar tables to the right and a restaurant to the left. They could eat and drink al fresco without leaving the hotel. Subdued lighting pervaded the lobby replete with tan leather sofa lounges, wood carvings of animals and native artifacts, marble lamps and ebony coffee tables. They felt they were in a congested African museum.

When they got to the registration desk, a chestnut-complexioned young woman in a maroon business suit smiled and asked if they had reservations.

"Yes," said Kelso.

"Name?"

"Mr. and Mrs. Kelso."

The clerk pushed keys on a CRT. "You have room 206."

When the clerk gave Kelso the key, hospitality and puzzlement seemed equally etched across her face. The man had said they were married, but she didn't see any wedding rings, and the couple hardly seemed like a couple. They certainly weren't romantic with each other.

The bellhop picked up the luggage and led Kelso and Evelyn away.

The room was spacious. Sunlight streaked in through sheer white curtains. Evelyn looked outside. Below was a courtyard resembling a rural college's quadrangle, containing fig trees, walking paths, a cage with birds, an empty oxcart and and an old cannon, surrounded by rust-colored, two story wooden cabins that looked like they dated from Hemingway's time. Evelyn could almost imagine wildlife scurrying to the cabins' doors. "We got quite a view," she said.

"It's very romantic," Kelso replied staring at Evelyn's doe eyes.

"Romance'll come later on." Evelyn patted his cheek and moved away. She placed her suitcase on the king size bed and opened it.

"How come I usually end up on pain's worst side when I'm with you?" Kelso asked.

"Do you love me?"

"What do you think?"

She put down a pair of khaki fatigues and turned toward Kelso. "You like me a whole lot. You've gotten a lot of satisfaction from what I do to you. I still don't know if you love me."

"Would I bring you here if I had doubts?"

"You might think of me as a bar bimbo who gives pleasurable pain."

"I'd do all this for a bimbo?" He spread his arms like a clergyman gesturing to his congregation.

"How many girls are you tight with who give pleasurable pain?" She sat on the bed.

"Why don't you stop trying to be a politician and speak in plain terms?"

"I don't know if I could fall in love with someone as obsessed with money as you."

"Money helped get you here."

"Look at how you go about earning it."

"Do I conduct my business any different than any major corporations?"

"Yes. A lot of corporations give something back to society - they sponsor scholarships, athletic events, make contributions to hospitals and museums."

"You think they do that because they really care, or it's good public relations?"

"Either way, it's more than you do."

"I helped a homeless family get a roof over their heads. The children who sell for me are less of a burden to their parents. Some even help their parents out."

They've had their morals corrupted."

"When you're homeless and broke, isn't someone going to try to corrupt your morals?"

"Sure, but does it have to be you?"

"They could do worse."

"They could do far better also." She saw his face fall. "Look, Kelso if I'm not the one for you, there's still someone out there waiting for you to sweep her off her feet."

He knew they weren't soulmates, but if he was persistent and applied his persuasive skills he hoped that could change. He found it gratifying she said there was someone else for him - he did have his doubts. He bent over. His lips tapped her forehead. "I'm going downstairs for a drink."

"After I'm done unpacking, I'll join you."

"No. I want to have this round alone."

"Suit yourself." She wondered if she had offended him. "When you're done, you want to go find a spice shop? We can buy fresh coffee beans to take home."

"Yeah. We'll do it before dinner. It'll help us work up our appetite."

His face appeared grave as he closed the door.

She paced, pondering what to do next. Maybe she had been too frank. If she immediately followed him, he'd probably think she felt guilty - which she didn't. If he didn't come back, her plan would be ruined. How would Rollo react to her not getting the job done? Would he still want her? How long would it be before Kelso found a new business where he could exploit, manipulate and commit murders in the name of profits? She stopped pacing and stood in the sun rays streaking through the window. She looked down at the peaceful courtyard, as a royal blue hummingbird sucked nectar from a flower on the balcony.

She moved to the telephone resting on the lamp table. She was ready to page him in the bar until her eyes fell on the room service price list, also on the lamp table. The prices were comparable to those in a Manhattan five star hotel. Suddenly, she grinned. Kelso wouldn't leave. He'd already paid for the room in advance. He'd lose money! His miserliness would overcome pride.

The ride through Nairobi National Park continued the reconciliation that had begun the previous evening when Evelyn joined Kelso at dinner. She had told him she did appreciate his splurging for the trip, that he was one of the few men who would have done it for her. She knew men who said they would do it, but they were just uttering male romantic fantasies. While it wasn't exactly what he wanted to hear, it changed his demeanor.

This morning he was acting like a sailor seeing land after an extended period at sea; he'd tap Evelyn's arms as he saw Impala, gazelle, giraffe, warthogs and zebra. The van they were in stopped near a pond and they got out, along with the other passengers, and walked along a path that led them closer to the pond. Vervet monkeys came up to them. They could have reached out and touched the grey, white and black primates; instead the animals and the humans carefully observed each other before the monkeys ran up their doum palm trees. Kelso decided he wouldn't shoot the little monkeys; they looked too much like domestic pets. He and Evelyn walked close to the pond. A middle aged woman approached and in a hushed tone said, "Do you see the hippopotamus?" The woman pointed toward a bush jutting out over the pond. "Thank God these animals are either in National Parks or game preserves now. That hippo would be dead meat if a hunter were here."

"Hippo. I didn't see any hippo," said Kelso, wiping his forehead

216

and neck. Heat and humidity made the air feel like sauna vapor.

"Keep looking," the woman whispered. "It's opening and closing its mouth."

A piece of flesh rose above the water line and went below again.

"It's smarter than us," said Kelso.

When they returned to the van, a troop of brown baboons were nearby running back and forth. All except one stayed near the road observing vans and cars drive by. One approached Evelyn and Kelso's van. It moved its head slowly, looking at the foliage by the pond, Kelso kept his eyes on the baboon. Kelso didn't want any nasty surprises. Kelso reached into his pants pocket to hide his trembling hand and moved closer. The baboon ran to the other side of the road with his friends.

"You big baboon. You scared the little baboon," said Evelyn.

Kelso turned toward her and grinned.

They waited near the van until the passengers returned and got on board. The tour guide drove toward the exit gate. Along the way Evelyn and Kelso saw vultures in thorntrees, cape buffaloes, wildebeests and hyenas. As the van past the gate, Kelso was happy he had seen the animals; he was formulating which he'd hunt. He had wanted to see big cats. Their tour had taken place during mid afternoon, a time when the cats were usually sleeping, but he had seen the results of lion kills: the bare bone carcass of a zebra and a dry impala skeleton.

"Hello, Basil?" Can you arrange a trip to a game preserve or a national park tomorrow?" Kelso asked and sat down on the bed. It had been a long day. The observation safari had taken all day.

"Which one you want to go to?"

"Any except Nairobi National Park. We went there today."

"Any specific animals you wish to see?"

Kelso thought. "Impala, wildebeest, zebra, wild dogs, big cats, rhino, giraffes."

"How far outside Nairobi do you want to go? Mount Elgon? It's a twelve hour train ride and more time on roads through rough terrain."

"Forget that."

217

"Let's see. Lake Nakuru is much nearer but mostly birds - flamingos and pelicans - and some marine wildlife."

"That's not what I want to see."

"How about Amboseli? Besides the animals you mentioned, you can see elephants and Mount Kilamanjaro. Only you might end up crossing the border into Tanzania and spending money on entrance and exit visas."

"Forget it," Kelso said.

"There's Tsavo. That's east of Amboselli. You'll see a lot of the animals you're interested in. One thing though, the lions there earned their nickname as the 'maneaters of Tsavo'."

He did want to see big cats but none with such an imposing reputation. "Anything west of Tsavo?"

"How about the Maasai Mara? All the animals you want to see and a virtual flat plain."

"Sounds good."

"It's a little bit closer to Nairobi than Amboselli."

"Let's do it."

"I'll pick you up at 6 A.M. With no problems on the roads, I can have you in a tented camp or lodge by nightfall. The following morning you can go on a game drive."

"We'll be ready." Kelso put the receiver down. "I'm going to an area where the wildlife roamed as if it were still in pre-colonial Africa. I'll be creating business for a taxidermist. I'll have trophies to put on my den walls." In addition to building businesses, he'd become an expert in killing animals. Which required more skill? Which required more ruthlessness? An intriguing look spread across his face.

"Why didn't you find out for yourself where we could go?" Evelyn asked, trying to muffle his enthusiasm. If his adrenalin overflowed, he'd again become eager for romance.

"I was busy with business arrangements before we came here, remember? I didn't have time to do any research. Why didn't you do any?"

"It's not as important to me to see wildlife."

"Fine. You could have looked for cultural sites and natural phenomena to look at."

I'm looking at a natural phenomena now, she thought. Evelyn

smiled. "You're right." She wanted to avoid another argument.

They were up at 4:30 A.M. getting ready to meet Basil promptly at 6 A.M. They took separate showers, put on khaki pants; Kelso wore a matching khaki safari jacket over a sky blue t-shirt and hiking shoes; Evelyn chose a kelly green polo shirt and aerobic sneakers. They packed overnight cases with a two day supply of clothes and toiletries. Kelso packed his firearms in a golf bag covered with a grey canvas. Kenya wasn't famous for golf courses, but he figured there had to be at least one there and if anyone questioned his bag, he could say he was getting in a round before leaving. Hopefully, there'd be no other golf enthusiasts who'd ask to see his clubs. By 5:45 A.M. they were ready. They went downstairs to the lobby to wait for Basil.

At five minutes to six Basil walked in. He smiled at the receptionist, then turned toward Evelyn and Kelso. They exchanged pleasantries.

When Evelyn and Kelso came outside with their luggage, Kelso noticed Basil was driving a Toyota Camry. He asked, "What happened to the Fiat?"

"It's at home. I have more than one car."

It was a late model car, though not the latest model. "How many cars do you have?" Kelso asked.

"Three. I also have a Volvo."

He had acquired one American tendency, thought Kelso as he began placing luggage in the trunk. "You use them all as taxis?"

"Sure." Basil smiled proudly, slammed the trunk shut, they were off.

"To get you to the rendezvous site as quickly as possible, I'm driving northwest to Kijabe," said Basil. When they cleared the city and reached a paved highway with very little traffic, Basil floored the gas pedal. The brilliant orange yellow sunrise, the foliage surrounding the road interspersed with trees and termite mounds were blurs.

"Are you going to get stopped for speeding?" Kelso asked.

"Do you see any speed limit signs?"

"Then see if you can go faster," said Kelso, tapping Basil on the shoulder.

Evelyn was mildly surprised; then she remembered Kelso was in a hurry - eager to get his first kill.

As the Camry sped along, there was a loud poof and screeching as the car's rear right slid closer to the ground. The wheel hit the tarmac. Basil put his right foot on the brake and the Camry slid to a halt.

"You have a regular spare or a temporary?" Kelso asked.

"Temporary," said Basil.

"Let's put it on. I'll help you."

He and Basil went to the trunk. Basil opened it, took out the luggage, then the spare and the jack. He carried them to the rear right wheel. Evelyn picked up the luggage and moved to the side of the road away from traffic.

Basil and Kelso knelt. Basil placed the jack under the underbody directly beneath the door. Kelso inserted the tire wrench in the socket and began turning. The right side rose. So did Maribou storks in a nearby thorntree. They peered at the large object below and the humans scampering about it. Two flew from the tree and landed on the side of the road opposite the Camry.

The car's right side was elevated enough for the flat tire to be removed. Kelso stopped turning the wrench, took it out of the socket and handed it to Basil. Basil put the wrench on a nut and began turning. Kelso moved around him and went to the spare. As he did, he noticed the storks on the other side of the road. The sun had risen, but the birds were still in silhouette. With their bony legs, feather-covered, bloated bellies, torsos and necks, skulls and beaks merged to appear as boomerangs. Kelso thought the storks looked like bald, malnutritioned children with overcoats on. He didn't know if they were scavengers, predators or herbivores. He stared at them, wondering what they would do next. He could go get a gun and use it, but he didn't want to - not yet; these weren't creatures he had planned on killing and he didn't want to reveal his weapons prematurely. The storks returned his stare, as curious about him as he was about them. As the staring continued, Kelso began to feel what it was like to be the prey rather than the predator: never able to relax one's guard, knowing as soon as he stopped being cautious a predator could seal his doom. Perspiration began trickling down his forehead.

Basil snapped his fingers in front of Kelso and pointed toward the spare tire. Kelso picked up the tire, moving as if he had just been awakened from a trance, placed it upright and rolled it toward Basil, his eyes shifting between the exposed wheel and the storks.

"Don't be frightened," Basil said. "You leave them alone, they'll leave you alone."

"Why are they staring at me?" Kelso asked.

"They probably have never seen an American fix a flat tire."

"What makes you so sure they're not sizing us up for the breakfast menu?"

"Look at their feet. Do you see any talons?"

"No."

"That would indicate they're not birds of prey."

"Look at those beaks. They look like hedgecutters."

"If by chance they do bite, you'll live."

"All right. Put on the spare and let's get moving. You want me to do anything else?"

"Go sit by the lady."

Kelso hesitated. He didn't know if Basil made his request out of concern for Evelyn, or because it was appropriate he sit next to the female after the way he behaved.

In less than fifteen minutes Basil finished putting on the spare. Kelso put the luggage back in the trunk. In another half an hour they were there.

Kijabe was a small town compared to Nairobi. Coke and Pepsi signs were displayed on walls everywhere and no buildings were above three stories high. It could almost pass for a small, midwestern American town, though the pace of life was drastically different, and Kelso was surprised to see few people moving about even with the sun having risen.

Basil drove the Camry to the hub of the town and parked in front of a grey, two-story hotel. "Wait inside the lobby and have some tea and honey coated wheat bread while I get you a tour guide to take you to Narok and the Maasai Mara," Basil said as he placed the luggage in the lobby. Basil pointed to a middle aged couple behind an austere registration desk before leaving.

"Do you want anything, my dear?" Kelso asked.

"Tea would be fine."

"What about the bread?"

"I'll pass." Evelyn went to sit down on the lobby's one sofa, a sagging black vinyl affair stuck in a corner.

Kelso approached the man behind the desk. He was as dark as Basil but stout and slightly shorter. "Can we have tea and honey wheat bread over there?"

"Sure mister."

"How many rolls do you want?"

"Rolls?"

The man pointed toward the bread. It was shaped like coffee cake buns.

"Three."

"I'll bring it to you and the lady," said the man.

"How much?" Kelso asked.

"Six and a half shillings," said the man. "Pay me when your through eating."

Kelso sat on a couch beside the coffee table opposite Evelyn's couch. He gave Evelyn a closer look to see if there were any bumps and bruises he had missed on the road. "You sure you're all right?" he asked.

"I'm fine. How about you?"

"I'm glad we're all in one piece."

Kelso looked out of the window facing them. Suddenly he got up excused himself and walked outside.

To the right of the hotel's front steps twenty-five yards away grew a thick fig tree. Standing in front of it was a Maribou stork. In broad daylight the bony legs, bloated belly and boomerang-resembling neck, skull and beak didn't appear as imposing. Kelso laughed. "Why I could have smacked you down," Kelso said. He wished he had a camera. No one would believe he saw a bird like this. He turned around and walked back inside the hotel. As he did, the stork flew off.

When Kelso sat back down, Evelyn had a half filled cup in front of her. One piece of bread and part on another were gone.

"I thought you didn't want any bread."

"I changed my mind?"

Kelso poured himself a cup of tea and took a bite. He understood why she had changed her mind. The bread was delicious. It was soft, easy to chew and had a mellow sweetness. He wolfed down the bread as if it were his last meal.

"You think that stork's going to come in here and take that bread from you?" Evelyn said.

"It isn't the stork I'm worried about. You want more?"

"No thanks. It's my responsibility to maintain my figure."

Basil walked into the lobby with a handsome man built similarly to him but without grey hair and wrinkles. They walked toward Evelyn and Kelso. Basil said, "This is Kushoto. He'll take you to the Mara. Your going to need four wheel drive from here on, and he has one."

Kushoto nodded at Evelyn and Kelso.

Kelso nodded and continued drinking his tea. For some reason, he didn't quite know why, he didn't know if he'd be comfortable with Kushoto taking him to the Mara, but he didn't have time to be particular.

Kelso got up and walked with Kushoto and Basil to a different corner of the lobby. "How much do I owe you?"

"One hundred ninety shillings," Basil answered.

Kelso gave him two hundred shillings, told him to keep the change, and asked how much Kushoto's services were going to cost.

"I got him to do it at a reasonable cost, three hundred shillings." Basil gave the same proud look as when he had mentioned his ownership of three cars.

"We should be back in Nairobi in two or three days. If we need you can we call?"

"Sure," said Basil.

Kelso and Basil shook hands and Basil left the hotel.

Kelso turned toward Kushoto. "You seem awfully quite," he said.

"Whatever you say, Mister," said Kushoto in a deep voice.

Kelso detected a tone of insincerity. "Call me Terry."

Outside Kushoto pointed Evelyn and Kelso toward a black Isuzu Trooper. Kushoto and Kelso put the luggage in the rear compartment. Evelyn got in the back seat. Kelso sat in the front with Kushoto. He figured he hadn't gotten as romantic with Evelyn as he would have liked to; the chances of him getting romantic with her while going to the Mara were remote; and he wanted to keep an eye on Kushoto.

The Trooper drove away, heading southwest. Kushoto didn't try

223

to be a speed demon, and the slower pace, along with the four wheel drive's heavier steel undercarriage, made the trip more comfortable than in the Camry. From Kijabe to Narok took close to an hour and forty-five minutes. Besides the open space they saw Harrier Hawks, Martial Eagles and Bateleur Eagles in the sky and in trees. At Narok they stopped in a Cantina and drank Coca Cola, ate pineapple chunks, used the rest rooms and then were back on the road.

When they got outside of Narok, Kelso and Evelyn found out why they needed four wheel drive. The road stopped being a road and turned into a shallow swamp. The Trooper's wheels would spin and propel the vehicle forward like a centipede climbing a sharp pebble. Several times mud splattered onto the vehicle's windows. Kushoto turned on the windshield wipers. The Trooper moved sideways almost as much as it did forward. Finally, the Trooper got stuck in a mud puddle it couldn't drive out of. Kushoto got out. A third of the Trooper's wheels were stuck in mud.

Kelso stuck his head out. "What are we going to do now?"

"Push."

"And if that doesn't work?"

"I'll try to find a farmer and see if he'll loan us oxen to tow us out."

Kelso shook his head.

"Come on out, Terry. Can you operate a stick shift, Miss?"

"Yes," said Evelyn. "You can call me Didi."

A smile as warm as the equatorial heat swept across Kushoto's face. "Didi, Terry and I are going to push. When you feel the vehicle moving, put it into second gear and floor the gas pedal."

Evelyn nodded and climbed into the Trooper's driver seat.

Kushoto and Kelso put their shoulders against the vehicle's rear and pushed.

The vehicle heaved but not far enough to escape the mud. They pushed again, using greater strength. The vehicle heaved again, this time higher, but was still stuck. Kelso had mud up to his belly button. "Look at the bright side: when I venture into the wild I'll have additional camouflage," he said.

Kushoto tapped Kelso's shoulder. "Turn around. We'll push using our backs."

They placed their backs against the vehicle and pushed, summoning all their back and leg strength.

Evelyn put the vehicle in third gear, floored the gas pedal and the vehicle jolted forward onto solid ground.

Kushoto and Kelso fell.

Evelyn put her head through the open window and laughed. Kushoto and Kelso were covered in mud. "You all right?"

"Outside of being wet and looking like mud wrestlers we couldn't be better," said Kelso, taking off his shirt.

"Then come on."

The mud track lasted until they were a few hundred feet from Cottar's, a tented camp on a large spring surrounded by acacia, croton and fig trees nine miles from the Mara's Sekenani gate. "Do you want to stay here while on the Mara?" Kushoto asked.

"How much does it cost?"

"A little more than 1,800 shillings per week for a double room with full board."

"That's about eight hundred-fifty dollars." Kelso had done a rough conversion of shillings to U.S. dollars.

The camp appeared spacious. Tents resembled canvas cabins and each had its own vegetation screen, making it appear they weren't too far apart. "How are the accommodations?" Kelso asked.

"Comfortable and the food is unmatched."

"Unmatched in quality or inedibleness?"

"Quality." Kushoto gave Kelso a look suggesting: "Why would I compliment the food if it was terrible?"

Kelso looked at Evelyn. She shrugged.

"We'll stay here," he said.

"Wait here." Kushoto got out of the Trooper. He went to a man in a maroon safari suit, standing near a large tent.

Kelso watched the men converse. He was glad he'd be staying outside of the Maasai Mara's gates. If he did kill an animal, he wanted to avoid anti-poaching rangers. Staying on the game preserve would make it easier for rangers to capture him. He'd have to maintain a constant vigil to make sure wild life observers who'd snitch wouldn't notice him. The tented camp provided the further advantages of being more open and was closer to the best game viewing sites.

Kushoto returned to the Trooper and drove about two hundred yards west and stopped in front of a tan tent approximately thirty feet long and fifty feet wide.

"This is your tent," said Kushoto. "It has a portable toilet in the rear as well as a stone shower stall fed by well water."

Kushoto got out of the Trooper and placed the luggage inside the tent.

"You want to go game watching before or after lunch?"

"Before," said Kelso. "Let us take a shower. Is there somewhere here where you can clean yourself off?"

Kushoto nodded.

"Come back when you're done and we'll go."

"Terry, why did you bring a golf bag?"

"I figured if the vegetation got too dense I could use my clubs for hacking."

"There are machetes for that and if you really wanted to play golf you should have gone to South Africa."

"Well, I'm here, and so is my golf bag."

"Not for golf but for another game?"

"You could say that."

"What do you want to shoot - Impala, Thompson gazelle, wildebeest, topi?"

"Those fit the bill. If we can squeeze 'em in, I'd like a shot at a zebra, wild dogs and jackals."

"The grazing animals you'll have ample opportunity for. The others aren't going to be easy. What are you going to shoot with?"

"A .22."

Kushoto nodded and walked through the screen door. "I'll be back."

Kelso looked at Evelyn. "You can take your shower first."

"Don't you need to clean yourself off right away?"

"Ladies first."

Evelyn opened one of her suitcases, took out her toiletries, grabbed a towel and washcloth and went to the showerstall via the tent's rear door.

Kelso sat down on his cot. If Kushoto revealed his hunting plans to the authorities and the golf bag containing two rifles, what excuse could he give? He heard the shower turn on. He decided if he was confronted he'd say the guns were part of an experiment to test a new animal tranquilizer. If asked to produce the tranquilizer, he'd say he was supposed to have received it in Nairobi, but it was late coming and supposedly on its way. Meanwhile, he'd decided to come here to look for suitable animals for the experiment. If he was asked why he had regular firearms for a tranquilizing experiment he'd say, without being too far from the truth, he had practically no knowledge of firearms and was told the weapons were suitable for the experiment. It wasn't an airtight alibi, but to disprove it the authorities would have to divert manpower from their anti-poaching patrols on the reserve. Would the authorities want to divert manpower from the field to investigate the story of someone who hadn't fired a shot and was willing to give up his weapons? He didn't think so. He hoped the alibi wouldn't be necessary, that if he had to, he could bribe Kushoto to keep his mouth shut.

Evelyn walked into the tent, a towel wrapped around her. He was no longer concerned with alibis. The towel didn't enhance her figure as much as skintight outfits, but it motivated Kelso. He wasn't getting on the plane home without having made love to her. In spite of disagreements, rebuffs and her sadism, he was in love for the first time since the early days of his marriage. He'd prove it was love by winning her over to his way of thinking rather than coercing her.

Evelyn saw the look in Kelso's eyes. "Go take your shower," she said.

"Maybe I should have taken mine first, after all."

"Should've, would've, could've, if only I'd have. You're not that type of guy. Go take your shower. You have more urgent concerns. I'm not running anywhere."

Kelso got up, gathered his toiletries and left the tent.

Evelyn put on another pair of khakis, a pink blouse, fresh sweat socks, and her aerobic shoes. She went to the golf bag and pulled out the Winchester and a box of .22 caliber bullets. She loaded the rifle's magazine, closed the chamber, locked on the safety, and leaned it against the wall in a corner. Then she moved to her cot and lay down. It was comfortable. The canvas supporting a two and a half inch thick mattress was durable. The mattress didn't cave in when she lay down. She

227

sat up as Kelso came back inside.

A few inches of flab were hanging over the towel he had draped around his midsection. He looked like one of Kehlmeyer's best customers. She watched him put on fresh clothes. Then they heard a horn honking.

Kelso went to the front door. It was Kushoto, honking for them to come out. As they neared the Trooper, Evelyn reminded Kelso he'd forgotten the Winchester and a pair of binoculars. He went back in the tent, approached the door with the items, looked to see if anybody was nearby, seeing no one beside Evelyn and Kushoto he scampered to the Trooper, put the gun in the back beneath Evelyn's feet and sat in the passenger seat.

Kushoto drove toward a semi-secluded exit. Once outside the camp Kelso asked, "How much do you want to keep your mouth shut?"

"An extra three hundred shillings," said Kushoto.

Kelso wanted to haggle, but was relieved that Kushoto hadn't told the authorities. "You got it," he said.

Kelso stuck out his right hand. Kushoto slipped his right hand, taking it off the steering wheel, under his left and shook Kelso's outstretched hand.

As they got closer to the Mara, using a dirt road, Evelyn and Kelso saw more wildlife. On either side of the road were gazelle, impala. About a quarter mile from the road were a pair of giraffe. Briefly, Kelso wished he had brought a camera instead of rifles. Taking pictures of animals used to fight or flight at the first sign of something strange was challenging too. And it was a lot easier to carry cameras, films and pictures than to conceal guns and carcasses. But guns made sure there was a victor and a victim. And he felt he had to be an unequivocal victor in order for Evelyn to change her opinion of him.

Kushoto took the Trooper off the road, bearing right and coming to a halt thirty feet before a ridge.

"What are you stopping here for?" Kelso asked.

"Get outside and I'll show you," said Kushoto.

Kelso wondered if he was being set up for a double-cross. He, Evelyn and Kushoto went outside and walked closer to the edge of the ridge.

It was as if every National Geographic special and Nature program outside of the polar regions were unfolding before their eyes - except this wasn't on a picture tube. Soon they'd be seeing close up the tree bordered rivers, massive ridges, savannah crowning mountains and stampeding wildebeest herds roaming far below. Suddenly, Kelso felt the significance of his business accomplishments diminished. In the business arena he dealt with people and through trial and error until he found what worked, though he couldn't control anyone - there being no such thing as a well adjusted slave - he could influence them. On the Maasai Mara he'd be dealing with nature - innocent and unforgiving. He was looking forward to the challenge. "Where do we go from here?" He asked, not entirely sure if he was referring to animal hunting or his life.

"Toward Kichwa Tembo. It's another tent camp. It looks out on the whole northwestern Maasai Mara. You'll have a better opportunity for the animals you want there."

"What's wrong with here?"

"Some of the country's largest lions live here. It makes the herbivores more skitterish, which doesn't make them any easier to shoot."

During the ride toward Kichwa Tembo they saw: a giraffe giving birth, warthogs hastily munching on grass, a martial eagle capturing a mongoose, a cheetah tracking down a baby impala and a pride of lions feasting on a cape buffalo. Looking at the lions devour the buffalo, Kelso found it hard to believe animals survived being anything less than aggressive. It reinforced his belief there was no viciousness or cowardice amongst wild animals - just survival instincts. He wished his father were alive to see this. Perhaps Edgar Kelso would have learned something that would have made a difference in how his life turned out.

When the Trooper got to Kwicha Tembo, Kushoto drove to a large acacia bush above a shallow lugga. Two maribou storks landed on an eleaodendron tree's thinnest branches. Kushoto lowered his voice. "We can wait outside the Trooper. Animals come here to eat. If no other vehicles come, we'll be virtually inconspicuous."

The trio resembled an infantry unit's forward scouts. They squatted low enough to hide and began to watch.

Two vultures stood on the branches of a pappea tree thirty yards east of the storks tree, waiting for a kill so they could partake of the leftovers. Finally, a herd of topi approached the lugga's edges and grazed on the abundant vegetation growth. Adult males were scattered around the herd's edges, keeping their keen eyes alert for predators. One noticed the humans but didn't seem alarmed.

"Would bagging one of these please you?" Kushoto asked.

"I don't see why not," answered Kelso.

"Then decide which one you want and shoot it. Soon predators'll be here, causing this herd to scatter. They won't appreciate us infiltrating their turf."

Kelso used his binoculars. Looking east two hundred feet away was an adult male. It resembled a cross between a deer and a goat with its pronged horns, drooping chin and mottled coffee brown skin. Kelso figured if he fired at this one and missed, he'd have an opportunity to get another of the fleeing animals, they being closer to him. Another vulture landed on the pappea tree. Kelso gave the binoculars to Evelyn. He picked up the .22, nestled it against his right shoulder, and aimed toward the unsuspecting creature. He wasn't using a telescopic sight, but figured he had the topi properly aligned. He released the safety, checked his aim, then pulled the trigger.

The loud boom had the same effect as a lion's roar. The topi scattered like gnats escaping a swinging hand, moving in every direction as swiftly as their limbs could carry them, all except the male Kelso shot at, who fell like a metal target at a carnival's shooting gallery.

That wasn't so hard, thought Kelso. There were now five vultures on the pappea tree.

"Come," said Kushoto. He got up and walked in the direction of the fallen beast, Kelso and Evelyn behind him.

When they got to the fallen topi, he was mortally wounded. "Finish him," said Kushoto.

"Can't I just wait for him to die?"

"No," said Kushoto. "If you do that you prolong his misery, give hyenas, baboons, vultures and every meat eater an opportunity to 'spoil' your trophy and allow anti-poaching rangers more time to catch us."

Kelso put the rifle's barrel beneath the underside of the animal's neck, at the top of its trachea. His index finger was on the trigger, but seeing the animal's eye in glazed disarray, as if it wanted to know how and why this happened, made it hard for Kelso to pull it.

"Go ahead," said Kushoto.

Kelso hesitated. He hadn't expected to gain such an intimate knowledge of slaughter. Target practice and shooting from a distance hadn't prepared him for this. From now on he'd be a better shooter. He pulled the trigger. The shot was muffled by the animal's neck. The topi became still.

Kushoto walked back to the Trooper, got a machete and a large plastic bag, returned and got on one knee, resting near the animal's forelegs. He raised the machete above his shoulder. With the precision of a prized meat butcher he chopped into the topi's neck, right above its shoulders. Blood splattered through the opening like water bursting through thin ice. Purplish red drops fell on Kushoto's arms and Kelso's clothes. Kelso pulled the head and neck away from the rest of the body. More blood flowed onto the lugga's black cotton soil.

Kushoto put down the machete, picked up the plastic bag, opened it wide and helped Kelso put the topi's head and neck onto it. He closed the bag and tied it tightly. "Let's go," he said.

Evelyn walked to the Trooper ahead of the men. The bloodletting was more gruesome than she had anticipated. She hoped she wouldn't puke before the day was over.

Having seen women act this way previously, he knew what advice to give. Breathing heat soaked air would add to her nausea. He turned on the air conditioner. "Lock the door and roll up the windows," yelled Kushoto.

"Why?" Evelyn asked.

"The animals coming might want to get in here."

Screams, giggles, growls and whoops of an approaching hyena clan, smelling fresh meat, got louder. To Kelso it sounded like a bunch a rowdy fans at the ballpark. Quickly, he and Kushoto, put the machete and topi into the rear compartment, got in the Trooper and drove off.

Three vultures had joined the five from the pappea tree and were circling above the carcass to see if the hyenas would leave any leftovers. They didn't. Once the clan found the carcass, they used their powerful forequarters to rip out chunks of flesh and swallow them. By the time the hyenas were done all that remained was blood soaked soil.

As the Trooper moved further from the kill, Kushoto said, "You won't be able to hunt here anymore. Your first shot had to have been heard. The rangers will be combing the area for the next few days."

"What about near where I'm staying?"

"The rangers will communicate. They'll increase patrols throughout the entire Mara. What you should be more concerned with is getting your trophy into Nairobi and finding a taxidermist."

"But we just got here. We were going to hunt all week. Is there going to be a problem?"

"There could be. Since Nairobi is more westernized than the rest of the country, it could be hard to avoid tattletales for free."

"How much do you want to take care of it?" Kelso didn't want to start spreading his wealth any more than necessary.

"Five hundred shillings."

"You got the job."

"Thank you. You expect to avoid detection until you gather every animal on your list?"

Kelso realized the tranquilizer alibi wouldn't work. The more animals he was found with would lead to harsher penalties. He was an American in a foreign country. He didn't want to spend time in jail - least of all a foreign one.

There was silence for the rest of the ride to Cottar's Camp. Evelyn and Kelso again took great pleasure in gazing at the abundant wildlife. What Kelso adored about the animal ecosystem was its simplicity: whether they were herbivore, omnivore or carnivore there was no haggling, bickering, complaining or appeals. The animals were either swift, strong or resourceful and survived, or weak, slow or lacked initiative and became meals. To an extent money couldn't compensate for the simplicity of animal instincts. In spite of their intelligence and sophistication, humans were mortal also.

They arrived at Cottar's Camp after dusk. Kelso was able to sneak the rifle inside the tent. Kushoto kept the topi's head and drove away.

The following morning Kelso, despite the previous day's lessons, wanted to continue hunting, but Kushoto convinced him to return to Nairobi and wait a week before he killed again.

They made only one stop going back to Nairobi the next day. Kushoto dropped Evelyn and Kelso back at the Norfolk, keeping the topi remains in the Trooper and helping the couple with their luggage. He saw them into the lobby, told them to contact him via Basil, got in the Trooper and left.

There she lay. A combination of passion and fury. Mysterious. He hadn't unraveled why she wasn't as madly in love with him as he was with her. He'd endured pain to be with her, taken her on a trip she should never forget and still hadn't touched her the way he wanted to. The zebra striped cotton bikini panties, bulging over her round derriere were too inviting an object for someone who felt he should no longer be denied. He reached out and placed his hand on top of the panties. No problem. Then slowly, as though creeping up on big game, he maneuvered his pinkie underneath the fabric.

Evelyn bolted out of bed. "What's on your mind?"

"It's about time we took our relationship to the next level," said Kelso.

"We've been through this. There's still a lot I want to learn about you."

"I can't go on like this much longer. We've been together three months. You'd probably treat a total stranger better than me."

She picked up a white pump from beside the bed and pointed the heel at Kelso. "I tell you what. You bag a big cat, and I'll fuck your brains out. Till then, keep your hands to yourself. So far you've been a bully. That topi wasn't in any position to fight back. Let's see what happens when you go after a hunter."

"Would a lion suit you?"

"It'd suit me fine. But lions usually hunt in prides - remember what we saw on the Mara? If you kill one, what's to stop the rest of the pride from getting you?"

"How about a cheetah? They're solitary hunters."

"They're also the fastest land animal. What makes you think you're going to find one standing still?"

"Damn. I knew I should have bought an automatic weapon." Kelso banged his fists against his thighs.

"A machine gun? A semi-automatic rifle? This is supposed to

competitive. Remember?"

"What is competitive?" A trace of exasperation was in his voice.

"Let's see. Do a leopard."

"How's shooting one competitive?"

"You'll have a gun. That's your advantage. It's difficult to spot. Its hearing range is twice yours. If it comes down to you stalking it in dim light - and it may - a leopard usually hunts at dawn and dusk - its eyesight is six times better than yours. And their hunts produce a higher kill ratio than those of a lion. So, who knows, it might have as good a chance of getting you as you do of killing it."

Kelso took a deep breath and lay down, resting his head against the fluffy pillow. "I'll get a leopard."

"When do you plan to start?"

"Tomorrow. Let's go to Aberdare. In the souvenir store I read there's a pretty good chance of seeing one there."

"Where do you plan to stay?"

"The Aberdare Country Club."

Evelyn rested the pump heel on the mattress. Hearing Kelso say he would splurge for a country club astounded her. Then she remembered he wanted to take their relationship to the *next* level; he was paying more than she had ever imagined he would to stay in the Norfolk.

She picked up the shoe and lightly tapped his leg.

Kelso sat up and leaned against the headboard. "You going to give me a sample of what's in store when I bag the leopard?"

Evelyn held the shoe's sole as if it were a hammer's shaft. "Does it look like it?"

He could've forced himself upon her. He was bigger, but he was out of shape, and she had the muscularity of a gymnast. He was certain he could overpower her, but it wouldn't be easy. He wasn't the type who fought to fuck. She's going to be mine willingly after I kill a leopard, he thought. He didn't want to waste energy nor create unnecessary hostility. He'd wait until a leopard was added to his tally sheet. As far as he was concerned, it was already done. He had always done what he set out to do; he had no reason to believe history would abandon him. He covered himself up to his shoulders and turned away from Evelyn. "Good night," he said.

Evelyn loudly kissed her fingertips and placed them on Kelso's cheek.

He was already asleep.

She turned out the light, but sleep did not come easily to her. Kelso's safari had to come to an abrupt end tomorrow. If it didn't, his advances would be less polite. She knew he would eventually rape her. Then she would kill him in cold blood, most likely get caught and sentenced to jail. She wondered if she could still execute her plan. It wasn't as easy as she had anticipated. Kelso had shown respect and sensitivity to the wildlife. She even noticed when he shot the topi he had seemed saddened by its agony. Her thoughts drifted to how Kelso might have turned out differently. If he had been raised in the African wilderness instead of the New York jungle, maybe he would have been a decent man. Not a tyrannical capitalist. The fact remained he had killed Severina. She knew facts couldn't change. She vowed tomorrow would be Kelso's last.

By 6:30 Evelyn and Kelso were ready, waiting in the lobby with their luggage when Basil walked in. "Today we can get a slight head-start." He and Kelso lifted the luggage and took it outside. None of Basil's cars were visible. The Trooper was. Kushoto was inside.

"I've got something for you, Terry." Kushoto got out of the vehicle, opened the rear door and took out a large box.

"Is this my trophy?" Kelso asked.

Kushoto nodded.

"I'll take it upstairs now, look at it when I get back." Kelso took the box to his room and was back in the Trooper in less than four minutes. He handed Kushoto five hundred shillings. They shook hands and Kushoto left.

"Where's he going?" Kelso asked.

"To my house," said Basil. "There's work for him there. It's best I be your guide from now on." He looked at Kushoto walking away, then Evelyn, smiled, and Kelso.

"Is he your son?" Kelso didn't comprehend the significance of Basil's glances.

"A nephew."

"You're a wonder, Basil. Sometimes I get the feeling you're

related to everything two-legged in Kenya."

Basil turned toward Kelso, grinned, turned the ignition and drove.

Aberdare was almost due north of Nairobi and reached by roads that reminded Evelyn and Kelso of the mud patch leading to Cottar's. The Trooper didn't get stuck; however, twice Basil stopped and he and Kelso helped people push their four-wheel drive vehicles. The second time they helped, being a good Samaritan paid a dividend. After helping a Swiss couple push their Nissan Pathfinder out of the mud, as Basil and Kelso walked back to the Trooper, Basil told Kelso to look to the left. Beneath bamboo stalks was a black panther. Evelyn, who had been watching the men from the Trooper, turned toward the direction they were looking and saw the rare creature also. The panther disappeared into the bamboo.

When Basil and Kelso reentered the Trooper, Basil told Kelso that sighting the panther was encouraging: it meant leopards were in the vicinity; but it was best not to hunt the black panther - they're so rare diverting other people's attention elsewhere would be difficult and killing one would be considered heinous - more so than killing the common pigmented leopard.

Basil asked, "Where do you plan to stay? You looking to save money? If so, I'll take you straight to the Ark."

"How come?"

"Low prices, a high concentration of predators and more comfortable than the country club or Treetops."

"How long is it going to take to get there?"

"Depends on the roads."

Going straight to the Ark meant driving through the two hundred thirty square miles Aberdare National Park. The peaks of Ol Doinyo Lasatina and Mount Kinangop, each higher than 10,000 feet - as is most of the park - offered magnificent views of Mount Kenya and the Rift. As they drove, Basil pointed to spots where elephants had dug into soil with their tusks seeking salt. As they climbed higher in the park, it was growing chilly.

"Can you turn on the heat?" Evelyn asked.

Basil laughed. "Sure. Did you bring sweaters and jackets? You'll need them if we hunt at night."

"Hunt at night?"

"Yeah, often the best game viewing is at night or dawn."

Kelso looked outside at the moorland with tussock and giant heath. If he hunted a leopard in darkness, the cat would have at least one advantage.

The Trooper pulled as close as it could to the Ark and stopped. Alongside the vehicle's right was a three hundred thirty feet long catwalk, with a gate leading onto the Ark, designed to resemble Noah's original.

"You like what you see?" Basil asked.

"It's beautiful," said Evelyn.

"Good we'll come back at dusk," said Basil.

"Why?" Kelso asked.

"If we go in now we can't leave until tomorrow. You can't hunt in there. By the way, what are you after this time?"

"A leopard."

Basil grimaced. "We'll see what we can do."

"What's the problem?" Kelso asked.

"Even though they're here, they're not easy to spot."

"That makes it more exciting. Even you were fascinated when you spotted the panther."

"It'll be exciting, probably long and laborious too."

"Take us to the best spot to see one."

Basil drove the Trooper to a grove of trees with under brush protruding from a bank of boulders. Between the boulders were dry water inlets leading to a cave. None of the channels was big enough for an adult human to squeeze through.

Basil examined the boulders, then moved the Trooper into bushes about thirty yards diagonally opposite the rocks. "Why are we stopping here?" Kelso asked.

"This is a good spot to observe the rocks. A male or a female with cubs might use it as a resting place. Mongoose, genets, civets, servals, foxes and hares also rest here. A leopard'll come for food."

The trio got out of the Trooper and turned toward the rocks. During the first two hours a baboon troop and a hyena clan passed through. Since those animals were primarily scavengers, Basil said they utilized the rocks as a source of food: leftovers from predators' kills and small animals they could slaughter.

"This stationery observation is ridiculous. I feel like moss," Kelso said.

Kelso grabbed a bottle of spring water, opened it and took a sip. He offered Evelyn the bottle. She took a sip and offered the bottle to Basil. He refused. Kelso returned his attention to the boulders. The rest of the afternoon was uneventful.

It was just as they were preparing to return to the Ark that Basil tapped Kelso's shoulder and pointed toward the rocks. Struggling to get into one of the inlets was a fur of yellow, white, tan and black spots with a long tail. The animal's continued struggle didn't get it into the cave. It stopped struggling, found enough space on another rock to sit on its hindlegs, catch its breath and looked for bigger holes.

The leopard was enormous. From the distance they were observing, the cat appeared to weigh at least one hundred fifty pounds and was lean and supple: a male. When it stood up and moved toward a bigger crevice, it measured close to seven feet and reminded Kelso of the South American jaguar he had once seen at the Bronx Zoo. The leopard had found an inlet it could squeeze its body through. It disappeared inside the cave.

"What do we do now?" Kelso asked.

"We could stay here, but it's getting close to dusk. We might have to fend off wild animals in the dark."

"Other options?"

"Go back to the Ark and register, but once that gate closes, we can't get out until the morning. By the time we get here tomorrow, it's doubtful your 'friend'll' be waiting for you. Since that's a male, it could have a range of up to sixty to seventy square miles. I suggest we stay at a tented camp, and get back here well before dawn and try to catch him coming from the cave. What we do from there depends on what he does."

Twenty minutes later they were at the Aberdare Fishing Lodge. It was a rugged setting. They rented a bunkhouse but would have to provide their own food and utensils. Kelso figured the Spartan accommodations would create fewer regrets when they left in the middle of the night. He and Basil put the luggage in the bunkhouse. Smoke was coming from another bunkhouse. The trio walked toward the smoke's source. Behind the bunkhouse was a couple slightly older than Kelso tending to a campfire. The man had black hair speckled with a few white strands - a wide and solid frame and wore a straw Spanish rancher's hat. The women had fiery red hair, freckles, a figure reflecting an enjoyment of eating and riding boots over jeans and a yellow t-shirt.

"Jessica, look! We got company," the man said.

The man's accent sounded either British or Australian. "Hi. How you doing?" Kelso said.

"Fine mate, care to join us?" the man asked.

"We wouldn't want to impose on you. And we got nothing to add to your cookout," said Kelso.

"No problem mate. You and the native can come fishing with me. I got a couple of extra poles. The lady can stay here with my wife and help."

"What are we going to catch?"

"Trout and perch," said Basil.

"Right-o," said the man. "By the way, my name is Conrad. This is my wife Jessica."

Kelso introduced himself, Evelyn and Basil.

Conrad got up, went inside his cabin and returned with three fishing rods and a tackle box. "Grab the rods and let's go."

Kelso and Basil each took a fishing rod and along with Conrad walked to the fishing lodge's pond: a small lake. It was well stocked. They returned to Conrad's cabin half an hour later with enough fish to satisfy everyone's appetite. Conrad offered Kelso, Basil and Evelyn, Tuskers beer to go with their fried fish. When they were finished eating Conrad asked, "You enjoy the meal, mate?"

"Indescribably delicious," said Kelso.

"You want to fish tomorrow morning for breakfast?" Conrad asked.

"No, we won't be here that long," said Kelso. "We're getting up real early to see some wildlife."

"Which animals?"

"Porcupines."

"You come all the way here to see porcupines!"

"We're working on a research paper to see if their quills are as sharp here as they are on porcupines in the States."

"What a strange project," said Jessica.

"What have you observed so far?"

"This is our first attempt to see porcupines. We've been on the Maasai Mara. There we saw some of the other species."

"Make sure you don't let the porcupines stick you. They might be carrying disease."

Everyone shook each others hands. Conrad and Jessica went to their bunkhouse, carrying dishes, pans and utensils. Evelyn, Kelso and Basil walked to their bunkhouse.

As Evelyn and Kelso entered the bunkhouse, they noticed they were alone. They turned around, saw Basil still inside the Trooper. "What are you doing out there?" Kelso asked.

"I'll stay here until we leave," said Basil.

"You'll catch cold."

"I have blankets."

Kelso walked toward the Trooper.

Evelyn remained in the bunkhouse. She looked over the Winchester to make sure it would function properly. While Basil, Conrad and Kelso were fishing she had excused herself from Jessica, returned to the cabin and loaded the rifle. The bullets she put in the magazine were slightly different than the ones she had previously used. The slight difference would be crucial to the outcome of her plan. She put the Winchester back in the golf bag and sat on a folding chair as Kelso entered.

"What's up with Basil?" Evelyn asked.

"He said, he'd feel uncomfortable staying in here with us. I told him he could stay in the top bed and we'd share the bottom."

"That was sweet of you," Evelyn said.

Kelso detected insincerity in her tone of voice. He didn't know if it was caused by her really not wanting Basil in the bunkhouse or a desire not to share the bottom bed. "I told you I have good points."

"You did," Evelyn said.

She took off her jeans, t-shirt and safari vest and put on sweat-pants and a hooded sweatshirt. She lay on the bottom bed.

Kelso took off his clothes, remained in his underwear, turned

240

off the light, got in the top bed and pulled the coarse military blanket the lodge provided over his body. "You want to share the bottom bed even though Basil isn't here?"

"What for?" Evelyn asked.

"Being close together our body heat'll keep us warmer."

Evelyn exhaled a breath that was a combination of a giggle and a sigh. She admired Kelso's coyness. "You want more than our body heat to keep us warm."

"I'd be lying if I said I didn't, but I can wait until the agreed upon moment."

Evelyn wasn't sure if she believed Kelso, but she figured she wasn't going to be seeing him such longer, she had put him through a lot and he deserved some solace. "Come on down."

It seemed like Kelso was in the lower bed before the invite was completed. Evelyn let him move behind her near the window. She remained on the side where there was clear space. Kelso pulled the blanket over them.

Kelso had said he could wait, but part of his anatomy Evelyn felt touching her rear wasn't quite as patient. She couldn't fault him for that. If a man could be so close to her and not have his reaction, what did that say for her femininity? She hadn't had a man since she and Rollo were at the Asgaard Chateau, and it was the time of the month when not having intimate male companionship was a test of her will.

She grabbed what was touching her rear. It wasn't particularly long, but it was hard and wide. She began stroking it, first softly, then harder.

Kelso was stunned. After all he had been through he felt he was going to the eventual gratitude prematurely. He pulled down his shorts.

Evelyn moved on her back, her hand moving with greater rapidity and clamped to Kelso's enlarged masculinity like a vice.

Kelso placed his hands on Evelyn's breasts. She didn't move away; she thrust her breasts further into his palms and worked her hand more feverishly.

Masturbation wasn't enough to satisfy her. She sat up, then bent over, and was about to place her lips where her right hand had been

- until she remembered who this man was. This was the murderer of Severina and her child. She stopped thinking of her needs and remembered her brothers and their killers; Rollo, what he meant to her and how what they had would be tainted if she finished what she was doing. Reason triumphed over instincts. She jerked her head back, pushed against Kelso's chest. His head thumped against the wall. She climbed into the upper bed and pulled the blanket over her body.

Kelso was dumbfounded. He was so close - closer than he ever expected to get before killing the cat - yet so far. Remembering how adamant she had been in her previous refusal made this denial more bearable. He forced himself to dwell on the positive: she had gone further with him than ever before.

At three A.M. Basil knocked on the door. There was no immediate response. He continued knocking.

Evelyn, in a groggy voice, asked, "What is it?"

"It's time to go," said Basil.

She didn't move with the swiftness and the confidence she displayed a few hours before, but she got up and tapped Kelso's leg.

"Get up," she said. "Basil's here."

Kelso sat on the top bunk, rubbed his eyes, then jumped to the floor. "Then let's get ready and go." The quicker he killed the leopard, the sooner he'd be enjoying what he felt he was entitled to.

When they were dressed she and Kelso left the cabin, the golf bag slung over Kelso's shoulder and walked to the Trooper. When they drove off, there was a full moon overhead and a creeping mist.

Basil parked the Trooper behind the shrubbery diagonally opposite the rocks where they had last seen the leopard. He and Kelso got out. Kelso put the binoculars to his eyes.

The full moon partially offset the mist and the darkness; there was enough light to notice what was happening around the cave. For what seemed like an eternity there was stillness. Then as the sun's glow gave a hint of appearing on the horizon, a figure came out of the cave. It moved to the apex of the rocks. Its silhouette resembled a stone cut crown as it peered at the surrounding habitat. It began descending the boulders.

242

"If it's leaving the cave what do we do?" Kelso whispered.

"Wait for it to return," said Basil.

"Are you kidding?"

"Remember what I told you yesterday about its range? Plus, I don't know if its spotted us yet. If we trail it, we run a greater risk of that happening. If it does, it'll be spooked. We might as well start looking for another leopard."

"We'll do as you suggest." Kelso sucked his teeth.

"Don't get upset. I told you it wouldn't be easy."

Kelso took another look at the leopard. The beast looked in every direction upon reaching the ground. Then it seemed to disappear. "I guess we'll be here the better part of the day," said Kelso.

"Maybe even return trips over the next three or four," said Basil. "He might stay in a tree, on top of a termite mound, another cave or other resting sites before coming back."

"We can't go to him? I don't want to wait three to four days for him to return."

"Finding him at another site might take longer. Might not work at all."

"All right! We'll wait."

"Calm down. Leopards are elusive because it's essential to their survival. Leopards conceal themselves out of necessity."

"What can I expect if I corner it? Kelso asked.

"If there's a means of escape, it'll run. If you do have it cornered, you'll have a fight. If it'll fight a lion knowing it can't win, it won't hesitate to fight you, too."

"How do you know so much about leopards? About wildlife."

"When you take enough people around who are satisfied shooting pictures of the animals, you learn a lot."

Kelso nodded. Taking pictures suddenly seemed the saner activity. Then he looked at Evelyn and remembered why he was stalking the spotted cat, but he wondered whether one less leopard was worth the reward.

Dawn turned into morning and morning to afternoon. All they saw were hyenas, baboons, lizards and wild dogs make use of the boulders. Seeing the different species use the rock formation gave Kelso a better understanding of the ecosystem and how it paralleled human

243

civilization: though he judged neither to be perfect, both sought to perpetuate themselves. He wondered if witnessing nature's beauty and simplicity would curb his ambition when he returned home.

Kelso took a nap during the afternoon. The singing of multi-colored warblers served as a wake-up call before the onset of dusk. He was restless. He didn't want to go through the same routine for possibly the next few days. Tracking the leopard was no worse than sitting around like old women gossiping on park benches.

For her part, Evelyn felt sick. She sensed impending disaster. It wasn't so easy to terminate someone's life - vengeance or not. If she engineered Kelso's murder, she'd feel contaminated. She put her hand on Kelso's arm. He turned and seeing the fear in her eyes, smiled. "Please, Kelso, this was a bad idea. Let's go back," she whispered.

Suddenly, Basil pointed toward the boulders. The leopard had returned.

Kelso, immediately grabbed the .22 and stood up. "Wait here."

"What are you going to do?" Basil asked.

"Get this over with. I'm not going through another day like this.

"But ...."

"But what? Yesterday and today were enough waiting and I'm not doing anymore observing with the cat within shooting range."

"Kelso, please. Listen to Basil." Evelyn said, holding his arm.

"What's the matter? Afraid you're going to have to deliver? You figured you'd get a free trip for nothing?" He pushed her roughly away and moved closer to the rocks.

The leopard was lying down. Kelso moved to within forty feet of the animal and knelt behind a thornbush. He reached into a vest pocket and pulled out a small box of bullets. He could have continued using the bullets Evelyn loaded, but the box in his hand contained bullets he thought were best suited for his purpose. He opened the box, placed it on the ground, opened the magazine and removed the spent shells Evelyn had loaded. It didn't occur to him Evelyn had loaded blanks. He didn't know what bullets were supposed to look like when they were spent. He placed the blanks in another vest pocket, then began placing the box's silver bullets into the gun.

Evelyn, seeing what Kelso was doing, gasped. The bullets he had placed in the .22 would kill the leopard. She no longer wanted him dead, but once the leopard was lifeless, she'd have to fulfill a promise she never anticipated having to fulfill.

"Oh shit," she mumbled.

Basil looked at her as if she were defiled.

"Sorry," said Evelyn.

"I'll get over it," said Basil. "Let me have the other rifle?"

"It's not loaded and its bullets are in Nairobi."

"You shouldn't have brought firearms period. People rarely make wise decisions when using them."

Kelso was finished loading the rifle. He unlocked the rifle's safety and cocked the trigger. The wee click alerted the leopard. It looked up, saw Kelso.

Kelso had the animal cornered and could have pulled the trigger from where he was, but he moved closer to show his machismo.

The leopard, enraged and frightened, resembled a spotted monster: ears back, green eyes glistening like crystal coals, teeth bared like fragmented glass between gnarled tarred lips. It kept its belly tucked close to the ground, a coil waiting to spring.

As he got to within twenty feet of the leopard, Kelso felt there was no place else he'd rather be - the leopard's valor inspired his. He placed the rifle butt against his right shoulder and aimed. What he saw made him shiver. He regained his composure and pulled the trigger. It *jammed.* For a never ending moment he froze. Then he pulled the trigger again. No bullets shot out.

The leopard jumped.

Evelyn screamed and sprang up.

Basil grabbed her. "Don't be a fool!"

"We can't let him die." Too late she realized no human deserved what Kelso was suffering. By planning this trip, she was as culpable as Kelso. She struggled, but Basil's grip was too strong.

Kelso grabbed the rifle's barrel and held it like a stickball bat. He swung. The rifle's butt smashed into the leopard's rump. The animal was more stunned than hurt. It landed on the ground, looked at its attacker again and eased its body backward to catapult forward.

245

Kelso grabbed the rifle and again tried to shoot, but the leopard was too quick. The cat pounced on him, knocking him over. The leopard pinned Kelso's shoulders and with its dagger sharp canines bit into Kelso's jugular vein. Blood shot from the jugular. The leopard's powerful neck and shoulder muscles smothered Kelso's throat.

The muted roar of the jet drowned all other sounds. Turmoil wrenched through her soul. Evelyn looked out the window. Though Nairobi was becoming a blur, what she had experienced in the wilderness would indelibly scar her. As much as she abhorred what Kelso represented, she had learned hatred could have bounds. You could hate a person's behavior and decisions, but it did not make sense to hate the person. Seeing Kelso's life snuffed changed her mind. In spite of his arrogance, wickedness and callousness, violent death was never justified. Only when she reminded herself that he changed the blank shells for silver bullets did she feel any less a murderer.

The plane would refuel in Dakar, the Senegal. She'd call Rollo from the airport. She wondered if he would want to be with someone he thought of as a murderer. Would anyone?

The 747 flew over the leopard's cave. He was gone, having taken his fill of Kelso's remains. Vultures had swarmed over the corpse to partake of the predator's largess, each doing its best not to be deprived. The bones they left behind were ground to dust by hyenas.

The phone beside Rollo's bed rang. His arm moved slowly. He reached for the television's remote control. He had fallen asleep with the television on. The cartoon: "Bunny Hugged," was playing. He muted the volume as the Crusher bit into a fuse lit stick of dynamite that had been Bugs Bunny's arm, put down the remote, and picked up the telephone receiver.

"You won't be seeing Kelso anymore," said Evelyn, her voice sounding very far away.

"How'd you do it?" Rollo asked.

"It was horrible. I'm not going to tell you over the phone. Let's just say I now see why you tried to get me to back out."

"When does your flight arrive?"

He heard her gasp what sounded like a sigh of joy. "Tomorrow. 9:45A.M."

Rollo grinned. He opened the lamp table's drawer with his free hand, then opened the little box containing a three carat diamond mounted on an eighteen carat white gold ring. "I got something for you and I'm not going to tell you what it is."

"What did you get me?" She sounded excited.

"You'll get it when you get back. And by the way, you ever been to the Statue of Liberty, Precious?"

-THE END-

BOOKS AVAILABLE THROUGH
Professional Business Consultants
By Dr. Rosie Milligan

Birth of A Christian $9.95

Rootin' For The Crusher, $12.99

Temptation - $12.95

Collection of Conscious Poetry - 9.95

Satisfying the Blackwoman sexually Made Simple - $14.95

Satisfying the Blackman Sexually Made simple - $14.95

Negroes-Colored People-Blacks-African-Americans in America-$13.95

Starting A Business Made Simple - $20.00

Getting Out of Debt Made Simple - $20.00

Nigger, Please -14.95

A Resourse Guide for African American Speakers & Writers - 49.95

......................................**Order Form**......................................

Mail Check or Money Order to: 1425 W. Manchester, suite B, Los Angeles, CA 90047

Name_____Date_____

Address_____

City_____State _____Zip Code_____

Day Telephone _____

Eve Telephone _____

Name of book(s) _____

Sub Total $ _____

Sales Tax (CA) Add 8.25% $ _____

Shipping & Handling $3.00 $ _____

Total Amount Due $ _____

❑ Check   ❑ Money Order

❑ Visa   ❑ Master Card   Ex. Date _____

Credit Card No. _____

Driver's License No. _____

_____   _____

Signature   Date